*A*
*MARK of*
*GRACE*

## Books by Kimberley Woodhouse

### SECRETS OF THE CANYON

*A Deep Divide*
*A Gem of Truth*
*A Mark of Grace*

## Books by Tracie Peterson and Kimberley Woodhouse

*All Things Hidden*
*Beyond the Silence*

### THE HEART OF ALASKA

*In the Shadow of Denali*
*Out of the Ashes*
*Under the Midnight Sun*

### THE TREASURES OF NOME

*Forever Hidden*
*Endless Mercy*
*Ever Constant*

SECRETS *of the* CANYON
—BOOK THREE—

# *A* MARK *of* GRACE

## *Kimberley* WOODHOUSE

BETHANYHOUSE

*a division of Baker Publishing Group*
Minneapolis, Minnesota

© 2023 by Kimberley R. Woodhouse

Published by Bethany House Publishers
Minneapolis, Minnesota
www.bethanyhouse.com

Bethany House Publishers is a division of
Baker Publishing Group, Grand Rapids, Michigan

Printed in the United States of America

Library of Congress Cataloging-in-Publication Data
Names: Woodhouse, Kimberley, 1973- author.
Title: A mark of grace / Kimberley Woodhouse.
Description: Minneapolis, Minnesota : Bethany House Publishers, a division of
    Baker Publishing Group, 2023. | Series: Secrets of the canyon ; 3
Identifiers: LCCN 2022031859 | ISBN 9780764238024 (paperback) | ISBN
    9780764241284 (casebound) | ISBN 9781493440597 (ebook)
Classification: LCC PS3623.O665 M37 2023 | DDC 813/.6—dc23/eng/20220817
LC record available at https://lccn.loc.gov/2022031859

Scripture quotations are from the King James Version of the Bible.

This is a work of historical reconstruction; the appearances of certain historical figures are therefore inevitable. All other characters, however, are products of the author's imagination, and any resemblance to actual persons, living or dead, is coincidental.

Cover design by Create Design Publish LLC, Minneapolis, Minnesota/Jon Godfredson

Baker Publishing Group publications use paper produced from sustainable forestry practices and post-consumer waste whenever possible.

23  24  25  26  27  28  29      7  6  5  4  3  2  1

This book is lovingly dedicated to
two precious women in my life:

My daughter-in-love
Ruth Woodhouse
We've been so blessed to have you as part of our family.
I love how you keep Josh in line. And how much you love him.
Your sweet spirit and joy for life are beautiful.
Here's to decades more of memories together.
Love, Mom

And to MY mother-in-love
Brenda Woodhouse
Every time I typed 1909, I thought of you.
It made me smile and giggle.
You have been such a gift to me for more than thirty years.
Thank you for loving me as your own.
Love, Kim

# Dear Reader

The Harvey Girls are one of my favorite parts of American history. Without them, would the West have been settled? Without Fred Harvey would we have the food and restaurant industry as we know it? What about marketing? Fred Harvey has been said time and again to be the father of modern-day marketing.

The more research I did, the more fascinated I became. With Fred Harvey, the Harvey Girls, the Kolb brothers, and Mary Colter. I could fill twenty books with all the interesting little tidbits.

What it all comes down to is this:

History is beautiful. And enlightening. And we have so much to learn from it.

It's amazing to see what shaped our country. What shaped *us*—and our society.

It is a privilege for me to bring *A Mark of Grace* to you, the end of the SECRETS OF THE CANYON series, and Ruth's story. I've had hundreds of you write to me about your hopes that she would have her own story. I pray that this story blesses you and reminds you of how valuable you are. No matter what stage of life you are in, you are still useful and needed.

Let's venture back to the Grand Canyon, the El Tovar, and the Harvey Girls.

Enjoy the journey,
Kimberley

# Prologue

**1894**

**PITTSBURGH, PENNSYLVANIA**

"I'm not interested in settling down right now." Ruth Anniston allowed the words to spill out.

Mother's gaze jerked up from the piano where she'd been working on a new piece for her music students. Her eyes widened.

Ruth watched. At twenty years of age, she had a close and beautiful relationship with her parents. Rarely did she ever surprise them because they knew her so well.

This was obviously one of those rare occasions. Had her words finally registered?

Mother put a hand to her throat and removed her glasses. "Wait . . . Ruth, are you saying you don't wish to get married one day? I thought you always wanted . . ." She swallowed. Blinked several times. "Forgive me. Tell me what's on your heart."

Ruth bit her lip. The intention hadn't been to drop the idea of becoming a Harvey Girl quite like this. But it had seemed like the perfect segue in the conversation and out it came. "I'm not saying that I *never* want to get married. Yes, I want a family. Just not now. I *do* want to help you and Dad out for as long as I can, and perhaps have a few adventures of my own along the way. You took me in—adopted me—and loved me when no one else did. I know what a sacrifice that was, especially on Dad's small salary. This is an opportunity for a good job for me. A reputable job for a woman these days. You raised me to think for myself. Research. Read. Be independent." She could ramble on forever, so she clamped her lips shut.

"But, sweetheart, just because we made the sacrifice— which was all worth it, by the way—doesn't mean we are destitute. The college is paying your father much more these days. And his geology lectures are gaining popularity every year. I have more students than ever. There's nothing disreputable about staying at home and living with us until God brings the right man along."

Ruth's shoulders fell as she let out a long sigh. "It's not good for any of us if I sit around here and take up space. You know me. I like to explore. Love hard work." Hopefully Mom wouldn't pick up on her real reason for wanting to go. "There aren't any interested parties offering marriage right now anyway."

That wasn't the *complete* truth. She wouldn't bring up the young man who followed her around everywhere and wouldn't leave her be. Mom would faint dead away if she heard some of the brazen things he'd said. At her age, Ruth longed for love. The kind she saw between her parents. But it wouldn't happen here. Of that, she was confident.

"You're such a pretty young lady, Ruth. Don't sell yourself short." Mom shook her head. "We'll speak about this over dinner with your father." She placed her spectacles back on the end of her nose and leaned over the staff paper. Her pencil didn't miss a beat as it drew several notes.

Just like that. The conversation was set aside. "That's not good enough. Have you listened to a word I've said?" Ruth shook her head and crossed her arms over her middle. "I can't believe you would say something like that. *Pretty? Don't sell myself short?* You and Dad raised me to care more about what was *inside* a person than what was on the outside. To value each and every person because God loved them, not because of how they looked."

Mom released an exasperated huff and looked at her over the rims of her glasses. "It wasn't meant as an insult, my dear, rather a compliment. You are beautiful. Always have been." She pointed her pencil at Ruth. "And don't even try to convince me there aren't any interested parties. Your father and I know better." She went back to her music. "Let's talk about it over dinner. I really must get back to work before my next student arrives."

With a deep breath, she shrugged. "All right." Her parents were the most wonderful people on earth. Perhaps she could spend some time working on a sound argument to present at dinner.

But by the time dinner rolled around and she forged ahead with what she thought was a well-thought-out argument, Dad wasn't easily convinced.

"I don't see how becoming a Harvey Girl will be good for you. There are plenty of suitors here ready and waiting to have the chance—"

"They've spoken to you about this? Why haven't you said anything?" Interrupting her father wasn't something she ever did, but her parents' attitudes were more than she could fathom. They'd never even broached the subject of multiple suitors with her before.

"Of course they have. You are quite the catch. I was hesitant to bring it up, feeling you needed some time. But now that you're talking about heading off to who-knows-where, it's my place as your father to speak up."

The discussion escalated and continued for well over an hour as Ruth—for the first time—felt like she was fighting with her parents over her future. How had they come to this place? Dad talked of how many interested suitors there actually were, then Mom made the comment about how pretty she was at least three more times. All it did was cement in Ruth's mind that she wanted to marry a man who loved her for who she was . . . not just her pretty face.

And as much as her parents disagreed with her, she wanted to head out on her own. Try something new. Experience life outside of the sheltered cocoon she'd always lived within.

They finally acquiesced. Albeit with tears and many cautions.

After long hugs with each of her parents, she headed to bed.

Her dream of becoming a Harvey Girl was about to come true.

1907
**Thirteen years later**
**El Tovar Hotel, Grand Canyon**

*"You're such a pretty young lady, Ruth. Don't sell yourself short."*

*Pretty young lady.* As the memories of the past washed

over her, Ruth couldn't believe how many years had rolled by since that day.

But now look at her. No longer did she have a pretty face. No longer was she young and eligible. Had she let her stubborn pride get in the way? Was she destined to be alone forever?

At this moment, the mirror across the room was the worst villain she could ever imagine.

The more Ruth thought about it, the more she wanted to throw something at it and make it shatter into pieces. But she wouldn't do that. *Couldn't* do that.

Because she was a Harvey Girl.

The head waitress.

In control at all times.

An example to all the girls under her. Mother hen. Mentor. Friend.

She couldn't allow herself to lose all command of her faculties just because her world would never be the same again. This had been her dream.

Even though she now faced the nightmare before her.

Ruth gingerly patted the bandage on her cheek. *Lord, give me strength to handle whatever comes.* She'd repeated the prayer too many times to count as she waited for the doctor to arrive.

She wasn't a vain woman. At least she hadn't been before a mountain lion mauled her face. Had she? Now she spent an agonizing amount of time consumed with her appearance and how it affected her future.

She was thirty-two—almost thirty-three. A veritable spinster. If she couldn't work, what was she to do? Where could she go? Working as a Harvey Girl had been her entire adult life. It had brought her so much satisfaction. Hopefully, she'd brought God glory through it all. And even when she was younger and struggled when all the other girls were getting married and settling down, the Lord had given her peace.

Now she was the headwaitress at the crown jewel of the Harvey Empire—an accomplishment she'd worked hard to obtain. It was all she'd ever wanted after donning her first black-and-white uniform. And after a year on the job, it had been easy to think she still had plenty of time for God to bring the right man into her life. She'd been completely content.

Being a Harvey Girl was the perfect job for her. More to the point, it was the only job she knew. What if she couldn't do it anymore? Harvey Girls made people feel comfortable. They were trained to be efficient. Pleasant. And spotless.

Without blemish, as the Bible verse went. Her soul might be spotless before the Lord, but people were far less forgiving than He. And she was no longer without blemish . . .

Mr. Owens—the manager of the El Tovar—had bent the stringent Harvey rules for Emma Grace in her time of need. Surely he would do the same for her. Only, Emma Grace could still do her job. Ruth *couldn't*. Not to the Harvey standard. Her leg would take a long time to heal. And she'd probably always walk with a limp. But that wouldn't be as visible as her face. She closed her eyes. What would she look like?

Reaching up with her right hand, she covered the bandaged area of her face. And for a moment, she looked normal again.

*Lord, give me strength to handle whatever comes.*

The prayer grew frailer with each repeat. It had started out sturdy and resilient but was now thin and ill-equipped to hold her together.

Against the doctor's orders, Ruth began to peel back the

edge of the bandage. She stepped close to the mirror, hoping the damage was far less than she feared.

"I asked you not to do that, Miss Anniston."

Ruth turned away from the mirror, her emotions a mix of chagrin for disobeying the doctor's orders and relief that she'd put off the inevitable for a few more minutes. "I'm sorry."

Dr. Collins' kind smile made the gray in his eyes blend nicely with the silver in his hair. He was such a nice-looking man.

*Nice-looking.* She cringed. No one would probably ever say that about her ever again.

"In truth, Miss Anniston"—he stepped deeper into the room and set his bag on the desk—"I'm surprised you haven't removed it already. How are you feeling?"

He wasn't asking about her pain, but she still didn't have a grip on her emotions, so she tempered her answer. "Fine. It's itchy more than painful at this point."

He narrowed his gaze. "All right. We'll leave it at that." He snapped open the black leather medical bag and peered inside. "I have an ointment that will help with the itchiness."

"Oh good, you're here." Mr. Owens strode into the room, a false smile on his face. "How are you feeling today, Miss Anniston?"

Unlike the doctor, Mr. Owens surely wanted assurance that she'd hold up under whatever the removal of her bandage revealed. So Ruth squared her shoulders and gave him her best Harvey Girl smile. "I'm fine, sir. Thank you for asking. How is the dining room?"

"Nothing to worry about. Miss Schultz will do a tremendous job in your stead, I'm sure."

*Oh, please. Don't let him replace me already!* She banished the selfish plea. "She will make the Harvey name proud." Her smile cracked at the edges. Her newest protégé had become a dear friend.

"She's been begging to see you all day. Shall I let her know that after the doctor leaves, she can come in?" The manager raised his eyebrows.

"Let's wait for visitors until later, shall we?" The doctor looked between the two of them. "I want to remind you both that Miss Anniston's wounds are still very fresh. They will be red and swollen today, far beyond what they will eventually fade to. I hope you'll keep that in mind."

*Lord, give me strength to handle whatever comes.*

The prayer was tissue-paper thin now. Barely holding her together. Her hands were damp, and her heart began to pick up speed. "I'm ready."

And she'd told Julia that lying wasn't the Harvey way. What a hypocrite she'd become.

"Have a seat, Miss Anniston." Dr. Collins pulled the chair out for her, the one not facing the mirror. Should she ask to be turned to face it? Or was it better to see the full damage at one time rather than in slow, tormenting pieces? But the doctor didn't give her a choice. He turned the chair away from both the mirror and Mr. Owens.

How bad did he expect this to be?

She wiped her hands against her skirt and, calling upon all her training, forced her legs to cooperate when they were dead set against moving. "Thank you." It was an automatic response to a man holding a chair for her, but was she thankful? No. Not for this.

But she was thankful for his many visits and his skill. She closed her eyes and focused on that while he eased the bandage away from her cheek.

While he worked, Mr. Owens talked. "I've been thinking about how to ease you back into working, Miss Anniston. I think it's best if we keep you off your feet as much as possible, don't you, Doctor Collins?"

"That's going to be a requirement until her leg fully heals, and that will take some time."

But that wound was hidden. It wasn't ugly and out in the open. Ruth cringed at her own thoughts.

Her manager was still talking. "I'd like you to keep training the new girls, of course, but perhaps it would be best to do that when the dining room is closed so you aren't interrupted by our guests. That way you can sit and not strain your injuries."

Ruth stiffened. Her fears were coming true. He didn't want her to be seen.

"I saw that, Ruth. I know what a workhorse you are, but you are too valuable to Harvey to not let you heal completely. It's for your own good," Mr. Owens continued. "I'm thinking we should keep you off your feet. But don't think we won't put you to work in other ways. I'd like you to take over some bookkeeping responsibilities. Don't you think that's a good idea?"

No. It was a terrible idea. She had no idea how to handle books. She knew how to handle people. But at least he was offering her work. "That sounds good, sir. Although I'll need to be trained on bookkeeping as it's outside of my—" She gasped as a piece of gauze pulled her tender skin. "Out of my expertise."

With the last piece of gauze removed, she took a shallow breath . . . then another one.

"Of course. I'm sure you'll be a quick study. Managing the dining room and kitchen alone are a huge undertaking.

With all your knowledge and skill as headwaitress all these years, perhaps we could make another arrangement. I find myself overwhelmed a good bit of the time."

Was he trying to make her feel better? It wasn't working. What she wanted was to be able to get back on the floor and do *her* job. Not the books. Not managing the dining room and kitchen.

"But whenever you're ready, my dear." The man's voice held a slight edge. Like he was tempering his tone. What did they see?

Ruth closed her eyes, forcing back hot tears. Mr. Owens was as no-nonsense as they came. He didn't believe in false hope or platitudes. He told it like it was. If he was calling her *my dear*, things must be worse than even he expected.

"I believe I should leave the stitches in for another week," the doctor said. "Even though they make the injuries look so much worse, it will be best for long-term healing. If you would like to keep it covered with bandages during the day, that is fine. But at night, it's best for the wound to be uncovered."

"All right." How bad did it look?

"I think we should leave Miss Anniston alone for a moment."

There was her answer. Yes. Things were much worse than expected.

Ruth opened her eyes and whispered, "Thank you."

Dr. Collins nodded once, his gray eyes wet with compassion. "Take your time. And remember, this isn't how you'll look in a few months. It will get better. I promise."

She swallowed and nodded. The tears she'd held back earlier leaked out, stinging her skin. She wanted to say thank-you again but couldn't get the words past the trepidation clogging her throat. She looked down at her lap.

He patted her hand, then stood. "Let's go, Mr. Owens."

"But I wanted—"

Ruth imagined the good doctor either grabbed her manager's arm or silenced him with a glare. Either way, she was grateful she didn't have to endure a gasp or horror-filled eyes or any other reaction. Dealing with her own was going to take every ounce of whatever courage she had left.

She stood, smoothed her skirt, and took one more shaky breath. As she turned to face the mirror, she whispered, "Lord, give me strength—"

But then she saw.

The prayer perforated, and she fell apart.

The next day, crisp air in the early morning hour gave Ruth a little jolt as she hobbled out to meet Frank Henderson. After pulling herself together yesterday evening, she'd scribbled a note to him and sent one of the girls to deliver it and wait for a response. If anyone would be honest with her and help her to sort through her feelings, it was her longtime friend.

For years, they'd both worked for the Harvey Company. Twice now, they'd worked at the same location. He understood the work she loved and understood her. Made her laugh. Challenged her in her walk with God. He was the one she trusted most.

She wanted to be respectful of his responsibility as a chef but knew that he loved to walk the canyon rim long before dawn. So, she'd asked to meet him. Early. Thankfully, he agreed to spare a few minutes for her.

It had taken everything in her to get up the stairs by herself. The crutches the doctor gave her to use were incredibly uncomfortable and awkward. She still hadn't mastered the technique, but she didn't want anyone else to know she was venturing out. The glances full of pity, the offers to help her move—even just across the room—well, they were more than she wanted to deal with for a walk out to the rim.

Her own emotions were tenuous at best, and she needed someone to help strengthen her fortitude. To stiffen her up. It was like she'd become a bowl of mush the past couple of weeks. That wasn't who she was. So yes, she would risk the consequences of coming out here by herself because something had to change. And soon. But the distance to their favorite bench loomed.

She lifted her chin. She would make it there. She would. And if she had to beg Frank to carry her back, so be it.

"Good morning, Ruth." Frank's mellow voice greeted her from the bench. He reached for her arm. "Why didn't you let me help you out here?"

With a shrug, she maneuvered over to the seat. "You know me. I'm stubborn and independent. I didn't want anyone to know. No one is out and about right now, and I was afraid of making too much noise and it making a fuss." The more she said, the less sense she made—even to herself. She sat on the bench and set the crutches beside her. That simple walk— one she'd made hundreds of times on two good legs—now took everything out of her.

It was a miracle she'd been able to keep her leg, she knew that, but oh, how she wished things were different. She swallowed her pride and touched his arm. "I might need your help to get back, though. I'm afraid I don't have much strength left."

"Oh, Ruth, of course I'll help." His eyes glistened in the first light of the day.

She pointed a finger at him. "Don't feel sorry for me, Frank. I don't need your pity."

"I most certainly do *not* feel sorry for you." He looked offended. "I'm hurt you would even accuse me of such a thing. After all we've been through. Tsk, tsk." He quirked one of his bushy red eyebrows at her. "You should know that you are my dear friend and I care about you. None of this pity nonsense. I know better."

The expression on his face made her laugh. "Thank you."

"Now, what is it that you needed to discuss? It must be of some import since you dragged me out here *so* early in the morning after you've been avoiding me for two weeks. My feelings might be hurt, by the way." He crossed his arms over his chest. But the twinkle in his eyes told her what she needed to know. He was her friend and wasn't treating her any differently than before her injury. Exactly what she needed.

Ruth swatted at his arm. "Oh, hush. I've never once seen you get your feelings hurt. Besides, I haven't been avoiding *you*. I've been avoiding everyone."

"Well, that explains *everything*."

"Don't take that sarcastic tone with me, Mr. Henderson." It felt good to tease and scold. Like she was still in charge. Like she wasn't an invalid.

"Yes, ma'am." His mustache wiggled with his lips, his humor evident.

"Thank you." She lifted her chin at him and grinned. What would she do without this man in her life? While she had always been so serious and a rule-follower, he'd continually made her laugh. "We've been through a lot, haven't we, Frank?"

He shook his head and let out a hearty laugh. "That's putting it mildly, yes. But the good Lord has seen us through, wouldn't you say?"

She nodded. But couldn't bring herself to affirm his statement with words. That was part of her struggle.

"Ah . . . so the crux of the matter." He turned to face her completely, his green eyes drilling into her. "Tell me why you asked me out here."

She broke eye contact and looked out at the canyon that was coming to life in brilliant colors with the sunrise. A strong scent of pine filled the air. "You've always been honest with me, and I'm asking the same of you today."

"Of course."

"I also know you well enough that I know your character. You won't judge me." Now that they were out here and the time was right, she couldn't quite get the words out. Why was she stalling?

"Heavens no."

Wringing her hands together, she took a deep breath and turned to face him again. "I'm worried about what this will do . . . how it will affect how people see me. Will I be able to do my job? You know as well as I do about Harvey's high expectations. My leg is going to make me limp for some time—at least that's what the doctor says—and my face . . . well, that's why I asked you out here."

His brows dipped as his forehead wrinkled. "I'm not sure *what* you're asking."

Without taking another second to think about it, she removed the bandage covering the wound on her face. "I need you to be honest. How bad is it, really? Will people ever be able to see past it? I know I can't." The last words slipped out before she could catch them. It was like baring her soul. If only she could take them back.

Frank lifted his shoulders and studied her face. With his

thumb and forefinger, he gently gripped her chin and turned her face back and forth.

It seemed an eternity passed while she waited for him to speak.

He patted her steel-gripped hands in her lap. "Ruth, you are beautiful. Inside and out. That mountain lion left its mark on your face, but that doesn't change anything. It doesn't change your beauty one bit."

She huffed at him and turned the mutilated side of her face toward him. "Look at this! You can't tell me this doesn't change things."

"You're still covered in stitches. Once those are removed, it will look a lot different. And over time, it will heal and probably not even be noticeable!"

"Frank, I asked you to be honest with me. Not try to cushion it with flowery words." She crossed her arms over her chest. What she wouldn't give to be able to jump up and stomp her feet.

"Ruth, you are the most stubborn woman I think I've ever met. I didn't give you any flowery words. I *am* being honest. Yes, you've been clawed by a lion. Yes, there are lines on your face. But I stand by what I said, it doesn't change your beauty. It doesn't change who you are."

*It doesn't change who you are.*

Oh, but it did. Couldn't he see that? Everyone had tiptoed around her, waited on her hand and foot, but she'd seen her reflection in the mirror. It was burned into her memory.

She would *never* be the same.

"I've always thought you were the prettiest lady I've ever met." Frank reached for her hand. "Bandage or no bandage, scar or no scar, I still think that. I mean it with all my heart."

She closed her eyes against his words. His intent was good,

she couldn't fault him. But it was exactly what she *didn't* want to hear. All her life she'd been told how pretty she was. And all her life she'd been taught to not look on outward appearance, but on a person's heart. She never thought she actually cared about what people thought of her.

But that had been because she *was* pretty. Now she wasn't. And it bothered her more than she cared to admit.

"Ruth?" Frank's voice pleaded with her. He gripped her hand tighter. "I need to tell you how I ca—"

"I'm not feeling too well. Would you help me back to my room?"

He let out a sigh and moved closer. "Of course. I'm sorry. I didn't mean to keep you out here so long."

Ruth struggled to her feet, but once the crutches were in place, she didn't have the strength to move.

"I'm right here if you need me . . ." He put a hand on her elbow. His words roared through her mind over and over again. *"I've always thought you were the prettiest lady I've ever met."*

Before the attack, she would have loved to hear those words from him. Why did things have to change? Why did her heart feel like it had been pushed through a meat grinder?

She took a step with the crutches before collapsing to the ground. Tears rushed to her eyes. Why did she come out here? What had she expected? Frank had been nothing but supportive and encouraging. Why did that hurt so much?

Without a word, Frank scooped her up into his arms. Ruth tucked her head against his shoulder, trying to hide her face and her tears.

Silence surrounded them, and all she heard was the beating of his heart, his steady breaths, and his steps as he carried her home. Her mind swirled with all the what-ifs from her life.

What if she'd stayed at home like her parents suggested?

What if she'd married one of the interested suitors?

What if she'd never been injured?

Her leg and face both throbbed against their stitches. Her heart felt like it was shattered. And she didn't understand why.

When they came close to the hotel's entrance, Frank veered down the hill to the left. "I'll take you down to the basement entrance and ask one of the girls to go back and fetch your crutches. I'm sure you just overdid it. Don't worry. Time heals all wounds. You're a strong and beautiful woman, Ruth Anniston."

At that moment, his words were like a knife to her gut.

No. She was sure time could *never* heal these wounds.

# 1

**MONDAY, MAY 3, 1909**
**EL TOVAR HOTEL, GRAND CANYON**

Spoons clattered against pots. Steam sputtered out from under lids. The scent of fresh-baked bread and brewing coffee filled the air.

Frank grinned to himself. He loved the hustle and bustle of this kitchen. It practically hummed with a symphony of culinary life.

Over the past twenty years, he'd worked for the Harvey Company in one capacity or another. But once he discovered the kitchen and cooking, he'd been hooked, and he'd been in a Harvey kitchen ever since.

Once he came to El Tovar . . . well, that had changed everything. The luxury hotel perched on the very edge of the Grand Canyon was a marvel, especially this far away from any city. Not only did they have electric lights powered by their own steam generator, but railroad tank cars brought fresh water in daily—120 miles—and the kitchen grew their own fruits and vegetables in greenhouses. Right here. Add to that their own dairy and poultry flock and they were set. It was a chef's dream.

Yesterday had been a huge success. Celebrating the opening of the official summer season at El Tovar had become quite the treat over the years, and the food only increased in volume and specialties. But when Chef Marques had been called away for a family emergency, the task of pulling it all off fell squarely onto Frank's shoulders. He'd learned so much from being the assistant chef under such an amazing mentor all these years that the event had run with precision and clockwork. But there was no time to revel in that. Another day, another crowd of people to feed.

"Chef Henderson!" Mr. Owens' voice rose above the kitchen clamor. "Might I have a word?"

"Yes, sir." Frank dipped his chin toward his manager and gave directions to the new hire beside him. He wiped his hands on his apron and headed toward the door.

Mr. Owens didn't stop there, though. He headed toward his office.

That was odd.

But Frank followed and hoped this wouldn't take too long. His bouillabaisse needed to be started for dinner.

When they reached the office, Frank saw Chef Marques standing beside the manager's desk, dressed in a suit. The man looked out of place without his chef attire. Derby hat in his hands, he nodded at Frank.

Mr. Owens closed the door and stepped behind his desk. "Chef Henderson . . . Frank. You have been an invaluable asset to the El Tovar since its opening."

"Thank you, sir." Hopefully that wasn't an opening for his dismissal.

"Chef Marques is needing to leave us."

The statement hit him like a cleaver chopping through thick steak bones. The man had taught him more than anyone else in his life. He couldn't believe it.

"I'm sure you are very sorry to see him go," Mr. Owens continued.

"I don't know what to say, Chef," Frank stammered. "You have been—"

"It is time." The man's French accent was thick, even though he'd been in the States for many years. He dipped his head and twisted his hat before lifting his head again, a sheen of tears in his eyes. "You will do me proud."

Frank swallowed hard. Blinked against the burning sensation in his own eyes. How could he say good-bye after all this time? How could he say . . . thank-you?

Mr. Owens gripped Frank's shoulder. "We will have an announcement with all the staff later this afternoon, but I wanted to inform you that as of right now, as long as you are willing, you are being promoted to the head chef position at El Tovar."

Frank gasped. Not what he expected. It was hard enough thinking of Marques leaving. "Head chef." He mumbled the words.

"You deserve this honor, Frank." His mentor patted his arm.

Their manager raised his eyebrows as if in anticipation.

Oh. He was supposed to accept. He pulled himself together. "Of course. I am thrilled and honored, sir."

"Good. We are thankful to have you here. We will hire a new assistant chef within the week, but you have enough staff to make it through, I presume?"

"Yes." Clearing his throat, he shifted his brain back to the schedule of the kitchen. "If we have everyone pull extra shifts, we will be fine."

"Excellent. Chef Marques needs to leave on the train today, so I'm thankful you've got it covered."

Frank looked from the manager to the man who'd mentored him the past four years. He could never repay him for all he'd learned. Fumbling around for words, he cleared his throat again to cover the lump that felt like rising bread dough. "I . . . um . . . that is . . . it has been a privilege to learn and work under such an amazing chef. I can't thank you enough for the knowledge and skill you poured into me."

Marques put a hand to his chest. "*Merci*. But it is I who should be thanking you. This is the first head chef position where I truly had an assistant—a right-hand man, as you put it. Most kitchens are full of egos and competitions, but *non*, we did not have that here. It has been *my* privilege, Frank." He bowed at the waist.

Frank held out a hand. But the former head chef held out his arms and embraced Frank instead of shaking. "I will write letters. We share recipes, *oui*?"

Frank patted the man on the back and released him. "Yes, Chef. It will be like old times."

With a nod, the man clamped his lips together, and headed out the door. But Frank had seen the heartache in the man's eyes. He'd truly loved his kitchen and the people he worked with.

"Those are some awfully big shoes to fill, Mr. Owens. But thank you for the opportunity."

"I'm confident you will do the Harvey name proud." The manager's broad smile was warm. "We've known each other a long time now and you're one of my most trusted employees. It's an honor to have you here, Henderson."

"Thank you. Again." He plopped his chef's hat back on his head. "I better get back to work."

As he left the manager's office and strode through the rotunda, he looked down the hallway into the dining room. Head chef! All he'd ever hoped for in his career, and it was now his. The steps through the dining room and into the kitchen made his heart pound. What an honor. And what a responsibility. *Thank You, Lord.*

With a glance at the clock on the wall, he went over the tasks for the day and looked at who was in the kitchen. Word would spread soon enough, so there was no need for him to say anything. Even though there was one person he wished he could tell before the news spread.

His face stretched into a smile. How would Ruth respond?

A pot clanked against the stove as one of *his* workers jostled about and brought Frank's thoughts back to the job—keep everything running smoothly, make sure delicious food was prepared, keep the guests happy and coming back for more.

The perfect job. Which he better focus on if he wanted to keep it.

Precisely at 10:45 a.m., Ruth walked into the kitchen. Every morning at this time, they went over detailed lists for luncheon and dinner. Secretly, it was the highlight of Frank's day.

With her dark hair piled on top of her head in that poofy bun that all the women wore these days, she was prettier than ever. The scars on her face weren't even visible anymore, but probably because she'd started wearing makeup as soon as she went back to work—something that Mr. Owens must have approved since none of the Harvey Girls had ever been allowed to do such a thing.

But she technically hadn't been a Harvey Girl since her

injury. As she'd healed, Owens had her doing tedious jobs with the books for the hotel and then had gradually given her more responsibility. Instead of being the headwaitress—of which she was the best Frank had ever seen—now she was the supervisor over the entire dining room and kitchen.

Her steps were a bit slow, but he didn't mind. After two years the limp was still there, but she covered it most of the time. Doc said that her leg would continue to heal but it didn't matter to Frank. She was still Ruth—feisty and accomplished and as pretty as ever.

"Good morning, Chef Henderson." Her hands were clasped in front of her.

"Good morning, Miss Anniston." He pulled the chart of workers and list of dishes from his desk on the side of the kitchen. "I have some big news." He couldn't help but grin like a silly schoolboy. He'd been wanting to find her and tell her ever since he found out.

"Oh? Do tell." She smirked at him and raised one perfectly shaped eyebrow. Her blue eyes sparkled in the bright lights of the kitchen.

"I've been promoted to head chef."

Her grin spread across her face, and she glanced around the kitchen before squeezing his arm. "I know! I'm so proud of you. Congratulations!"

Of course she would know. She was in charge of the kitchen and dining room, after all. "I can hardly believe it. I mean, I hate that we had to lose Marques, but this is a dream come true for me."

"You deserve this, Frank. And I couldn't be happier for you." She leaned in close and squeezed his arm again before glancing around and resuming her stiff posture. Miss Professional Supervisor. "Is there anything important we need to cover today? Because I'm sure you have your hands full."

While he'd hoped to chat as friends for a few minutes after he shared his news, he could see the trepidation on her face. The longer she stood here, the harder it was for her to sneak back to her office without a lot of eyes on her, which was her habit, even though she'd never say it aloud. The dining room opened again at precisely eleven in the morning. He handed her the chart and list. "Thanks for believing in me to do this job."

"You completely earned this on your own merit, Frank. As much as I think you're the best chef in the world, I didn't need to put in my two cents for Mr. Owens to make the decision." She waved the papers and turned. "Thanks. I'll see you later this evening."

With a swish of her skirts, she was gone. Head held high. Shoulders straight. Trying her best to keep her steps smooth and steady as she exited the kitchen. He'd watched her do the same thing every day for the past two years. Never allowing himself to tell her what was in his heart. And the couple times he'd tried when they weren't working, he had been interrupted. Which made him think God was having him wait.

Until when? Neither one of them was getting any younger. But Ruth wasn't ready. Not since the accident.

When would she see how valuable and cherished she was? That scars and limps didn't matter? That she was the most beautiful woman in the world?

The way *he* saw her.

⊣ ⊢

**MAY 5, 1909**
**KANSAS CITY, MISSOURI**

Uncle Melvin would be proud.

After years of meticulous research and planning, Oliver had figured out a way to put his plan into action. A way to tarnish the Harvey name. And not just tarnish it but ruin it. For good. That would be the ultimate win for his family. To make up for the decades of disgrace and loss. The empire that should have been O'Brien. *Not* Harvey.

While the rest of the family wallowed in self-pity and poverty, sitting around rehashing the story, he'd made a name for himself and was determined to reclaim what should have been theirs. Uncle Melvin should have never gone into business with Fred Harvey. They'd had a thriving restaurant and saloon until that thief took off with every cent they had. All because he disagreed with Uncle politically. What a slimy, backstabbing wretch.

Oliver walked over to the chessboard under the window and looked at the pieces in play. He'd practiced his moves over and over again. Until he could capture the king each and every time. Perfect.

Granted, his initial attempts to put a dent in the Harvey Empire had been chaotic. Half-hearted. Not well thought out. He'd been young, stupid, naïve, and poor. It not only took money to make money, but it took money to *steal* money.

Things were different now. He was older . . . wiser. Richer. He knew his opponent better. He had a saboteur in place. Just like in studying the game of chess. If he had to lie, cheat, steal, even kill to accomplish his goal, he didn't care, because he would do whatever it took. Every time he heard of Harvey's success, it dug the knife in a little deeper. His family could whine and complain all they wanted, but it wasn't helping them. He, on the other hand, had allowed the rage to boil inside him until revenge was the only way out.

He looked out the window and straightened his collar. This quick trip home would be his last until it was all over. The busy street before him would soon bear his family's name. It wouldn't be such a dingy place. He could turn everything around. His cousin's little restaurant, started by Uncle Melvin, could become something bigger. They would expand across the country. Just like Harvey, but they would do it better. And use *their* own name.

It would all come out. People would hear the truth.

It had taken a lot of time to learn the inner workings. To analyze the Harvey Company. The food. The Harvey Girls. The standards. To understand how the El Tovar succeeded. How a luxury hotel could exist in the middle of nowhere. The supply chain alone was outrageous. But because the wealthy wanted the best at one of America's wonders, Harvey made it happen.

Well, money could disappear.

Supply chains could be disrupted.

Accidents could happen.

Rumors could spread like wildfire.

People could even get sick.

Which would mean guests would stop coming.

Newspapers would write about the demise of Harvey's Crown Jewel and predict that the empire would fall.

And in time, it would. Just as the O'Brien Empire rose.

Wouldn't be long now until all the pieces would be captured. He'd take the queen—the El Tovar—and then?

Checkmate.

# 2

**MONDAY, MAY 24, 1909**

Another disappointing visit with the doctor. Would she ever get back to her normal self?

Another long day as supervisor of the dining room and kitchen. Would things ever change? Or would she be in this job for the rest of her life?

Ruth gave herself a lecture. She should be proud of such a position. Management like that had always been considered a man's job. Mr. Owens and the Harvey Company obviously believed in her.

So why was she still struggling with these feelings of inadequacy? No matter how much she fought against them, day in and day out, they plagued her.

Probably because she didn't feel comfortable being in front of people anymore. And yet that was exactly what she *wanted*. After all these months, every time she left the security of her closed office, she double-checked the mirror to make sure her scar was covered, and she slid her injured leg under her skirts rather than stepping to try and hide the

36

limp. It took far more effort and time than it should, but she was determined to make everything appear . . . normal.

Normal.

Such a strange word. It carried a different meaning than ever before.

Ever since that day, she'd wanted things to *get back to normal* so people would stop hovering and worrying over her.

Then she begged God for her to *look like her normal self* again.

To *walk normal* again.

Now, she found herself pleading to *feel normal* again.

So much time had passed that she didn't even know what that meant anymore.

Enough was enough. Rather than going back to her room, which was her regular routine, she should do something different.

Ruth left her office and limped her way out to the rim. It had been far too long since she'd enjoyed a sunset. And there was no more beautiful place on earth to watch it than here.

Forcing herself to do this was harder than she imagined. As much as she hated for people to watch her struggle to walk, it was good for her.

At least that's what she kept saying to herself.

But she wasn't convinced.

The voluminous clouds in the sky turned deep shades of orange as they chased the setting sun. The canyon below deepened into a dark rusty color in the shadows and lit up like gold where the sun still caressed its ridges and folds.

This. This was something to be thankful for. People all over the world would never have the opportunity to see this amazing piece of God's handiwork.

She could see it every day.

There was much to be thankful for. Every day.

But as she scanned the rim and saw couples walking with arms linked, and children skipping and laughing, faces aglow with awe and wonder—her heart felt broken. Unwanted. Unworthy.

Finding a place to settle herself away from gawking eyes, she lowered herself to a large rock and breathed deep.

*Father, I'm struggling. Not that You don't already know that. But it's been two years. When Doc examined my leg today, I was hopeful. Just like every time I've seen him. Hopeful that there would be some good news. Some turn of events that meant I would improve and walk normally again. But no. He said I need more time. Time. Always more time. Hasn't it been long enough?*

She looked down at her hands. It wasn't her place to question God. She'd been pouring out her heart to the Lord for so long. Time was always the word that came to her. *Time* and *wait*. Was she being horribly impatient?

Two long years had passed since the attack of the mountain lion.

Two years since her leg had been shredded by the fierce beast. Her face imprinted with deep gashes from its paw.

Two years since she'd felt like herself and knew who she was.

Two years since she'd thrown herself in harm's way. At the time, she hadn't thought twice. To lay her life down for her friends was what she was supposed to do. Especially when the question of a friend's eternity was uncertain.

Every day for two years, she'd told herself she would do it again.

And she would.

Wouldn't she?

Of course she would.

Julia hadn't known the Lord then, and if Ruth hadn't stepped in front of her friend on the trail in the canyon that day? The thought made her stomach turn. They could have lost sweet, vivacious Julia.

Mr. Owens had been gracious about giving Ruth book work to do and having her still train the incoming waitresses the first few months. But oh, how she'd second-guessed herself. In fact, she'd been determined to leave at one particularly low point, after a little boy asked her what happened to her face.

He'd held no guile or malice toward her. It had been a simple question. But it had torn her in two. Whenever she was discouraged, his words came back to her.

*God, I'm so sorry I'm complaining. Thank You for keeping me here. For Mr. Owens giving me this position. Please show me where I'm failing. I should be grateful I'm alive. That even though I'm a single woman, You have provided for me. Thank You.*

A tear slipped out and made a slow trail down her scarred cheek. She reached up and patted it away gently, hoping that the makeup was still there to cover the ugliness.

Makeup. A few years ago, she would have scorned the thought she'd ever need to use it. Then again, she never thought she'd still be single as she faced her thirty-fifth birthday.

As each one of the girls in her care had married over the years, she'd longed to find love herself. Knew that if she stayed focused on the Lord that He would bring the right man to her. Someday.

That dream died a slow, excruciating death the last two years.

*Stop it*. It was time to stop feeling sorry for herself. This was where things took a turn for the worse. Every time. How many girls had she guided and advised over the years? Whenever any of them would wallow in self-pity, she was quick to nip it in the bud. Turn their focus around. Get them to think on all the things they were grateful for and look toward the positive aspects of their lives.

Taking her own advice seemed like swallowing a bitter pill at the moment, but it was better than this seesaw of emotions.

Grateful. There was so much to be grateful about—more than just the view.

The wounds on her face had healed nicely. Sure, there were scars, but she could cover them up.

Her job at the hotel was prestigious. It gave her purpose. She still had both of her legs. And she could walk.

Yes, she was grateful for that. But was it so wrong to want more?

Lifting her shoulders a touch, she watched all the people walking in the distance.

Maybe it was time to stop hoping that the doctor would say something different. Maybe she should try to see another doctor in Williams. Or even Flagstaff. It might be embarrassing to show someone else her scars, but perhaps there was some new medicine that could help. Or perhaps exercises to make her leg stronger. It couldn't hurt to look around and at least try, right? Her heart lifted with the hope.

"Miss Ruth! Miss Ruth!" The young voice called to her from the Hopi House. Ruth turned her gaze and watched Sunki run toward her. The beautiful young girl was growing so much.

She held out her arms. "Sunki, it is so good to see you!"

The girl ran into her outstretched arms and hugged her. With her hands on either side of Ruth's face, she looked at both sides. "Your scar is going away." The little girl frowned.

"Why do you look sad about that?"

"I liked it. It was pretty."

For a moment, Ruth was taken aback. What was pretty about a scar?

"But you're still pretty." Sunki shrugged. "Will you come weave baskets soon? Or make jewelry? I can teach you. Mr. Chris says I learned real good."

"I would love to. But it will probably need to wait a bit. I have a lot of work to do."

The girl's face fell.

"But don't worry, I'll let you teach me."

"Okay." Sunki turned on her bare feet. "Mama will look for me. Bye!"

How long had it been since she'd even gone into the Hopi House? Too long. Which meant she hadn't seen Chuma or Humeatah, and both women had become dear to her. Her heart twinged with guilt. She'd seen the children playing a few times and had waved, but that was it. And after all the women had done to help take care of her . . . she hadn't shown her appreciation very well, had she?

"Why, good evening, Ruth." Frank's familiar voice floated on the air behind her.

It sent a little shiver up her spine. Was her scar hidden? She adjusted her skirts and pasted on a smile. "Good evening to you, Frank."

"It's nice to see you out here. It's been a while." He sauntered closer and pointed to the boulder she sat on. "May I?"

"Of course." She scooted over to give him plenty of room. "How's the job of head chef treating you?"

He grinned so wide it almost touched his ears. "Fabulous. Better than I ever imagined. Can't believe almost a month has passed."

"You're an excellent chef, Frank. Yesterday, I tried the new beef tips recipe you said you were working on. Delicious." She licked her lips just thinking about the savory dish.

"I'm so glad you enjoyed it."

"The addition of the pearl onions and whole mushrooms made it one of the best things I've ever eaten."

"High praise indeed. Thank you." He turned his face to her, his cheeks ruddy. "What brings you out here this evening?"

She stiffened. Frank knew her well. Probably better than anyone else. But she wasn't ready to admit to the constant turmoil inside her. "I forced myself to come out here. It had been too long since I watched God paint the sky with one of His sunsets."

"How's your leg feeling?" Leave it to Frank to ask the question that no one else dared ask.

"Same as always." She shrugged.

"Didn't you see Dr. Collins today?"

"Yes, but nothing new." It sounded depressing as soon as she said it. "I'm thinking of trying to see another doctor."

"Oh?" He tipped his head back and forth. "Might be worth it to get another opinion."

"Really? You agree?"

"Of course. It's a wise idea." He lifted his foot to the boulder and wrapped his hands around his bent knee.

She raised her chin a bit. "Good. Then I'll do it."

"Other than that, how are you doing?" His deep green eyes drew her in.

"I'm fine."

"Ruth." A shock of reddish hair fell across his forehead when he tipped his head. "Is that all I get? Fine?"

This man had been with her through many ups and downs. Why was she holding back? The prodding inside her to open up to him made words gush out. "I'm feeling stuck, Frank. With my wounds, with my position here at the hotel, even with God." She shook her head. "Something needs to change. Like I need to shake things up somehow . . . do something to make it all better."

"Makes sense to me." His gaze went back to the sunset.

"It does?" All this time, she'd thought she was crazy for feeling the way she did.

"Sure. You're pretty amazing. I've always thought you were feisty. Taking the bull by the horns, proverbially speaking." He held up both of his hands like he was surrendering. "Don't get mad, just being honest."

She swatted at his arm. One of their regular habits. He teased. She swatted. "I'm not mad. I thought maybe *you* thought I was too proper to do something different . . . or drastic."

He chuckled. "As long as you're not thinking of leaving *here*"—he pointed to the ground—"I'll stand beside you and cheer you on while you try whatever you think you need to do to shake things up."

"You're a good friend, Frank."

He shrugged. "Eh, maybe mediocre . . ."

Laughter bubbled up as she swatted him again. It felt good to laugh with him. In fact, it felt . . . *normal*. If only she could revel in it forever.

"So, what's making you feel stuck with God?"

Once again, he made her feel comfortable and then asked the hard question. Their relationship had never been one to chat about the weather and all the social niceties. Ruth took a long inhale. "I opened the door for that."

"Yep. But I'm always here for you . . . ready to listen."

The sun was almost down now, so the light wouldn't last for long. Best to get it all out. Frank would understand. He always did. "My feelings go up and down every day. I try to be grateful and positive, and then I feel sorry for myself and feel down. I'm tired of the constant uncertainty. Nothing is the same as it was before. Like I said . . . I feel stuck. I pour everything out to God and then feel horrible for complaining. I know I should be grateful to be alive and to have both of my legs, but I miss who I used to be and what I used to look like and what I used to be able to do."

"You worry about what people think of you."

Yep. He understood. "To put it bluntly, yes."

"It's a trap we all fall into."

She got to her feet and wobbled back and forth to gain her balance. "But I didn't used to have this struggle. I'm about to turn thirty-five, Frank. I've always wanted to be married and have a family and now I don't see how that can ever happen."

Once the words were out, she couldn't take them back. She'd never told *anyone* that.

"Don't put limits on God, Ruth. His timing is always perfect."

"Your words are sincere, and I know they're true, but to be honest, they sound like Christian platitudes at the moment." She placed her hands on her hips. "I never thought that my whole perspective would change like this."

"You went through a traumatic event—"

"I know. Everyone knows." With a hand pointing to her heart, she looked down at him. "But no one knows what the outward wounds and scars have done in here." She shook her head. "Not even me."

More than anything, she wanted to be back out on the floor in the dining room as the headwaitress. Make sure things ran smoothly, help her girls. Guide them. But that wasn't meant to be anymore. The thought crushed her.

Frank's face softened in the waning twilight, and he held her gaze. Coming to his feet, he took one of her hands. "Then let's figure it out together. You're not alone, you know."

Staring into his green eyes, she actually felt like there was hope to make it through this storm of life. "I—"

"Miss Anniston! Miss Anniston!" One of the newer girls, Jennifer, waved an arm as she walked briskly toward them.

Ruth released Frank's hand and stepped a pace back as her heart raced. What could be wrong?

The girl put a hand to her chest as she got close and took several deep breaths. "Mr. Owens has been looking all over for you and Mr. Henderson. He needs to see you immediately."

---

Emma Grace Watkins rushed to the front door, opened it to the Millers, and held out her arms to Julia. "It's been way too long!" Hugging her friend, she heard the husbands greet each other with claps on the back and most likely a hearty handshake.

"Thank you for allowing us to invite ourselves over." Julia squeezed her shoulders and then pulled back.

"We're glad to have you. With everything going on, we tend to let too much time slip between visits." Emma Grace's husband, Ray, smiled at their guests as he held out a hand toward the parlor. "Please, come in. Make yourselves at home."

Her heart swelled as she watched Chris and Julia chat with her husband. Every day there was another reminder of how much she had to be thankful for—and how grateful to God she was that He had led her here to the canyon.

Julia's voice brought her attention back. "Let me see how the little one has grown." She clasped her hands together.

"She's asleep at the moment, but probably not for long. For some reason dinner wasn't to her liking and she made sure to let us know. Fell asleep right there at the table in the middle of a fit." Emma Grace took a seat next to Ray. He put an arm around her shoulders. "I wish I'd known how difficult a toddler can be." She let out a sigh and rolled her eyes.

"You two are doing a wonderful job." Her friend sent a sympathetic gaze. "Hopefully Chris and I don't spoil her too much when she comes over while you two are in Williams."

That made her laugh. "Goodness, I'm sure you do, because she loves nothing more than when we hop on the train. Auntie Julia and Uncle Chris are her favorite people. But we wouldn't have it any other way. We can't thank you enough for all the times you've taken care of our little scamp."

Julia leaned forward. "Well, I'm sure you're probably wondering why I asked for us all to meet like this."

Ray's low voice rumbled beside her. "Whatever it is, it's a welcome chance for us to see our friends."

"Agreed." Emma Grace raised her eyebrows at their friends. "I completely forgot to offer you anything. Coffee? Tea?"

Chris waved a hand at them. "We don't want you to go to any trouble. We are fine."

Julia bounced a bit on her seat. "I'll get right to it. I can't believe it's already the end of May. Ruth's thirty-fifth birthday is in less than two months."

Why hadn't she thought of that? Her insides swirled. Just the thought of her precious friend and how little time they'd spent together since Emma Grace had given birth made her grimace. "You're right. I completely forgot."

"Well, I'd like to throw her a big surprise party. A picnic." The grin that stretched across Julia's face practically lit up the room.

"What a wonderful idea." Ray leaned forward. "How can I help?"

"Since you go back and forth to Williams so much, it would be great if you could start bringing items back with you. I've already begun to gather supplies, but we need to get them up here. She won't suspect you to be our party smuggler." Julia looked at Chris and then back at them. "I know how instrumental Ruth has been in all of our lives, I'd love to have a special gift from the four of us. To thank her for everything she poured into us."

There was something special about their connection. The relationships they'd shared with Ruth were deep. The older woman had been much more than just a friend. She'd been a mentor, a confidante, a loving shoulder, an encourager, and like a big sister. "Could Chris create something for her? A broach, perhaps?"

Christopher Miller was an incredible jeweler. If anyone could make something unique for Ruth, it was him.

He leaned forward. "I would be honored to do that. Any particular color?"

"Blue." Emma Grace piped up. "To match her eyes. Ruth has the most beautiful eyes."

"Oh yes!" Julia clapped her hands together lightly. "That will be perfect."

For the next several minutes, Julia regaled them with all the ideas she'd had. It would be a lovely picnic. Hopefully Ruth would be surprised.

But a niggling at the back of Emma Grace's mind wouldn't let her go. When was the last time she and Ruth had a real heart-to-heart? Married life had never kept her from her friend before . . . but having a child definitely had. Guilt settled on her chest. Ruth had been through a lot.

Then Emma Grace had the baby . . . and well, she hadn't been there. At least Julia had.

"Emma Grace?" Julia broke through her thoughts.

"I'm sorry. What did you say?"

"I didn't mean to take the conversation on a downturn, but I'm worried about Ruth. I hardly ever see her anymore. Neither do any of the other girls. They say she stays in her office almost all the time. . . ."

"Really? She doesn't even help with any of the training?"

"No. Tessa handles all of that. Ruth will come and say a few words here and there, but nothing like what we were all used to." Julia sniffed. "Tessa came to me in tears the other day because she feels so alone. It's hard being the headwaitress without support, and she has had another unruly group. Several girls have been let go, and she's having to replace them and train the new girls in record speed."

Emma Grace frowned. "Ruth always made it look easy, but even with both of us, it often felt like an impossible job."

Julia's eyes widened as she gave an emphatic nod. "I know! I'll never understand how Ruth handled everything that she did. And she loved it. Loved teaching us and training us. I feel like something must be very wrong for her to sequester herself away like this."

The guilt deepened in Emma Grace's chest. That wasn't like the Ruth she'd known at all. The question that plagued her earlier returned. When was the last time they'd taken the time to chat? *Really* chat? She couldn't even recall.

Had she completely missed that her friend had spiraled?

# 3

Holding on to Frank's arm, Ruth walked alongside him as fast as she dared. Thankful for her companion's steady and slow stride, she tried to rein in her emotions. After all she'd shared, she felt better, but they hadn't finished their discussion. What did Frank think of her now? No. She had to put that aside. The real question was, what could their manager want?

He hadn't seen them talking together and thought something was . . . going on? Did he? The Harvey rules were very strict about employees courting one another.

No. That was ridiculous. She and Frank had been good friends for years and had spent plenty of time chatting together. Mr. Owens knew that.

So what was it?

"Don't worry." Frank's calm voice failed to soothe her rattled nerves.

"Why do you think I'm worrying?"

"Because you have a death grip on my arm, and you're biting your lip." He sent her a side grin.

He knew her too well. Loosening her grip, she licked her lips and clamped her mouth shut so she wouldn't be tempted to go back at it.

"Am I going too fast?"

"Not at all. But thank you for asking." In another time and place, she would tell him how much it meant to her. Somehow he seemed to know the perfect pace where she could walk and not feel like she would tumble over at any moment.

They walked the rest of the way in silence. Not an awkward silence, but the good kind, the kind that between friends felt comfortable. Right.

He patted her hand that gripped his arm and then opened the door for her to enter the hotel. "Let's go find out what Mr. Owens needs."

With a dip of her chin, she entered the hotel and headed toward the manager's office. When she tapped on the door, it opened almost immediately.

"Oh good. Jennifer found you." Mr. Owens let out a sigh. "Please, please. Come in."

She walked in and took a seat in one of the chairs. Her leg ached from the walk, but she couldn't say anything. Neither of them needed to be burdened with her struggle. Her weakness.

Frank took the seat next to her, and Mr. Owens closed the door and then walked around the desk and stood looking down at the papers in front of him.

"I need your help. But first, I need both of you to give me your word that you will speak of this to no one." The expression on his face was serious. Much more so than normal.

"Of course, sir." Ruth nodded at him.

"Anything you need. You have my word." Frank lifted an ankle to settle on his other knee. He put a hand to his face and rubbed at his mustache.

Their manager placed both of his hands on his desk and leaned toward them. "I believe someone is stealing from the hotel."

Her eyes widened. That wasn't what she was expecting to hear. Never had she worked in a place where there had been thefts. At least not that she knew of. "Are they stealing from the guests?"

"No." Mr. Owens shook his head. "Thankfully, no. But for several weeks now, the books haven't added up. I haven't had enough time to investigate thoroughly since Mr. Hammond, our bookkeeper down in Williams, died. His replacement hired by the company got sick as soon as he came here and had to move back to California, so I'm waiting for yet another replacement. Apparently, the area is not enticing for most men with families."

He paused and took a deep breath. "I have been doing my best to stay on top of everything. As long as all the big numbers add up with the bank, everything's fine. But they don't. At first, I was certain it was a clerical mistake. But now that I've spoken with the bank and have taken a closer look, I'm certain that someone has either made a huge mistake, or someone *is* stealing from the hotel. The deposits don't line up with what is on paper."

"How do you need our assistance?" Frank leaned forward. Mr. Owens took his seat and wiped a hand down his face. "You two are my most trusted employees. You have been with the company the longest and understand the inner workings. I need you both to keep your eyes open for anything amiss. Be on high alert and let me know if you see anything—anything at all—that is out of the ordinary."

He looked straight at her. "Ruth, I know you won't be thrilled with this, but I need you to go back to double-checking the books. It has been wonderful to have you take over the supervisory role for the kitchen and dining room, but my duties have continued to grow as the hotel has gotten busier and busier."

She swallowed. Bookkeeping had never been her favorite, but she could do it. "Of course I will help. Do you need me to stay later each evening?"

"I know you are already very busy. But yes, if you could put in some extra time, I would be forever grateful. I'm sorry to ask such a monumental task of you, but I trust you." Mr. Owens turned to Frank. "You've just taken over as head chef, but I need you to go back over the past six months of orders for the kitchen. It might seem a bit hefty of an ask, since there weren't discrepancies before Mr. Hammond died, but if we do have someone nefarious behind all this, I want to be thorough. It's hard for me to imagine that it started all of a sudden. Check for any discrepancies. And if you could assist Ruth once a week in doing a triple-check of the books, I would greatly appreciate it. At least until a new bookkeeper is found."

"Yes, sir." Frank nodded.

"When do you have to report this to the Harvey Company?" Ruth grimaced and twisted her hands. She would hate to be in the manager's position at a time like this.

"Wishful thinking would be never. But that could only happen if we discover that it has been clerical mistakes along the way. We're all busy, and sometimes our handwriting is rushed. I can't assume that, though, because that would mean multiple mistakes were overlooked. We've been perfect in our records since we opened, so I can only presume there's something more to this. I'd like to have a handle on it before I have to alert the company, but if it continues, I will have no choice." Once again, he plopped down into his chair.

"I'm sorry, Mr. Owens. Rest assured, I will get to work

on it right away." She reached for the books. "Let me take them back to my office now."

"It's late. It can definitely wait until morning. You both need your rest." The manager handed the books over. "Your schedules are already very full, I know that, but I appreciate your willingness to help. Since we don't know who could be behind this, I will remind you of the need for confidentiality. Only speak to each other or to me about anything amiss. Understood?"

"Of course, sir. We'll get this figured out." Frank stood and took the books from Ruth. "Let me carry those to your office for you."

"Thank you." Coming to a standing position wasn't always the easiest especially after a long day, but she managed it without too much trouble.

"One more thing, Miss Anniston."

She turned. "Yes, sir?"

Mr. Owens looked away. "The discrepancies are all with the dining room and kitchen. You are excellent at what you do—rest assured, I know that. But if we can't figure out who is doing this and *how* they are doing it, then I will have to report it. . . . The last thing I would ever do is blame you . . ." He clamped his mouth shut and didn't finish the thought.

But she got the point. Loud and clear. No woman had been in such a high role of management in the Harvey Company before. No doubt, the blame *would* be thrown at her feet, whether it was her fault or not.

A month at the El Tovar Hotel had helped Charles Goodall learn all the names of the staff. Every one of them was kind, courteous, and top-notch. It was the best experience he'd had so far. And that was saying a lot. He lived at luxury resorts. They were his bread and butter, after all.

After spending the winter at the Monteleone in New Orleans this past year, he wasn't sure anything could top the food or service. There, he'd only had to complain about a couple of staff a handful of times.

Let's see, which resort would be next as top on his list? The Crescent Hotel in Eureka Springs?

No. Now that he thought about it, the food hadn't been up to snuff.

The Grand Hotel on Mackinac Island had certainly poured on the charm. He'd had plenty of customers for his enterprise, that's for sure. But the maids hadn't given him the attention he desired.

Last summer at the Mount Washington Hotel in New Hampshire had been superb, but many of the staff had been snippish.

Ah well, it didn't matter. He was here now.

Flicking his newspaper open, he peered over the top at the dining room full of socialites. Yes, it had been a good idea to summer at the Grand Canyon. A little remote for his taste, but stunning nonetheless.

Simply amazing how Harvey had done it. Convincing the railroad to bring the tracks out here so he could build a hotel. Now the wealthiest and most elite were all clamoring to stay here. Smart move.

Miss Rand, his waitress this morning, appeared at his right elbow and refilled his coffee cup. Her given name was Charlotte, and she always blushed when he complimented her. How long would her innocence last? Surely she'd been tempted by one or two roguish aristocrats along the way.

"Thank you, Miss Rand. Perfect timing as always." Covering his grin with the paper, he took a sip of his coffee. As she walked to the next table, he watched the pink creep into her cheeks.

Observing people—more specifically, the clientele—was his specialty. At this point, he knew everyone who would be staying for the season. The ones who only came for a few days weren't worth his time for the most part. But a well-planted bribe in a valet's pocket could get the tongues to start wagging and keep him busy for months.

Now that he was well established here, it was time to search for his next prey.

"Mr. Goodall? How lovely to see you again." A man in a fine-tailored suit stood next to his table. "Might I join you for a moment?"

Ah. Yes. He recognized the fellow now. "Mr. Lindsey. How are you, old chap? Enjoying the dry air?" Holding out his hand to the chair across from him, he laid his paper down with the other. Last time he'd seen the man, they were at . . . the Palmer House?

"It is good for the lungs." Lindsey adjusted his waistcoat. "After that thick, humid air in Chicago, my doctor thought this would be a nice change of pace."

"Wonderful." He took another sip of coffee. The man had sought him out, so he'd wait for him to continue. Surely this would be beneficial.

Just as expected, Lindsey leaned forward on the table, did a quick check around the room, and spoke in a more hushed tone. "I hate to bother you while you are on vacation, but I recall you helping one of our fellow gentlemen back at the Palmer House."

"I will help if I can." Charles kept his tone relaxed and leaned up against the back of his chair.

"This past spring, our neighbor's dog bit my arm. It has given me a nasty scar that my wife finds quite repulsive. I believe you had a cream to remedy such a thing?" He tilted his head ever so slightly and squinted at him.

"Would your guest like some coffee, Mr. Goodall?" Miss Rand appeared out of nowhere.

"Nothing for me, thank you." Lindsey waved his hand at her.

Charles watched the waitress walk away with a nod and then looked back at the man. "Well, we do want to keep our women happy, don't we?" He tapped the table with a finger. "It may take some time for me to acquire what you need. The ingredients are quite rare."

"Don't worry about the cost. Just tell me what you charge. I'll pay extra to expedite the process. We'll be here until September." Lindsey stood, tucked the chair back under the table, and straightened to his full height. "Thank you, Goodall." With a dip of his chin, he walked away.

Charles leaned forward and took a last swig from his coffee cup.

The games had begun. This summer would be most profitable indeed. In more ways than one.

---

**TUESDAY, MAY 25, 1909**

Didn't take much for Frank to be wound up this morning. Proof of that was in the time it took him to whip the bowl of eggs and milk in front of him into a frothy mixture.

His thoughts spun as the sounds of his kitchen accompanied them. Their rhythm was like the beating of his heart. Scraping, stirring, pounding, kneading. Something was always in the process of creation.

Ever since their conversation last night with Mr. Owens, he'd been on edge, especially after the manager mentioned the discrepancies being in the kitchen and dining room. Which meant if the Harvey Company needed someone to blame, it would be Ruth. For sure there would be comments made about a woman being in a management position.

None of which would be good for her fragile mindset.

Thinking of Ruth as fragile was hard to swallow. But now that he knew how she was really feeling, it made his heart ache even more for her.

Over the last year, he'd watched in agony as she withdrew into herself. Oh, they still saw each other every day and chatted, but she'd put up a wall between her and everyone else. The other Harvey Girls. Emma Grace. Julia. Even him.

And when she'd finally started to open up last night, of course that was when Mr. Owens called them to his office.

He just couldn't win.

He whipped another bowl of eggs with a frenzied hand on the whisk.

Last night had been different. He felt like Ruth had come really close to sharing her deeper feelings. Frank hoped with everything in him that she could care for him. But maybe he'd never know. Two years ago, he'd convinced himself to ask her to consider courtship. It would take all manner of coercing for certain, because of the permission they would have to seek from their boss. But as soon as he'd gathered up his courage, the horrible incident with the mountain lion had occurred. Ever since, he'd waited patiently. And died a little more each day watching her wither away inside herself.

She struggled with feeling unworthy now that she was injured. Her dreams of marriage, though, weren't gone. How could he help her to see that?

It was a lose-lose situation in his mind. If he told her how beautiful she still was, she'd tell him he was simply feeling sorry for her. And if he told her he cared about her, she'd tell him he was simply feeling sorry for her. No matter that he'd had feelings for her since long before the accident. It was too late to tell her. If she hadn't seen it back then, why would she believe him now?

Frank let out a long, frustrated sigh. It was his own fault he was in this mess. Trying to be a good employee, following the rules, keeping his heart in check. Isn't that what the Lord asked of him? And now there was no chance with the one woman he cared about.

He shook his head and tried to focus back on work. His specialty sauce for the pork cutlets wouldn't make itself.

"Chef Henderson, the first dozen quiches are in the ovens." Howard, his new assistant chef, stood in front of him. A lanky thing, the man knew his way around a kitchen and had been a valuable asset.

"Good, good."

"Did you need me to do anything else before I start on the second batch?" The poor guy looked scared of him. Everyone had noticed Frank's intensity that morning. It couldn't be avoided because he was normally so easygoing.

Throwing a towel over his shoulder, Frank aimed a smile at the younger man. "Go ahead with the second batch. Thank you." Somehow he needed to tame his emotions. This wasn't like him. It didn't do any good to have everyone in the kitchen on edge. That's how accidents happened.

Howard nodded and walked away. When he'd first arrived, he told Frank that he dreamed of being a head chef one day. Most chefs did. And competition could be fierce between kitchen staff, but the young man had proven himself efficient and loyal. Always willing to help another of the staff if someone was behind. Not afraid to get dirty and do any of the other jobs in the kitchen if it meant that the guests would be served the very best.

He was exactly what Frank had hoped for in an assistant chef.

Which meant he *could* entrust him with extra responsibility.

As the head chef, Frank had a bit more leeway and could delegate more often, but he didn't want to be out of *his* kitchen more than he had to. Especially since he hadn't been in charge all that long. Definitely not enough to establish his leadership. It was important for him to set the tone and standards as head chef.

He stopped what he was doing and looked around. What was he thinking? His pride was getting in the way. Plain and simple. It was selfish of him to worry about losing the position. No matter how long he'd worked for it.

The kitchen crew respected him. They'd worked together for years. He'd been the second-in-command since the hotel opened, so it's not like he was the new guy who had to prove himself. Why was he hesitating?

Mr. Owens told him he could take off two days a week from the kitchen to help out with the investigation, rather than the normal schedule of one day off. It was *that* important. And Ruth needed him. It's not like he would be giving up his new position.

Glancing around the busy kitchen, Frank looked at each man who worked there. They were all capable. And he trusted them.

The hesitation was totally personal.

Ruth.

Truth be told, he'd been trying to convince himself that he didn't care for her as much as he did. Because watching her for two years had been sheer torture. So, he'd told himself all kinds of untruths. Like, he wouldn't want to ruin their friendship. Or the company would never approve of their courting. Or they were both already so set in their ways.

But last night, it was clearer than ever. He had deep feelings for her.

If he told her now, it would be a disaster. That wouldn't do. Besides, she never gave him any indication that she was interested in him. They weren't supposed to.

There were rules.

Which brought him back to the dilemma at hand. To do what Mr. Owens asked, he'd have to spend even more time with Ruth Anniston. Time that could very well make it even more painful to keep his feelings hidden.

Was he up for that?

The fact of the matter was, her job might be in jeopardy. Where would she go . . . and what would she do if she didn't work for Harvey? It had been her life.

Frank *needed* to help her.

He'd fulfilled his dream of being head chef. Shoot, even if he had to give that up, she was worth it. It was the right thing to do. He'd sacrifice whatever he needed to for her.

# 4

As the train began to slow, Ruth thanked God for the lack of passengers and took the time to massage her leg. While it didn't hurt her in a seated position, it always became stiff after sitting for too long, and she was facing a good deal of walking this morning if she wanted to make it to the bank and to her doctor's appointment before heading back on the afternoon train.

The past few days had given her a lot of time to think about the situation. So far, she couldn't find any mistakes in the ledgers, but that didn't mean they didn't exist. After she looked at the deposits today, hopefully she'd have a better idea of what she should look for in the books. Mr. Owens obviously thought it had something to do with the kitchen orders, since he'd asked Frank for the last six months of them. But they were so complicated and large, she'd need Frank to help her decipher what she was reading. It was almost June. The next three months were their busiest by far. None of them had time for mistakes or discrepancies. Or for someone to be stealing from the hotel.

The thought made her shiver. Who would do such a thing?

The train came to a stop, and she eased herself to her feet. After making sure that her leg would hold her up, she reached for her leather satchel filled with her papers and stepped into the aisle.

Grateful for the handrail on the steps, she took one step at a time, using her good leg for leverage, and made it to the platform without falling on her face. Always a positive.

She didn't have time to cover her limp like she did at the hotel. At this point, she'd be happy to make it to the bank without incident. People didn't know her here like they did at the El Tovar. But her face still flushed every time she noticed someone glancing at her in her periphery.

Praise God the bank wasn't far.

Fifteen minutes later, she entered the bank with sweat beaded on her upper lip. She dabbed it away with her handkerchief and smiled at the manager, who waited for her at the front counter. "Mr. Ackerman. It's lovely to see you again."

"And you, Miss Anniston. When Greg phoned me this morning, I was thrilled to hear we'd get the pleasure of your presence." His broad smile took the attention away from his shiny, bald head as he turned and led her down a long hallway.

Over the past two years as she'd taken on a supervisory role, she'd visited the bank several times. Mr. Ackerman, thankfully, was a man who didn't have a problem with a woman in her position. Unlike most men. Not that she was one to stand up and shout for her rights to have her job, but she did appreciate being able to work as a woman. Since every dream of marriage had vanished, she was forever grateful that the Harvey Company made it possible for women to gain respectable work. Who knew, maybe even one day women would have the right to vote.

Mr. Ackerman led her to a small room at the back of the bank. "I believe I've prepared everything you need, but be sure to let me know if you require any other documents. We are proud to have the El Tovar's business." He held out an arm toward the open door. "Feel free to use this space for as long as you need."

"Thank you." She walked past him to enter the room and found a tray of fruits, pastries, a pitcher of water, and coffee service all laid out in perfect order. "This is lovely, Mr. Ackerman."

He reached for the door handle. "My pleasure." Pulling the door closed, he gave her a slight bow.

It always made her grin when men were gentlemanly. Something that was definitely changing in the modern times. Thankfully, she worked in a place where manners and chivalry were paramount, but every time she ventured out of her little hamlet at the Grand Canyon, she saw the real world with wide eyes.

An hour and a half later, she'd copied down all the numbers and dates she needed and put the papers back in order. Mr. Owens was correct. Things didn't add up. The actual amounts deposited didn't match the numbers between all the ledgers and orders. But prayerfully, between the three of them, they'd be able to figure the puzzle out.

Even though there was no one else in the room, she rubbed her leg while it was hidden by the table still and prepared for another walk. Oh, how she wished she didn't have the telltale limp. For the most part, the severe pain had subsided—other than when she was on her leg for too long—and she didn't fall down as much as she had the first few months. But what she wouldn't give to walk like she used to before that fateful day. To run even.

With a shake of her head, she stood. All the what-ifs in the world couldn't change things. That's why she was taking action.

Time to head to the doctor's office.

Chin lifted ever so slightly, she pasted on a smile and headed back out to the bank lobby. With a nod to the receptionist, she shuffled her way to the door and exited.

Out on the boardwalk, the dust from a passing motorcar caused her to cough. But she waved the brown cloud away and continued down the street. If only Arizona wasn't so dusty and dry. Or if all the streets were paved. Wouldn't that be a wonder?

Her skirts would definitely benefit from that. Not to mention her boots that had to be shined at least once a day. Even more so if she ventured out to the canyon—which she used to do almost every day.

Oh, to get back to that. She wouldn't even mind having to polish her boots more often.

That was the spirit. The fighting spirit that made her Ruth Anniston. She needed to hold on to this feeling and keep it at the forefront so that she could keep the negative ones at bay.

When she entered the small building that was the doctor's residence, a lovely woman around her same age with a navy skirt, white shirtwaist, and light blue ribbon around her collar came to greet her. "You must be Miss Anniston."

"Yes. I am Ruth Anniston." She nodded.

"I'm Anna. My husband is Doctor Newport. But he prefers everyone to call him James. Follow me to the examining room, please." The woman was gracious and warm. It instantly set Ruth at ease.

*Lord, please let this doctor have some answers for me.*

The room Anna led her to was a simple one, with cheery yellow curtains at the window and a raised couch covered in a clean white sheet. "Would you like to change out of your clothes into a robe, or would you prefer removing your stocking on the injured leg?"

Ruth gripped the front of her skirt in a fist. This was the part she hated. The slashes the mountain lion made had been deep in her upper thigh. "I think I would prefer removing my stocking and then I can lift my skirt."

"Whatever is most comfortable for you. Let me move this screen over to give you a bit of privacy." The foldable white screen opened up and blocked the door.

"Mrs. Newport?" Ruth cleared her throat, trying to get rid of the hesitation she heard in her own voice.

The woman peeked around the screen. "Please, call me Anna."

"Anna. I know I told you the story of my injuries over the phone. But would you mind staying with me while your husband examines my leg?"

"I don't mind one bit. You let us know if anything at all makes you uncomfortable." Anna stepped back behind the screen. "Let me know when you are ready and I'll go get my husband."

Removing her boot and stocking didn't take much time. Ruth positioned herself on the couch. Back ramrod straight. "All right. I'm ready."

It had taken every ounce of willpower she had to call the new doctor in Williams and ask to see him. Anna had answered the phone, and it had made it much easier for Ruth to convey everything to the woman. She was as warm and genuine in person as she had been over the phone.

But now that footsteps sounded in the hall, Ruth put a hand to her heart. She'd never met Dr. Newport, and it made her nervous. What if he didn't give her good news?

"Miss Anniston." The doctor walked around the modesty screen and nodded as he entered. His dark hair was speckled with gray. "It's nice to meet you. I'm Dr. Newport, but please, call me James."

She swallowed and sent him a nervous smile.

"Anna has filled me in on why you are here today. I am sorry to hear about what happened to you, but I am very thankful you are alive and have all your limbs." He paused and stared. Raised his eyebrows.

This was where she was supposed to say something. She cleared her throat. "Yes. Me too."

He stepped closer. "It's been two years since your injury?"

"Yes." Her mouth felt like it was filled with cotton. She swallowed again.

Anna seemed to understand her distress. "Let me get you a glass of water."

Dr. Newport stepped another foot closer. "I can barely see the scar on your face. That's quite a stitching job Doctor Collins did."

Instinctively, she put a hand to her face. "He said he made them as small and as close together as he could so that it would heal better." Deep breath. "I do wear makeup to cover it up."

"There's nothing wrong with that. I wouldn't even know it was there if my wife hadn't told me."

That was encouraging. But every day when she looked in the mirror, she could see it. It was the first thing she *always* saw. Raging and red. Screaming that she was deformed and ugly. "I would like to not have to wear all the powder to cover it."

"Scars do fade with time."

Anna returned with a glass of water, and Ruth took it with a shaky hand. After she took several sips, she handed the glass back. Straightened her shoulders and lifted her chin. "I'm really hoping to get your opinion about my leg. Doctor Collins believes that I need to continue to rest it so that it can heal, but I was hoping there would be something— anything—that I could try that would help me to walk better."

The doctor nodded and moved closer. His brows had dipped. "I will gladly take a look at it."

After several agonizing moments of him poking and prodding her leg, he let her skirt fall back over her legs. "Would you walk a few steps back and forth for me? Don't try and hide the limp. Walk as naturally as you can."

She slid off the couch and gained her balance. Then walked across the room. Then back.

The doctor's mouth was pursed, and his eyes narrowed as if he was thinking with great intent. He tapped his chin with a finger.

"Is there a chance my leg can get better?" Desperation pushed the words from her lips. "That I'll be able to walk without the limp?"

Doctor Newport appeared to weigh the question for several moments. "The human body is incredible and amazes us at every turn. The wounds appear to be very deep and that takes time to heal—knit back together. Doctor Collins' advice to rest and let things heal *was* good."

"But . . . do I still need to be resting it?"

"Miss Anniston, have you heard the term *atrophy*?"

Ruth shook her head. "No, I don't believe I have."

"People who are in serious accidents and find themselves

unable to use their arms or legs after a long recuperation have a condition that we call atrophy. It's where the muscles and tissue decline because they haven't been used. Now, since you are still walking on your leg, you haven't had a severe case of it, but there is a big difference between the muscles in your left leg and the muscles in your right. Your left leg has taken the bigger burden of carrying your weight since your right hasn't had the strength. In fact, your left leg is almost twice the size of your right. It shows great strength and muscle."

Ruth glanced down. With her legs under her skirts, she couldn't see them, but was her left leg really that much larger?

"There are cases where patients have gained a good deal of mobility and strength from exercising. Most of the cases have been men, which is why Doctor Collins probably hesitated from prescribing any other treatment. Women and men heal differently. On top of the fact that it will be a great deal of work. Especially with as much muscle mass as you have lost."

"I'm not afraid of hard work, Doctor." She'd held on to every word he said. Dare she believe it could be true? She bit her lip. And then barreled on with her questions. "Tell me about the exercises. How many of them? Are they difficult? There's truly hope for me to improve? For my leg to get stronger and possibly close to normal?"

A soft smile covered his face while he chuckled. "I can understand your eagerness, Miss Anniston, I can. And while I can't say that it's certain, I do believe that if you begin to exercise your leg to make it stronger, there is a good chance that it will improve."

The smile that stretched across her face made the scar pull, but she didn't care. "Can you show me the exercises?"

"Yes."

After twenty minutes, Ruth felt like she had an understanding of what the exercises entailed.

"There is one more thing I might suggest."

Eager to hear anything else that might give her hope, she bit her lip again.

"I met a man a few weeks ago who had used a treatment with great success from someone he'd met down in Louisiana. He had a sizable scar over his lip that healed quite nicely. The reason I bring it up is because the man who sold him the treatment is staying at the El Tovar, I'm told. I've heard he only sells to the wealthy because the treatments cost a good deal of money, but his name is Charles Goodall. I've thought of contacting him myself but haven't had the time yet."

Ruth had met Mr. Goodall on several occasions. He was quite a wealthy man himself by all appearances and was there to "summer" at the El Tovar like so many of the other people of influence.

"You're thinking it might help the scar on my face?"

"Perhaps. But again, it's barely visible as you have it covered, so maybe that's not an option worth looking into." He shrugged. "It could help the scarring on your leg, though."

Ruth looked over to Anna, who sent her another warm smile. "You're a lovely woman, Ruth."

Said the *very* lovely woman who didn't have a scar on her face that she had to hide with thick makeup. Ruth closed her eyes against the ugly thought and opened them again, determined to smile at the compliment. "Thank you, Anna." Ruth turned to the doctor. "And thank you, Doc—uh, James. You've given me lots to consider."

The busiest rush of the season was about to start next week, and Frank and Ruth hadn't been able to find much of anything. Most Saturdays, like every other day, he was in the kitchen. But today was his day off, and he'd promised to help Ruth all day. She'd been determined that if they put their heads together and examined everything, they could figure it out.

Easier said than done.

Frank puzzled over all the books in front of him. For three hours, they'd been quoting numbers to each other and trying to check between books. But he'd looked at them so much that he was confused. Shaking his head, he turned to Ruth and grimaced. "Tell me what each of these are for again?"

She put her pencil down and gave him a half-laugh. "I know exactly what you're thinking, Frank. You're about as into the math and numbers all in neat little rows as I am, aren't you? Who am I kidding? I can barely remember which number should be where, so you probably are ahead of me at this juncture."

A long, exasperated sigh left her lips. "All right. Let's start again." She pointed. "This one is all the deposits and with-drawals from the bank. It *should* line up with the actual deposit sheets from the bank." Her hand went to the one on the right. "This one is for all income for the hotel. The red one next to it is for all the expenses of the hotel. The smaller one next to it is for the payments to the employees, although this number is included in the expenditure ledger."

She stood up and reached for another one across her desk. "Then this one is the one that is used at the front desk. It shows all the guests, their names, how many per room, how long they are staying, et cetera, et cetera. Total end charges."

"What about the green and blue ones over there?"

"Green is for all supplies ordered for the hotel. Blue is orders for the dining room, which includes the kitchen. This smaller blue ledger is also for the dining room, but for income. All guests of the hotel are on the American plan, which pays for their food, but we feed a lot of people *other* than guests staying at the hotel. *Everything* has to be itemized."

He squinted and then rubbed at his eyes. "The goal is to make sure that the deposits and withdrawals from the bank line up with everything else in these ledgers. But I'm getting confused about which one goes to which."

"I know." She stood and stretched, then placed her hands on her hips. "Let's see . . ." She moved the books around on her desk. "Ideally, this one that shows the deposits and withdrawals from the bank has to line up with the income ledger and the expenditure ledger." She lined them up, then pointed. "Then the employee pay ledger, the green ledger, and the large blue ledger all need to add up for the expenditure ledger. While the front desk ledger and the smaller blue ledger need to add up for the income ledger."

"All right. I think I've got it." He raised his eyebrows and took a sharp inhale. "That's a lot of comparing."

"Yes." She let out a long sigh, and her shoulders slumped. "It's so very tedious. It's a big hotel with a lot of staff, and every time I think I have it figured out, I realize that all the numbers are blurring together."

Frank leaned back in his chair and studied her face. "Let's say there *is* someone stealing from the hotel and this is not all a big mistake. Would they have to understand how the books work? Or could someone have gotten to them and tried to change them?"

Leaning back in her chair as well, she stared at the ceiling.

"You know, I don't see how anyone could access the books. Mr. Owens keeps them locked up. Well, other than the one at the front desk and the one at the dining room. But they are watched. Someone is with them at all times—that is, until they are locked up at night. Those ledgers don't contain the overall big numbers."

"Hmmm. All right. So let's put those two aside." He held his hands out and widened his eyes. "At this point, there are too many things to look at. We need to simplify, don't you think?"

She nodded and sat up straight. "That's a good point. We should take one thing at a time instead of trying to look at the big picture."

"Exactly." He picked up a pencil again and took another deep breath. This one long and steady. "So, where do we start? Where are the discrepancies, exactly?"

"The expenditures for the kitchen and dining room. In the ledgers, they're smaller than what has actually been paid out."

Frank reached over to a pile of papers beside him. "Okay, well, I brought my handwritten lists of what I had Howard order for the kitchen. Let me go through these and look at the expenditures."

"Then I will go through all the lists of items ordered for the dining room, like service ware and linens. Then there's all the cleaning of the linens." She sifted through piles of paperwork. "This could take a while to put together and double-check."

"That's why I'm here. We can do this. One small chunk at a time, right?"

A knock to Ruth's door was the precursor to Mr. Owens poking his head in. "How are things going in here?"

Frank let out a laugh and looked at their manager. "Math. Lots of math. Exactly how I wanted to spend my day off, sir."

Ruth swatted at him. But the tired lines around her eyes spoke volumes. They'd been at this for a long time without any indication of an end in sight. In fact, they'd barely begun.

"Any chance there are any other ledgers we're missing?" Frank shifted in his chair.

The manager shook his head. "That's all of them. I know it's daunting, and I apologize, but we have to find the issue. June tenth will be a month since I found the first discrepancy. If we can't figure it out and fix it by then, I have to report it to the Harvey Company."

Today was the twenty-ninth of May. That didn't give them a whole lot of time.

The manager swiped at his face. "I'll go get us some lunch and coffee. I have a couple of hours that I should be able to spend with you in here unless there's some sort of emergency. Every set of eyes should help."

"Thank you, Mr. Owens. That sounds wonderful." Ruth already had the pencil back in her hand as she studied the papers in front of her.

But Frank's stomach felt like a ball of dough had dropped down into it and was trying to drag his gut to his feet. May tenth was just a week after he became the head chef. His face heated up. This couldn't be his fault, could it? What if *he* messed up somewhere?

There was a good chance he wouldn't have his job for long. No matter how much Mr. Owens liked him.

# 5

Now that Ruth knew the word *atrophy* and what it meant, she *really* disliked it. Especially after everything it took for her to even attempt these so-called exercises. Doctor Newport hadn't been kidding when he said it would hurt.

Hurt was too mild a word. Multiply that by one hundred and it might be in the same realm of what she was feeling. She'd had to stuff a rag in her mouth to bite on so she didn't cry out and have any number of girls come running down the hall thinking she was in distress.

She let out a huff and sat back down on her bed. For two days, she'd tried to move her leg the way he'd instructed her.

Each time, it discouraged her more because it simply wasn't working. Why hadn't she noticed how much movement she'd lost? Maybe if she'd tried sooner, or if Doctor Collins had told her about this at the beginning, maybe things wouldn't be so bad two years later.

With sweat across her forehead, she shook her head. No. That wasn't kind. Dr. Collins had saved her leg. It wasn't his fault.

She needed to try harder now that she knew what to do. Even if it took another two years, she had to be willing to try. There had to be hope.

Testing her leg while she sat down, she lifted her knee an inch or so. While she could do that movement, her leg also felt like it had a basket of stones on top of it. And she couldn't move her leg to the side. So she stood up. She could slide her foot and leg forward and backward. Like a step. But not out to the side.

Ruth rubbed at the scars. The lion's claws had ripped through her leg from her hip on the side, around the front of her leg, and then down to about four inches above her knee. Dr. Collins had lectured her over and over about how much tissue and muscle had to heal. Every time she'd begged to be allowed up on her feet. Patience had not been one of her virtues back then.

Apparently, it still wasn't.

But she would always remember how sad his voice had been when he told her that parts of her leg would never be the same again because of scar tissue. Did that mean there wasn't any hope? Was she fighting a losing battle?

The clock on the table by her bed chimed. It was late, and she was tired. Maybe she should try the exercises in the morning rather than after a long day.

The only problem with that was her leg was always so stiff when she first woke up that she had to rub it down for several minutes before she could even stand.

Either way, tomorrow was another day.

Tap tap tap.

The light knock on her door brought her attention back up. Even though she was no longer the headwaitress, the girls still often sought out her counsel. Although she'd kept all of them at arm's length and sent them on to Tessa most of the time. Swiping a hand over her hair, she made her way to the door and opened it.

"Charlotte!" Seeing her friend brought a smile to her face. "Come in." Ruth waited for the charming brunette to enter and then shut the door. "How are you doing?"

The girl leaned in for a hug. "I'm doing well. Busy, as you can imagine. But doing very well."

Ruth stepped over to her bed and sat down, pointing to the chair with her hand. "Please, sit. That is, if you have a minute."

"I signed up for the bath, and my time is in a few minutes, but I've been wanting to tell you about something that I overheard."

Oh boy. The last thing they needed was another girl who loved to gossip and stir the pot. "From one of the girls? You need to report it to your headwaitress immediately."

Charlotte waved her hands in front of her. "Oh goodness no. Nothing like that. This has nothing to do with another Harvey Girl."

"Good." That eased a bit of her tension.

The other girl noticed the papers on the table. The exercise instructions.

Ruth instinctively reached for them. "I saw another doctor down in Williams, and he gave me exercises to try and strengthen my leg." Why she felt the need to explain herself, she had no idea. It's not like she was trying to hide anything. Fumbling with the pages in her hands, she set them on the bed next to her.

"Is it helping?" The expectation on Charlotte's face couldn't be missed.

Ruth let out a long breath. "No. At least not yet. It's only been a couple of days."

"Well, not to be nosy or anything . . . but that is why I came. One of the guests had another guest come to his table the other morning. In hushed tones, he was asking for a treatment to help with a scar." Charlotte bit her lip.

Ruth perked up at that. "Was the guest Mr. Goodall?"

"Yes. How did you know?"

"Doctor Newport just told me about him! But when I asked Mr. Owens about him, apparently Mr. Goodall is on vacation. He's not here on business."

"Oh. Well, I thought it was worth a try. If the rich people seek him out to help, what he sells must be really good."

Charlotte wasn't wrong about that. It was amazing what you could buy if you had money. But the thing was, Ruth had been working for a long time. She'd saved up a good bit, hoping that one day she'd be able to get married and help make a home with it. It didn't look like that was much of an option right now, so it wouldn't hurt to spend a little of her hard-earned money on something that might help her. . . .

"I couldn't believe how amazing that new dessert was. What did Chef Henderson call it? Croquettes of apples?" Charlotte had obviously continued talking. She licked her lips. "Yum. I told his assistant chef that I wouldn't mind giving my opinion on any of the new desserts they want to try."

Laughter bubbled up. The girl had always had a sweet tooth. "I haven't tried the apples. I'll have to tell Frank that I need to."

"I better get to the bath before I lose my slot." Charlotte hopped up and then hugged her again. "I hope it wasn't silly of me to tell you about Mr. Goodall."

"No. Not silly at all. Thank you for caring." Ruth returned the hug.

"Next time we need to have a longer chat." Charlotte quirked a brow.

"I'm working on a pretty big project for the hotel right now. Perhaps later this summer?" She knew that the girls had been talking about her not having time for them anymore. While it pricked her heart, this was for the best. Besides, they had a headwaitress to turn to.

"All right. I'll hold you to it."

"Sounds good." She let her friend out, closed the door behind her, and leaned against it.

There were a lot of reasons why she needed to keep her distance. Her heart ached to be among the women called to the same position that she had loved for so many years.

With a shake of her head, she limped her way back to her bed. Goodness, the exercises hurt.

It couldn't be a coincidence that she'd been told about Mr. Goodall and his treatments by two different people. It was very unlike her to go and ask for help—especially from one of the guests. Was she brave enough to do it?

—  —

**MONDAY, MAY 31, 1909**

Metal clanking on metal was one of the finest sounds in a kitchen as far as Frank was concerned. Especially first thing in the morning.

It meant clean pots, pans, and utensils were being gathered. Fresh ingredients were being prepped for the next meal. It meant fresh starts. New creations. Savory and tasty food.

It was always invigorating for him to get started in the morning. As the day went on, the temperature would rise. Their aprons would get many spills on them. And the number of dishes used would increase every minute. But he loved it. Every aspect of it.

It was time for the first inspection of the day, and he waited for each man to finish gathering what he needed for his station and then line up for the day's roll call.

Frank had worked with all of these men for many years. Except for Howard. The assistant chef was new, but he was a hard worker and a talented chef. Howard was at the head of the line, with his hands clasped behind his back.

"Good morning, Chef." Howard nodded toward him.

"Morning, Chef Monroe. I would like to see you immediately after roll call, please. Over at my desk."

"Yes, sir."

"Is everything in order?" Frank looked to his second-in-command.

"Yes, sir. All stations are checked, prepped, and have their list of assignments."

"Perfect." Frank walked down the line. "Gentlemen, it's another day that you have the privilege to cook for the best hotel in these United States."

"Yes, Chef." The group's answer was in perfect rhythm.

"And our guests expect the very best from each and every dish we serve them."

"Yes, Chef."

"Let's have another stellar day, shall we?" Frank made it to the end of the line and turned back to face all of them.

"Yes, Chef!" Each man scurried to his station and went straight to work.

The almost military-like morning drill and roll call was something Chef Marques established when he arrived, and it was appreciated by all the men, so Frank didn't have the heart to change it, even though he was much less marching-order oriented. The respect that he had for his mentor was above and beyond his own likes and dislikes.

Chef Marques kept order, and the kitchen ran like clockwork. *That* was something Frank wanted to make sure he continued. It was necessary in an establishment such as the El Tovar.

Frank walked over to his desk, where Howard waited. The younger man looked a bit timid and almost scared. "Howard, I hope I didn't make you feel like you were in any sort of trouble. Rest assured, you're not. But I need all of the orders you've made for the kitchen since you've been here and the receipts you've gathered from any of our suppliers."

"Yes, Chef. It may take me a bit of time to gather up everything properly. When do you need them by?"

"Tomorrow morning, first thing. I have my handwritten notes to you about what needed to be ordered, but I don't have the actual slips. It was an adjustment for me to go from assistant chef to head chef. I had a system for how I did the orders, and I'm sure you will establish your own system. But I need the paperwork from you so that we can accurately balance the books. Not to worry."

Howard nodded. "Of course. I will have all of it ready for you first thing in the morning."

"Most of the time, you only need to keep a file and we will go through everything every three months. Since you started in the middle of the year, I know you probably haven't gotten your feet quite under you yet, and paperwork is never a chef's favorite thing, but I appreciate you gathering it together for me."

"Yes, Chef."

"You may go ahead and attend to your duties. It's going to be a busy day."

Howard nodded and walked away briskly. The thin man could fit almost anywhere.

Just give him a few more years in the kitchen and that would change. Frank patted his thicker girth and laughed. Now if he could get this mess figured out with the discrepancies. He hated that Ruth was having to deal with all her regular duties and now *this* was hanging over her head.

Maybe it wouldn't be a risk for him to take another day out of the kitchen like Mr. Owens suggested. If the manager over the entire hotel thought it was a good idea . . . it couldn't be bad, right? Howard seemed to be loyal and content to be in the prestigious position he'd earned here. What was Frank so worried about?

No one was gunning for his job. The men in the kitchen were all devoted to him. That had been proven time and again over the years. The years of him being in the competitive, cutthroat kitchens were behind him. He was the head chef at the El Tovar now. The most amazing hotel in the whole Harvey Empire!

If Mr. Owens thought he could spare his head chef in the kitchen two days a week so that they could figure this out, then Frank should be willing to do it.

It was for Ruth, after all. And he would give everything he had for her.

It was coming together exactly as Oliver had predicted. The years he'd put into this plan would all be worth it. The O'Brien family name would finally be restored. He would see to that. *After* he took the El Tovar down.

Oliver took a sip of his evening brandy and watched a lovely blonde sashay her way to the stairs. A quick glance out of the corner of her eye made him smile. She *wanted* his attention.

Of course she did.

Perhaps later, he could find her. Ask her for a walk . . .

One of the boys from the front desk stepped up next to him. "I have a letter for you, sir."

"Thank you." He picked up the envelope, dismissed the young man, and opened it.

*Meet me at our designated location—H*

Taking the last swig of his drink, he looked around the room and shoved the missive into his coat pocket. After he set his glass down, he headed out the front doors of the hotel.

It was late, so there weren't a lot of gawkers about, but Oliver kept his eyes alert to make sure that no one was watching him. *He'd* expected to be the one to make the summons, not the other way around. Because it wasn't a place people would go to chat or take a gander at the canyon, they'd chosen the area around the water tank to meet. The entire vicinity wasn't touristy at all. Simply the place where the train brought in water each and every day. Another of Harvey's extravagant ways to keep the luxury hotel here—hauling in water to this desert land. Every single day. Outlandish is what it was. But they'd made it work. Much to Oliver's annoyance.

He rounded the hotel, and sure enough, his thin little accomplice was waiting for him under the massive frame of the tank. With a few more glances around, he picked up the pace. He couldn't risk being seen.

"Howard. What is this about?"

The young chef shifted from one foot to the other. "I can't be padding any more orders out of the kitchen."

"Whyever not? I thought you were in charge of all the ordering. And it's been working brilliantly."

"I *am* in charge. But I think they're onto us. Sooner than expected. Chef Henderson has asked me for all the orders and receipts. That means I'll be spending the entire night having to cover my tracks and fudge all the paperwork so I can give it to him in the morning."

Hmmm. That was a problem. "Well, then we will move on to the next phase. Like we planned, just a little sooner than expected."

"Hopefully they won't figure it out for a while. I don't want to lose my job."

"Don't worry. I'll take care of you, Howard."

The man looked like he had more to say but clamped his mouth shut. What was going through the little man's mind? When he'd signed on, he knew everything up front.

"You're being handsomely compensated, Howard. You're not getting cold feet, are you? Need I remind you that there's a head chef position waiting for you if you succeed?"

He lifted his chin. "No, sir."

"Good." Oliver shoved his hand into his vest pocket. "I'm going to head back to the hotel now. Make sure you stay out of sight for at least ten minutes."

Silence was all he heard as he turned on his heel and headed back.

Time to step up the game a notch or two. He'd seen Mr.

Owens' face the past few days. The man couldn't hide his concern. At least not from him.

Now that the manager was scrambling, wouldn't it be awful if several newspapers got word of scandalous things happening at Harvey's fancy hotel? Owens wouldn't be able to keep his financial problems a secret because Harvey would send people out immediately to investigate. That's how they stayed so squeaky clean. They took care of things quickly and quietly.

Well, Oliver could ensure that things would neither be quick nor quiet.

And in the process, he could find out exactly what he needed for his endgame.

# 6

Frank entered the kitchen as the bakers were placing the first bread of the day into the ovens. Four o'clock in the morning wasn't a time most people wanted to see, but this was his normal routine and he loved it. It would be another hour before the majority of the staff would enter, ready to start the breakfast dishes, and then roll call would kick them all into high gear.

These first few moments were his time to focus in on the specialties of the day. As head chef, it was his honor and privilege to use his own recipes to give the guests something new and unexpected. All other recipes had to be Harvey-approved so that they were up to the standards. But once a chef made it to the top, he was given leeway and was often *expected* to come up with new and tantalizing dishes that would keep the crowds talking and coming back for more. Everything he'd presented so far had been met with great success, which brought a good deal of relief, but also kept the pressure high for him to continue. Every day negative thoughts could wiggle their way in and bring with them the fear of preparing something subpar.

He kicked those thoughts out of his mind and focused on Ruth instead. Ruining their friendship was the last thing he wanted to do, but more than anything, he wanted to tell her how he felt. Now that he'd conceded in his own mind and heart, it was hard to shove it back down. Like trying to stuff the genie back in the bottle—it simply couldn't be done.

But he needed to tread carefully. The time wasn't right. Not in the middle of them trying to figure out what was happening at the hotel. Tensions were high. For all of them. He'd spent more time on his knees praying about the whole situation than he had for anything else.

Once they got past this bump in the road, he would tell her. Then he could face the battle he was sure would take place trying to convince her that he loved her and wasn't feeling sorry for her. That was a worry for another day.

Howard entered the kitchen and plopped his chef's hat on his head. "Good morning, Chef."

"Morning, Howard."

"I placed all the orders and receipts on your desk last night."

Relief filled him. "Thank you." Maybe, just maybe, they could get to the bottom of this. And prayerfully, it wasn't Frank's fault. "I need to ask something of you. Let's step outside for a moment." He didn't want any other ears listening in.

His assistant chef followed him out the side door. "I haven't done anything wrong, have I?" The man's cheeks were red.

"No. Not at all. In fact, it's the contrary." Frank crossed his arms over his middle and took a deep breath. "You see,

I've been impressed with your attitude and hard work in the kitchen. In addition to that, your loyalty and management skills are commendable. It has been good to see you take a leadership position and help defuse any squabbles and disagreements as they arise. It has helped keep our kitchen atmosphere positive and uplifting."

"Thank you, sir." Howard looked down at his feet. Perhaps the man was even more humble than Frank thought.

He continued on. "I need to ask you to keep something confidential. Just between the two of us. You cannot speak a word of this to anyone. Understood?"

"Yes, sir." Howard met his gaze.

"Mr. Owens has asked for my assistance. I will be leaving the kitchen under your command two days a week instead of one."

"Is everything all right, sir? Anything I can do to help?"

"No. Just you taking the reins is help enough. I've come to trust your impeccable work, and I know that you aren't trying to undermine me. Thank you for that."

"Of course. I will do whatever you need me to do." Howard tilted his head. "Is something wrong at the hotel?"

Frank couldn't divulge the reasons why. "We're double-checking some things. Making sure all is in order."

Howard's head tipped up and down in a slow nod. "Ah. That's why you needed all the paperwork."

He couldn't keep it completely hidden without lying. "In part, yes. But not to worry. I'm sure we will get it figured out straightaway."

The man stood tall in front of him. "Rest assured, you can count on me."

Frank reached out and shook the man's hand. "I knew I could. Thank you. I'll go look at the schedule and see which days are best for us to work this out. I appreciate your help."

"Not a problem, sir."

Frank turned and opened the door to the kitchen. Soon it would be time for roll call. He'd best get all the papers to Ruth before then and tell her his good news. Hopefully the idea of help two days a week would relieve some of the strain that he saw in her shoulders each day.

And it didn't hurt that the thought of spending more time with her lifted his spirits to new heights.

If only they could figure out the discrepancies at the hotel.

Charles adjusted his cutaway jacket over his high-buttoned waistcoat. Must make a good impression on Miss Anniston, now, mustn't he?

He attempted to keep his smile at bay, but his plan—as usual—had worked like a charm. A note was waiting for him under his room door this morning, requesting he attend a private meeting with Miss Anniston in her office.

Taking his time down the beautiful red-carpet staircase, he examined all the woodwork. It really was a unique building.

He nodded and smiled at several other guests, keeping up all the social niceties.

This was his world.

Living among the rich. Pretending to be but a humble man of means whose business was selling high-priced, hard-to-obtain, sure-to-cure treatments and remedies. Oh, he used the ruse that he was on vacation. Needing some time for himself. But he was always on vacation. People sought him out when they heard who he was and what he offered. He'd quietly and graciously assist them, which only made word spread like wildfire.

Funny how he didn't have to do much to get that first spark started. The guests' maids, valets, and companions were the perfect grapevine. And he'd been at this so many years, everywhere he went people knew who he was and what he had to offer.

The rich would do almost anything to stay in their prime, look younger, have energy, get rid of scars or unsightly spots, or aid in healing a sprain or break. And he delivered what they wanted: creams and elixirs that made them feel better about themselves. They worked well enough. Made his customers feel better. And so they came back for more. Paid a pretty penny too. Told their friends.

Which gave Charles Goodall a solid reputation.

He'd made hundreds of thousands of dollars with his business over the years. Enough to make him wealthier than many of his clients.

Gaining the rotunda, he turned toward the desk and asked for Miss Anniston.

A young man promptly led him down a short hall. He stopped in front of a door. "Here you are, Mr. Goodall." He bowed, pointed toward the door, and headed back to his station at the front.

Charles touched the bow tie under his high-wing collar and then rapped on the door.

"Come in," a feminine voice called.

He reached for the knob and entered. "Mr. Charles Goodall at your service, Miss Anniston. I believe you requested a meeting?"

She looked up at him from her seat behind the large desk and closed the book she'd been writing in. "Yes." She held a hand toward a chair but didn't come to her feet. "Please, make yourself comfortable."

He left the door open as a proper gentleman should, but took his time as he fully expected her to ask him to shut it.

To his surprise, she did not. "Mr. Goodall." Her voice was quiet. "I asked you here on a confidential matter."

"Yes. Indeed. How may I help?"

"It has come to my attention that your business is in medicines. Treatments?" One of her eyebrows quirked up with the question.

Exactly what he'd hoped. If he could get *her* in his corner, this summer would go better than planned. Putting on his most humble face, he nodded. "You are correct. But I'm not here on business. I am simply here to vacation at the hotel."

"I didn't ask you here to reprimand you in any way, Mr. Goodall. Rest assured. You are our guest, and we are blessed to have you here."

"Thank you." The bait had been taken.

"I asked you here as a personal request."

"Oh?" The hook was set.

"You see, two years ago, I was . . . injured. And I hear that you have many treatments that help with scars and healing of muscles, tissues, and bones." She folded her hands on the desk in front of her. "I apologize if this is in any way offensive to you. My wish is not to take advantage of your presence here at the El Tovar, but I was wondering if you have anything available . . . that might . . . assist me in my recovery."

The woman had guts. He had to give her that. Normally it was the husbands who came to him and asked on behalf of their wives. But Miss Anniston was obviously single. "Miss Anniston, I would love nothing more than to help you. And you haven't offended me one bit." He put a hand to his chest.

"Please accept my sincerest apologies, but the treatments that I provide are very expensive because the ingredients are rare and hard to come by. I didn't bring anything with me on this trip and it would cost a great deal to get any of them shipped here."

"But you *do* sell something that could help my scars to heal? And something that would help with a leg injury?"

Persistent. He'd give her that. Which was exactly what he hoped for. "I do. But again . . . they are *very* expensive." He stood. "I'm sorry, Miss Anniston."

She stood as well. Her fingers steepled on the desk in front of her. "How much?"

"Twenty-five dollars." He put on his sad face. The one that showed he felt the utmost sympathy to his client and then turned on his heel and left the office.

He'd reel her in later.

---

Twenty-five dollars for a treatment. And that was for something Ruth knew nothing about. Would that be one of the creams? How long would it last? Or one of the elixirs? What were the ingredients? And how long would it take to see results?

Goodness. Twenty-five dollars was almost an entire month's salary for one of her girls. Of course, the rich could scoff at that and throw it away in a second. But she wanted to be a good steward.

Still, she did have a lot of money saved. A lot. What if the treatments worked and she regained even a part of her normalcy back? Wouldn't it be worth it?

God had certainly seemed to put Mr. Goodall in her path.

Dr. Newport had heard good things about him. And the guests were all talking about Mr. Goodall and how he'd helped people for years.

With a reputation like that, he had to be a good man. With reputable products.

The clock chimed, and she went back to the ledger she'd been inspecting. The dining room would soon close after breakfast, and she'd be expected in there to address the girls. Once a week, on Tuesday mornings, she did an inspection along with the headwaitress. Each day, the girls had a different inspection at different times. It was all to keep them on their toes and exemplary in every way. It worked well, and this group of Harvey Girls was one of the best. If only they didn't lose so many of them each year to marriage.

But she couldn't blame them. Marriage and family were a wonderful thing. She couldn't deny any of them happiness.

Thoughts of Emma Grace surfaced. She hadn't seen her friend in a few days. And that had just been in passing. A wave back and forth. Which had happened a lot lately.

Sure, she was busy with hotel business and Emma Grace was certainly busy with her little one, but the distance had been growing between them for a while now.

Ever since her accident, if she was honest with herself.

A knock at her door brought her out of her thoughts. Before she could say anything, the door whooshed open. "Julia!" She couldn't help but smile.

Her friend's red hair was piled atop her head and bounced with her as she entered the room. "I hope I'm not interrupting anything desperately important, but I simply couldn't wait to come see you and tell you the news."

Ruth braced herself. All the girls sharing good news lately had done a number on her own heart. Not that she didn't wish them all the very best . . . but it hurt. Slipping a smile into place, she stood and limped around her desk to hug her friend. "I can't wait to hear."

"Chris's parents have decided to move to Williams!"

"That's wonderful news! I know you've been praying about that for a long time."

"Well, Chris had to finally resort to the fact that we want to start a family and basically said that he wanted our children to be raised with their grandparents close." Julia beamed.

"Wait a minute, does that mean . . . ?"

Her friend's head shook back and forth. "No. Not yet. I would have led with that news first, if that were the case. But we are hopeful." Her smile made the dimples in her cheeks even more prominent. "I know that God's timing is perfect."

How many times had Ruth heard that phrase—or even said it herself? Hundreds, most likely. She glanced down at the watch pinned to her shirtwaist. "I only have a few minutes before I'm needed in the dining room."

"Ah yes, it's Tuesday. Your inspection." Julia nodded and crossed her arms over her chest. "Well, I'm here all day. We're at the Hopi House, helping Chuma with the new line of Hopi jewelry. I'd love it if you could come visit. Even for just a few minutes?"

Why did her friends' invitations now feel like she was being backed into a corner? Ruth couldn't take the way it made her feel trapped. Out of breath. She looked down at her desk and riffled through some papers. "I've heard the jewelry is quite beautiful and each piece has its own story. You two have been busy." Needing a distraction, she straightened the ledgers and tidied up her workspace. "If I have time, I'll try to come by, but I have been very busy." She forced a smile. She couldn't tell Julia about the extra work on her plate, nor could she open up about what held her back. As much as she *wanted* to re-engage with her friends, there was a huge wall standing in her way. What if she couldn't tear it down?

Julia's face fell a bit, but she kept the smile up. "I understand."

Best to keep the subject off visiting, chatting, or anything personal. "Tell me more about the jewelry."

"One of the elders tells me a piece of their history for each new design and I write it into a story. The guests have loved it so far. We can't seem to keep the pieces in stock for very long."

"I'm so glad the business is doing well."

"And how are things here? Seems I hear that you're holed up in your office far more than usual these days." The scolding in Julia's tone wasn't to be missed.

Ruth waved her off. "Things are incredibly busy. Lots of books to double-check as well."

"I didn't think Mr. Owens was having you do all that bookkeeping anymore."

She headed to the door, needing a way to navigate through the hurdle that was Julia Miller. "It's some necessary work for right now, but hopefully it won't take too long."

"Good." Julia stepped out into the hall while Ruth shut her office door and locked it. Then she linked arms with Ruth. "Have I told you lately how thankful I am for you?"

The sentiment pricked Ruth's heart. Why would anyone be thankful for her now? She shrugged off the question. "Have you written any more on that children's book you were working on?"

"A little. I'm almost finished, and once I'm done, I'll want you to read it first."

"Deal."

"Would you like to come to dinner at our house next time you're down in Williams?"

Ruth's heart cinched. "I would love to . . . but things are so busy right now."

"I understand. But don't think you can put me off all summer."

"I won't—"

"There you are, Ruth!" Frank's voice echoed down the hall to her.

She turned toward him, thankful for the interruption. "I need to get to the dining room."

Julia hugged her and winked. "I'll come look for you around lunch, okay?"

With a nod, Ruth cringed inside. She'd have to find an excuse at lunchtime. What was wrong with her? She missed her friends. Desperately at times.

"I have all the orders and receipts here for the kitchen." Frank rushed to her side and walked a slow pace with her toward the dining room. "Hopefully we can match these up with the ledgers."

"Oh good." While Frank's interruption had been perfect timing to rescue her, she glanced over her shoulder. Regret and guilt pushed their way to the surface. Julia stood at the desk, smiling and chatting. How long could Ruth push them all away before they stopped checking in on her? She hadn't been a good friend in a long time.

"I'm going to do what Mr. Owens suggested and take two days off a week until we find the problem."

She stopped in her tracks. "What?"

Frank crossed his arms. "I had a feeling you weren't listening. I said, I'm going to take Mr. Owens' suggestion and take two days off a week until we find the problem."

"Really? You would do that?"

He appeared shocked that she would ask.

"I mean, I know your new position as head chef is what you've always wanted. And it's got to be hard to not be in your own kitchen. In charge." She bit her lip.

"Sure. But helping you is more important right now."

She wanted to throw her arms around his neck but refrained. "Thank you, Frank. I will gladly take all the help I can get." A new energy filled her. "I better get to the inspection."

"All right. Want me to put these on your desk?"

"The door is locked." She changed directions to head back toward her office.

"No problem. I'll slip them under the door."

"Thanks again, Frank." The fact that he would save her the extra steps meant more than she could say in that moment. After trying the exercises that morning, she'd cried for a good fifteen minutes, and now her leg screamed at her as she put weight on it.

"If I don't see you before then, I'll see you in the morning." He waved at her.

On her good foot, she turned around once again, but when she stepped, her bad leg wouldn't hold her weight.

In front of guests and staff, right there in the entrance to the rotunda, Ruth tumbled to the floor.

# 7

Emma Grace sat outside the Hopi House, watching her husband set up his new camera. Her heart soared thinking how far God had brought them over the years. How He had transformed each of them and then saw fit to bring them together. It truly was a miracle.

The sun warmed her face, and she closed her eyes. Times like these were few and far between now with a toddler in the house. Thank goodness for Chuma offering to play with their little one this morning. It had given her and Ray some time for long conversation, which they'd sorely needed.

There were days she missed being a Harvey Girl. Working side by side with Ruth as headwaitresses. But she wouldn't trade her life now for anything, even though the philanthropic work they'd been doing with the fortunes from their fathers took up way more time than she'd ever anticipated.

She cast a glance over to the El Tovar. Julia's words from the other day had done nothing but haunt her thoughts. Was she really that horrible of a friend that she hadn't seen what had happened to Ruth?

"I can see you haven't heard a word I've said." Ray stood in front of her, his arms across his chest.

"Oh! I'm so sorry, my dear. What were you saying?"

He reached out a hand to her. "I was saying that I needed a subject for my photos. Will you do me the honor?"

She lifted her hand to his and allowed him to pull her to her feet. "Isn't the canyon enough of a subject?" With a wink, she sent him what she hoped was a flirtatious smile.

"You should know that *you* are my favorite subject." Ray pulled her close for a quick kiss and then led her in front of the camera. "This will make the picture perfect."

As soon as he was back behind the apparatus, her thoughts went back to Ruth.

"What's got your brow furrowed?" His voice was a bit muffled by the camera.

Releasing a long breath, she let her shoulders drop. "I'm worried about Ruth."

He stood up and came toward her. "I know. Ever since we visited with Julia and Chris, I could see it."

"Have I been too busy to notice that she's hurting? Struggling? Am I so caught up in myself?" Tears squeezed out of the corners of her eyes. "She's the dearest friend I've ever had, and I feel like I've failed her."

"Ruth is an incredibly strong woman. She's also taken on even more responsibility. You are both busy with very full lives. Could you possibly be worried about nothing, my dear?" He wrapped his arms around her, and they stared out at the canyon.

Here she was, with the most incredible husband in the world, and she was ruining their brief time alone together with her melancholy. "Perhaps you're right." She pasted on a smile. "Where do you want me to stand?"

He turned her around and beamed at her. "Right here." He shifted her a bit, lifted her chin with his finger, and then jogged back to the camera.

But as Emma Grace's gaze lay firmly on the hotel, that sinking feeling in her stomach wouldn't go away.

After several moments, Ray was back beside her. "Look, we still have plenty of time to spend together this morning. I'd like to get a few more shots, so why don't you go inside and see if you can snag a few minutes with Ruth?"

"Really? You wouldn't mind?"

"Not at all." He kissed her on the forehead. "Now go, so you can hurry back."

"I won't be long. I promise." With a giggle, she kissed his cheek and then scurried off to the hotel's entrance. Ray knew her so well. The fact that he would sacrifice their precious time together so she could go check on their friend meant the world to her.

As she climbed the steps to the front doors, Emma Grace slowed to a fast walk and put a hand to her chest. Now where would Ruth be at this time? She checked her watch. Most likely back in her office. That seemed to be where she spent most of her days.

Emma Grace acknowledged several of the guests she'd met and headed toward the rotunda when she spotted Ruth. A storm was brewing on her face as she headed away from the dining room. "Ruth!" Emma Grace called out across the large room.

Her friend stopped. When their gazes met, Emma Grace couldn't help but notice the redness to Ruth's cheeks. The anguish in her eyes.

She rushed to her friend's side. "What is it? Are you hurt?"

Eyes darting to the guests around them, Ruth yanked her

arm and limped to the corner with her in tow. "I'm fine. Please keep your voice down."

"I'm sorry," she whispered. "I didn't realize I had been loud."

"It hasn't been a good morning, so I'd like to keep attention off of me, if that's all right with you." The words were a bit frosty.

This was not the Ruth she knew. Something must be terribly wrong. "I had a little time and thought I could come see you and chat for a bit."

A long sigh escaped Ruth's lips as she started toward her office. Her steps were slow. Forced. "I'm sorry. I don't have time for a chat today. Perhaps another time?"

Emma Grace followed. She couldn't abandon her friend when something was clearly upsetting her. "I could help you. Obviously you have a lot on your plate. So put me to work and we can catch up while we do it."

Ruth stopped in front of her office door. "I appreciate it, I do. But now is not a good time. I don't need help."

She reached for Ruth's hand, desperate to bridge the gap between them. "We haven't had a good talk in so long. I'm so sorry if I have neglected our friendship. Is this all my fault?"

"Things have changed. You and I—we're no longer head-waitresses working side by side. I don't need help. I can't deal with this right now, all right? I have work to do, and I need to be alone." With that, Ruth turned, unlocked her door, walked in, and closed the door with a firm push.

---

"I can't do that." Howard shook his head.

Oliver forced his voice to stay low. "What do you mean, you can't do it?"

"Don't you see? Frank has given me his trust now and I've shown him full support. I can't undermine him in the kitchen like that. It'll be too suspicious. But you have another way to do things. I'll have inside knowledge."

"Has he actually shared anything useful?" Oliver tried to keep the sarcasm out of his voice, but the young man was getting entirely too cocky.

"Well . . . no. But over time, I'm sure that he will. He's putting me in charge of the kitchen for two whole days a week. That's unheard of."

Oliver paced in the cool night air. "I am paying you handsomely to do what I ask."

"But what you're asking isn't feasible. You never said I would have to sabotage my own career to help you. In fact, you promised me a head chef position after we were done. And there's no way you can promise me that if I'm tainting the food and getting people sick. I won't do it." Howard crossed his arms over his chest, his face set.

Oliver studied the younger man for several moments and weighed his options. "Since Frank has opened the door to let you into his confidence, I'm sure there's a clever way we can use that information." Howard wasn't the key to the whole plan, but Oliver needed him inside. Even if he didn't agree to do the next step. "I suppose I can come up with another way."

Howard let out his breath. "Thank you."

The younger man was smart to not want to give himself a bad name. But that didn't mean that Oliver still wouldn't allow him to take part—or all—of the fall. He didn't care how many people he had to ruin in the process. But for now, he needed Howard on his side. Let him think he could call the shots this once. "All right, but I need you on the inside reporting absolutely anything and everything of value. There has to be a way to blast the Harvey name and I'm expecting you to find it."

"You got it."

It had been one of the worst days since *it* happened.

Ruth lay on her bed with an arm over her forehead. The pain in her leg had only gotten worse as the day went on. Now her head was pounding. All the crying this evening probably hadn't helped.

How Frank had gotten to her side so quickly after she fell, she'd never know. And she'd been grateful for his help. How he shielded her from the crowd and assisted her to her feet. But the pitying glances from everyone were more than she could handle. It took far too long for her to gain her balance. After excusing herself to the ladies' room, she lost her breakfast and then was ten minutes late for the inspection.

The inspection where *she* was in charge. Where all eyes were on her. And for certain, her blotchy face and shaky frame hadn't helped matters. There'd been no time to go back down to her room and reapply the makeup, so her scar had been plain for everyone to see. Her tearstained cheeks gave away the fact that her fall had bruised not only her body but also her ego.

Because every Harvey Girl in that room had looked at her with pity.

More *pity*. It disgusted her.

*Poor Ruth.*

As she'd instructed the girls to walk in front of her, their pristine black dresses with their crisp white aprons practically flowed and swished with the taunt that the girls could walk without a limp. They were without blemish. Their hair was perfectly coiffed with the huge white Harvey Girl bow. Everything was perfect and in order.

Except for Ruth.

And yet, every one of the waitresses continued to stare with pity. Oh, they smiled at her. But she knew what they were thinking.

*Poor, poor Miss Anniston.*

But it had been Frank's words that kept coming back to her. *"You're all right. Chin up."*

He hadn't hovered over her and babied her. Hadn't asked if she was okay. No. Instead, he'd hidden her from view as best as he could, cleared the people back, and then helped her up. Had stood with his back to the crowd as she steadied herself. Then said those words.

*"You're all right. Chin up."*

It had been exactly what she needed to hear. No matter if she was all right or not. He'd helped protect her dignity and she would be forever grateful.

When she thought about it, she couldn't imagine her world without Frank in it. He'd been her friend for so long. But now? He was so much more than a friend. If she were honest, she *wanted* him to be much more . . . but it would never be. How could he ever feel anything for her? Not in her condition. What man in his right mind would want a woman scarred and broken like she was?

Many times over the years, she'd allowed herself to think of Frank as a potential beau. He was someone she could always talk to, speaking her mind as well as her heart. Before her injuries, she'd thought of it more often. Had often wondered if Mr. Owens would give permission if Frank asked

. . . but they'd not spoken of such a thing. And Frank had never asked.

As that thought sank in, she sat up on the bed. Her whole world was at the El Tovar. Had been for more than four years. These people were her family.

*Why, God? Why would You deform me after You haven't given me a husband? I thought marriage and a family was Your plan for me, at least one day. But I've been waiting so long. And now look at me. Who could care for me now?*

Her heart hurt after lashing out at the Lord like that. But nothing made any sense. What was she to do with herself now? She'd always said appearances didn't matter. She wanted to be loved for who she was, not for her pretty face.

But oh, she learned the hard way that appearances *did* matter. Very much so. Harvey Girls were supposed to be pristine and flawless. And she'd heard enough comments when the scar on her face had been much more visible . . . Yes. Appearances mattered.

How she hated that she'd become so accustomed to being pretty. Why couldn't she have been born plain? Then the scars wouldn't matter so much.

She shook her head. What an ugly thought. Ungrateful for her looks. Ungrateful for her life. Ungrateful for everything.

When had her thoughts taken such a cynical turn? This up and down of her emotions. It was like she was on a constant roller coaster.

Shame washed over her as she recalled her words to Emma Grace. The woman held no ill intentions, and Ruth had snapped at her and brushed her aside. As much as she hated how she'd reacted, she couldn't change it. It was better for everyone if she kept them in the dark. How could she talk about how she was doing when she didn't even understand that herself?

Ruth got up and stepped over to her small desk. The latest letter from her parents was there, filled with news of all of Mother's piano students and their antics and Dad's favorite quotes from the books he'd read. They were enjoying the new pastor of their small church and the study of the book of Isaiah. Oh, how she missed them. When she was first injured, she refused to let Mr. Owens telegram them until she could send one herself. Then she demanded that they stay at home. The cost to travel was too great, and she was fine.

Hundreds of times she'd regretted that decision. But she'd written more letters home than ever, hoping to convince them that she would come home to visit soon. Which she never did.

But they'd spoken via telephone twice, and it had been wonderful to hear their voices. Dad had some health issues of his own that they didn't want her worrying about. And since she hadn't been forthcoming about everything, she couldn't scold him for doing the same.

The only thing that kept her from thinking the worst was that every month, she could count on the same tidbits of their lives. It was warm and genuine, predictable and even a bit boring. But she loved it.

She picked up the sheets of paper and skimmed them. She hadn't had the heart to speak to her parents about how she was really doing. They were simply proud of her for her promotion. Glad she was on her feet. And they were praying for her.

It seemed too weird to think that when she left home over fifteen years ago, she'd been adamant about marrying for love.

Men wanted a pretty face. They wanted a wife. That was about it.

Her heart's longing for love, marriage, and family disintegrated after the first hundred or so marriage proposals as she waited tables. Add to that the long work hours and the fact that she didn't have the desire to get to know anyone outside of her circle, and well . . . here she was. Almost thirty-five. Unmarried.

Scarred.

Unwanted.

Unworthy.

Would it have been so bad to marry a man she knew little about? At least then she wouldn't be alone.

How many of her girls had gotten married since coming to the El Tovar? The number was higher than she could even count at the moment.

Emma Grace and Julia and a number of others had married for love—and Ruth wouldn't wish to deny anyone that. But it didn't work out for everyone that way.

She set the letter down. This train of thought was getting her nowhere. She was either going around in circles or up and down the same hill over and over again.

Time to do something about it. She couldn't keep headed down this same path.

With a new resolve, she lifted her chin.

Ruth left her room and headed down the long hallway toward Charlotte's and Tessa's rooms. If she were going to change things, she had to stop withering inside herself.

The two girls had worked at the hotel for more than two years now, and they were precious. Tessa had been Julia's hiking partner and was one of the quietest girls Ruth had ever met. But my oh my, she could be feisty and protective.

One of the many things she loved about the girl. As a head-waitress now, she was one of the best Ruth had ever seen.

Then there was Charlotte, who was always an encourager.

After Ruth had pushed Emma Grace away today, she needed to know that she was not a complete and utter mean-spirited hermit.

Ruth tapped on the first door.

It opened, and Charlotte sent her a smile. "Ruth! So good to see you." She yawned behind her hand.

"I know it's getting late, but I was wondering if you or Tessa might be up for a short walk?"

"Sure. As long as it's not far." Charlotte shrugged. "Tessa was just here visiting." She looked behind her. "What do you think?"

The other girl was already on her feet and headed toward the door. Guess there was their answer. It made Ruth smile.

If she was going to change the way she was feeling, she needed to get out more. She'd been hiding in her room or her office for far too long.

She'd declined invitations by the Watkinses and the Millers—and they were her closest friends. Well, other than Frank. But he didn't count. She saw him every day. Although their chats had changed over the years. If only she'd paid attention to her feelings and done something about them before . . .

"How is your leg feeling?" Charlotte took the lead down the hallway to the basement exit.

Her first instinct was to cringe and try to dodge the question, like she'd made a habit of doing. But no more. "It hurts. I'm trying to strengthen it with exercises, but they make it hurt worse."

"Are you sure a walk is a good idea?" Charlotte's tender

heart was beautiful, but she always spoke her mind nowadays.

"I'm sure." Ruth's steps were much slower than the others', but they didn't seem to mind. "I don't want to go far. Just need some fresh air."

Tessa didn't say anything but stepped beside Ruth and linked arms with her as they exited the building.

The gesture of friendship brought the sting of tears to Ruth's eyes because it was so much more. Stability was always troublesome and to have someone else to hold on to was simply a relief.

Charlotte led their little band and turned around to walk backward. "You know, the Bible study has had some great discussions the past few weeks. We've missed having your input there, Ruth."

That's right. She'd missed Bible study. "I'm sorry. I got behind on my paperwork in May and had to stay late several times to catch up. Now I'm working on an extra project for Mr. Owens' and I'm afraid it's slipped my mind. What are you studying now?"

"We've been in the book of James, and it's brought up quite a debate about works." Charlotte turned as they went up the hill.

No one said anything for a few moments as they worked their way up the hill around the hotel.

Ruth pointed to a bench. "Why don't we sit there a few minutes before we head back?"

"Sure." Charlotte shrugged. "So, what do you think about the topic of works, Ruth? Some of them say that if you're not doing good works, then you must not be saved. You know . . . that whole passage about faith without works is dead."

As she settled herself on the bench, she looked up at the stars. "I bet that is an interesting discussion. My whole life I've thought that the fruit of the believer showed their salvation. Does that mean works? I think a lot of people believe that way. Frankly, I don't know what I believe anymore. Ever since the accident . . . there are a lot of things that I grapple with on a daily basis."

"Like what?" Charlotte might be the one doing most of the talking, but the look on Tessa's face showed how intently she was listening to them.

Ruth tipped her head back and forth as she weighed her response. "We are so ingrained with the idea that good behavior equals good results and bad behavior equals bad results. But what about bad things happening to good people? And good things happening to bad people?" She took a long inhale. "Then I think about the thief on the cross next to Jesus. Jesus told him that on that very day he would be with Him in paradise. To me that proves it is faith in Christ alone that gives me—us, anyone—eternal life. But then what do we do with all the passages about walking worthy, walking blameless, or faith without works being dead?"

Tessa piped up. "I think it all comes down to grace."

All eyes turned to their quiet friend. Ruth chewed on that for a few moments. "I've tried to wrap my mind around God's grace a good portion of my adult life. It seems unfathomable to my human mind."

"Exactly." Tessa stood. Her hands lifted to the incredible starry sky above them. "Like trying to count the stars. We can't do it. I think the part that is unfathomable is that we want to *do* something for it. To somehow earn God's favor. So that we feel worthy. Because we *are* unworthy until . . . His grace. And it's completely and utterly by His grace alone.

That any of us are here. That we are breathing. That we have the chance at eternity with Him."

"Which goes back to good behavior equaling good results." Ruth shook her head. "But you're right. It's grace alone."

Tessa smiled at them both. "Grace . . . plus nothing."

Huh. She'd never thought of it that way. And couldn't quite wrap her thoughts around it.

Charlotte jumped to her feet with a gasp and broke the serious moment. "I just looked at the time. We better get back before curfew." She giggled. "Well, *Tessa and I* better get back before curfew. You're the supervisor, so I doubt you have to worry about that."

As they headed back down to the basement together, Charlotte prattled on about how many aprons she'd gone through that week, and Tessa admitted that she'd stayed up too late reading one night and had been chugging coffee ever since.

Their light chatter helped Ruth focus on careful steps down the hill as her leg burned with pain.

But as they entered the building, said their good-nights, and headed to their rooms, Ruth couldn't let go of the words *grace plus nothing*.

# 8

Frank glanced across the desk at Ruth. She looked like a young school-aged girl as she leaned over the ledger with her pencil stuck between her teeth.

It made him grin as he went back to the order sheets.

Everything Howard had given him seemed to line up with his handwritten notes about what needed to be ordered. Not that he wanted to blame the new guy, but it sure would be easier if someone had just made a mistake. The receipts from all the vendors seemed to line up as well.

"These look to be accurate. I've gone through every one of them." He grimaced as he looked at her.

She released a long sigh. "Mr. Owens wanted us to go back six months. So let's do that. We'll start with the kitchen orders from six months ago and work up to today. Let's compare them to the expenditure ledger. It's going to take some time to find each line, but if you call it out and the amount, then I can check it in the book." She scooted her chair over to the side. "Why don't you come over here so we can compare columns? I'm not good at reading upside down."

Frank picked up his chair and carried it to the other side of her desk. He quite enjoyed sitting across from her so he could sneak glances at her from time to time. But now he'd be closer.

Much closer.

He settled in beside her and they went back six months, calling out amounts, dates, and vendors to each other. An hour and a half later, they had made it through one week. One. Single. Week.

With a groan, he stood and stretched. "Goodness gracious, I had no idea what it took to keep a place like this running. My brain can't quite fathom all the numbers."

Ruth set her pencil down and laughed. "Math was *not* my favorite subject. And yet here I am. Trying to reconcile all these numbers." She pinched the bridge of her nose. "When I first started helping with the books after I was injured, it was simply to double-check the bookkeeper's work. He always helped. Now I wish they would have hired someone else right away for that position. Because this is way too many numbers to have to go through and not lose my mind."

"I hear you. I'm a chef. Not a number cruncher." He reached over and squeezed her shoulder. "But Mr. Owens needs our help. I can understand him not wanting to bring anyone else in on this. I mean, this could be big trouble for the hotel. He needed people he could trust. And here we are."

Ruth rose to standing as well and rubbed a hand down her leg. "I know. I'm glad we can help. But that doesn't make the work any more fun."

"Yeah, if it were fun, everyone would want to do it." Frank winked at her.

She smiled back and lifted her hand and made a swirling motion. "I need you to turn around so I can massage my leg for a moment."

The fact that she felt comfortable enough to even say that to him meant a lot. Frank turned. "Is it hurting you more than usual?"

Her exhale was so big, he heard it—and the frustration behind it. "Just between you and me, I did go see Dr. Newport down in Williams. Apparently, my leg has lost muscle and tissue from not being used over the last two years. The doctor even said there was a great deal of atrophy. And if I want to have any chance at walking a bit more normally, I'm going to have to work for it. He wrote down some exercises for me to try every day."

"Is it helping?"

"Not that I can tell. It actually makes it hurt more. But I'm going to keep trying."

"Doesn't sound like a whole lot of fun."

"Which brings me to my next question . . ." She poked him in the shoulder. "Thank you. You can turn back around."

He shoved his hands into his pockets and faced her. "Sure. What's on your mind?"

"Do you think you'd have the time—and energy, for that matter—to walk with me in the evenings? Once it's dark and there are not a lot of people out and about to watch the crippled woman try to walk?" She bit her lip. "It's the only way to get stronger. No matter how hard it might be. I've tried to keep my injuries and limp hidden, but walking from my room to my office each day isn't enough to get the muscles working and growing again."

"It'll be quite late. You know the kitchen schedule. But I'd love to walk with you."

She patted his arm. "Thank you so much, Frank. That means a great deal to me. It's embarrassing enough to walk in front of people. I'm hoping the cover of dark will help me not feel so . . . exposed. I'll clear it with Mr. Owens so he's aware."

His heart clenched. All this time . . . she'd been embarrassed. Ashamed to even walk in front of people? No wonder she worked so hard to hide her limp.

"There's nothing to be embarrassed about, Ruth."

"Says the man who can walk without a limp and without falling on his face." Her laughter sounded forced—like she was covering the hurt behind the truth.

"Hey, you haven't seen me fall in the kitchen. We all have. Let me tell you, at least two of us a day take a tumble. Especially in the evening once the ovens and stoves have been going all day and the steam builds up and covers everything. Those floors get slick."

"Exactly why I avoid walking in the kitchen anymore, I remember."

"Now it's tradition to applaud when one of us slips since we know it's inevitable."

Her cheeks tinged pink. "I definitely don't want to be applauded for falling down."

He should have kept his mouth shut. Falling because of a slippery floor and falling because you were injured were two entirely different things. But he'd wanted to make the conversation lighter. When would he learn? *Get back on track, Frank.* "Would you like to start with the walks this evening?"

"That would be nice." She pushed him toward the door. "Would you mind getting us some lunch? I lost track of time."

He glanced at the clock. Ah. The dining room would be packed. Her window of getting in and out unnoticed had passed. "Sure, what would you like?"

The door burst open, and Frank jumped.

Mr. Owens stood there, his face a deep shade of red. He stepped into the small office and slammed the door behind him.

Tension radiated from him and filled the entire room. Frank felt Ruth's hand on his forearm. Her grip tightened. Was she afraid? With everything in him, he wanted to protect her. But from what?

"I thought I asked both of you to keep this completely confidential?" Mr. Owens' voice boomed.

"We did!" Ruth's voice squeaked.

"We would never betray your confidence, sir."

"Well, someone said something! Look at this!" He shoved papers toward them.

Frank grabbed at them, but one dropped to the floor. He flipped open the folded newspaper in his hands and read aloud, "'Financial Woes at Harvey's Grand Dame?'"

Frank's heart sank. "Sir, we haven't said a word to anyone. I assure you." He bent down and picked up the other paper. *Will Harvey's Era of Perfection Fold?*

"I . . . I don't understand." Ruth stepped out from behind him. "What do the articles say?"

Their manager crossed his arms over his chest. "That via an 'anonymous and credible' source, they've learned that Harvey Company has been riddled with scandal and dishonest practices since the death of Fred Harvey. It says that the El Tovar is having financial difficulties, and it warns readers that if they've made plans to vacation with us, they better beware."

——| |——

**WEDNESDAY, JUNE 2, 1909**

Life had become entirely too stressful.

Not only had Ruth and Frank spent an hour trying to calm their manager down after his explosive revelation, but then they'd read the actual articles. *"Yellow journalism,"* Frank had called it. And he was right. Not a bit of substantiated evidence. It was simply a ploy *someone* was using to attack Harvey.

They were going to great lengths. That must be why there were discrepancies here. Someone had gotten inside. But who? It couldn't be a coincidence.

The Harvey name was squeaky clean, thanks to Fred Harvey. He set the standards. And they were high.

In fact, most people didn't even realize that the great icon and founder of the company had died in 1901. Because the Harvey Company had done a fantastic job of using the legacy and brilliant advertising of their namesake. Most ads, posters, flyers, and pamphlets were all signed, *Fred Harvey.*

Because people trusted Fred. They'd come to know great service, terrific food, and wonderful accommodations at Harvey establishments. That everyone assumed Fred ran. Himself. Right?

The rest of the day had passed in a blur of checking ledgers. Brainstorming with Mr. Owens and Frank about who could either be tampering with the books or stealing money. And how they were accomplishing such a feat.

Frank had been on edge. Probably because Owens was on edge. Which made her on edge.

It didn't help that Owens now had to deal with the people

who had seen the papers and were demanding answers. The staff had been rounded up and given phrases to use to answer any of the guests who questioned them.

*"It's sensationalistic journalism."*

*"Everything is top notch here at the El Tovar."*

*"Don't worry. The management assures us that everything is just as it should be."*

But the staff were worried. And why wouldn't they be? Whenever there were headlines plastered across the tops of newspapers, people paid attention. Even if they were found out later to be inaccurate. They were all just going to have to live through this storm.

By the end of the day, she wanted to pull her hair out and run away.

Frank held up his end of the bargain by coming to escort her for a walk. But that had lasted all of ten minutes before her leg gave out from under her and she collapsed. At that point, she was on the verge of tears. He didn't say a word, just helped her up and back to the basement door. They'd said a simple "good night" and "see you in the morning." But she couldn't look him in the eyes.

Then she'd sat in her room, wallowing in how horrible the day had been while she went through her mail. A letter from her parents.

She ripped open the letter, hoping for some lighthearted news to take her mind off her troubles. But as she scanned her mother's beautiful penmanship, she sucked in a breath.

They were coming for a visit.

Ruth hadn't seen them since right before her injury. Now was not a good time to be having company, but they'd already purchased their tickets. Probably to keep her from convincing them otherwise.

The date of their arrival was less than two weeks away.

At that moment, she determined to convince Mr. Goodall to help her. No matter what. She needed help.

All night she tossed and turned. Going over what she could say.

Morning came all too soon. The culmination of yesterday's events had been the proverbial straw that broke the camel's back. With little to no sleep, she now paced her room. Dressed for the day and resolved that she wouldn't take no for an answer from Mr. Goodall. She tapped the missive she'd written him in her palm.

It just needed to be delivered.

She couldn't seem to control anything else in her life anymore. Well, that was about to change.

The stories he could tell.

How many times had Charles let it play out almost exactly like this? He couldn't even count. But oh, how it brought him a smile. And a hefty profit to boot.

With his briefcase tucked under one arm and a hand to his waxed mustache, he lifted his chin and then knocked on Miss Anniston's office door.

"Come in."

Setting his features to convey his deepest empathy, he opened the door. "Good morning, Miss Anniston. I received your note."

"Thank you for coming, Mr. Goodall. I know your time is very valuable." This time she stood at her desk. Shoulders back. Chin up. Fingers steepled on the desktop in front of her. "I'll get right to the point. Like I said in my note, I have the money required. I'd like to order whatever treatments are necessary."

"Could you tell me a bit about what it is you need?" He already knew, but it always made the customer a bit more vulnerable when they had to say it out loud.

"I was attacked by a mountain lion. As you can probably see, I have a scar on my face. There's an even larger one on my leg. I obviously would like to diminish the appearance of the scars, but even more than that, I am looking for ways to heal the injuries to my leg. The wounds were deep, and the doctors have told me that much tissue and muscle was damaged." Her words were matter-of-fact. Rehearsed almost. But she didn't flinch. Didn't show emotion of any kind.

He was impressed. For a woman of such slight stature—he guessed she was barely even five feet tall—she displayed a lot of grit.

He liked that.

For more than one reason.

"I see." He reached into his briefcase and pulled out a dark bottle with a gold filigree label. It looked expensive. Intentionally. "I must admit that I was deeply moved by your letter this morning. I would like to help. While the cream for the wound on your leg won't be here for a few days—possibly even a week or more—I do have this."

Her eyes widened as she reached for the bottle and examined it. "What is it?"

"I call it the miracle elixir—which is silly, I know—but it has a much longer medical name. The ingredients are the very finest to be found. Natural, healthy, and good for you. It is guaranteed to help with your healing from the inside out. Filled with vitamins and nutrients, it helps our bodies with their God-given ability to knit themselves back together. It has also been proven to boost your energy, help you to sleep better, and make you feel better all around." He pointed to the bottle. "My recommendation is to take a teaspoon of it five times a day. I know that is a lot, but I promise you will feel better almost instantly. You will need to continue with the elixir once the creams arrive. Stay off your leg as much as possible for the first few weeks—it will aid in the healing process. Once the creams do arrive, one will be to put on the leg wound first to help restore your muscles. Then, an hour later, you'll need to put on the other cream—which you can also use on your face. It will help the scars to diminish."

"Each one of the treatments is twenty-five dollars?" Again, she didn't flinch, but he did see the hint of trepidation in her eyes.

"For you, Miss Anniston, this bottle is a gift. I'd also like to thank you for the impeccable service you provide here at the hotel by offering the creams to you for half. Providence has blessed me, and I'd like to pass that on."

"That is very generous of you." This time her lips trembled just a touch. But she held her composure.

"I'm not here for my business or to make money. I simply want to help you."

She pulled an envelope out of the top drawer. "Please take this as my payment for the first treatments, then. As soon as they arrive, I would appreciate you letting me know. I'm anxious to feel like my old self again." This time she smiled.

He could see what a beautiful woman she'd been. Even the scar on her face didn't diminish it much. Especially when she smiled. "I'm honored to assist you." He put the envelope in his briefcase, closed it, and then turned toward the door. "Don't hesitate to let me know if you need anything else."

"Thank you." Her voice was soft, but her gaze was already back on the bottle.

People were so easy to manipulate. Such a shame that he was so good at what he did.

He pulled the door closed behind him and chuckled as he walked down the hall. Oh, the plans he had for this place.

# 9

The morning meeting with Frank was in a few minutes, and Ruth couldn't keep herself from smiling. One, because she'd taken the elixir and felt great. Amazing what one little teaspoon could do.

Two, because she was actually looking forward to the day. Thanks again, most likely, to the elixir. The thought of a nice walk with Frank that evening made her happy and gave her something non-stressful to look forward to.

Three, because in Mr. Goodall's instructions, he'd said to stay off her leg the first few weeks. Even though she didn't have the creams yet, she'd decided against the exercises at least for a while. While she wasn't sure if they had begun to help or not, the thought of avoiding the pain during this stressful time made everything a little bit sweeter.

She made her way to the kitchen and passed the girls polishing the silver. The expectations at every Harvey establishment were high, but at the El Tovar, they were the highest. No one seemed to mind, especially since being chosen to be a Harvey Girl here meant you had reached the top.

Not being headwaitress the past two years had put distance between her and the girls, though. She didn't know the majority of them all that well. They didn't need to come to her for guidance or to have someone to confide in. She missed it.

But did she really? How many times had she been relieved to be by herself so no one else would see her pain? Could it have contributed to her keeping more to herself? More than just her injuries?

Probably.

Wait. She wasn't going to allow herself to meander down the road of mixed emotions. Not anymore.

Charlotte made a beeline for her from across the dining room. Ruth braced herself, and the younger woman gave her a big hug. "It's so good to see you smiling."

The words made her pause. Had she not smiled? "It's good to see you too, Charlotte. How's your shift going?"

"Just fine." She looked around the room. "Look, I know you've needed time to heal and we've all wanted to respect that, but . . . I really need someone to talk to. May I come talk to you, maybe Friday night?" The twinkle in the girl's eye gave her away.

Once again, the words hit Ruth square in the chest. What did people think of her now? She brushed off the thought. She'd determined to do things differently. "Have you met someone special?"

"I think so." Charlotte bounced on her toes.

"Friday it is. Come see me at curfew. I'll wait up for you." Ruth squeezed her friend's hand.

As she walked into the kitchen, she went over Charlotte's words. All this time, Ruth hadn't wanted people to see the scars. The injuries. Wanted to be looked upon as the same person she'd always been. Because she wanted to *be* the person she'd always been. And yet . . . in keeping to herself she'd become a different person. That's why she didn't know many of the girls well at all. That's why Emma Grace was so persistent the other day. That's why Frank probably didn't care for her anymore. Maybe it hadn't been the scars. Maybe it was because she'd changed.

Her heart sank a bit at the thought. Then she shook her head. No. Just a little bit ago she'd felt great. If she wanted to truly turn things around, she had to follow through. So what if she'd handled things differently for a while, kept a wall up? The people who knew Ruth Anniston knew her. She could get back to that person. That was what she wanted, wasn't it?

Turning her thoughts back to Charlotte's request, she felt a burst of encouragement. See? The young woman still needed her, still thought of her as a confidante, someone she could go to for help. The thought of helping another of her young wards through the courtship process didn't make her cringe. It made her happy for her friend.

Things *were* turning around.

"Miss Anniston!" Mr. Owens' voice greeted her instead of Frank's, though the two men stood together.

"Good morning, Mr. Owens. Chef Henderson." She walked toward them.

"Let's step outside." The manager opened the door for her.

Oh boy. What had happened now?

Once they were all outside, their manager clasped his hands behind his back. "The Harvey Company is sending two men to audit. Apparently, they've been inundated with phone calls and letters since newspapers across the country ran those slanderous stories." He paced a couple steps back and forth. "I know we haven't been able to find the discrepancies yet, but I'm confident you two will be able to figure it out or help the men to get to the bottom of it once they arrive. But everything will go on as normal. Top notch. Cream of the crop. We are the best of the best." He looked at both of them and nodded emphatically.

Was he giving himself a pep talk? Or them? Either way, he didn't seem to need any response from them.

"I have the utmost of confidence in both of you. I'm certain that the Harvey men will see there is no need for alarm." Mr. Owens turned to Frank. "I would appreciate you helping Miss Anniston those two days a week until the men arrive, and then I will need you back at the helm of the kitchen seven days a week until they are gone. I know that puts a lot of undue pressure on you. But I need my best man at the job."

"Of course, sir. Whatever you need."

"Miss Anniston, I'm sure I can rely on you for making sure that the kitchen and dining room are in tip-top shape. You've always been one to go above and beyond the call of duty. I'm positive I will need that in the weeks ahead. Thank you once again for your service."

"Yes, Mr. Owens." She kept her hands clasped in front of her. Sounded like they wouldn't have any days off for quite some time. But they were well compensated, so she really couldn't complain.

Wait. Uh-oh. "Um, I haven't told you because I just found out myself, but my parents are coming for a visit in less than two weeks' time."

The older man huffed. "We'll deal with that when the date arrives. I can't promise you any time off, but I will make certain that they are well taken care of. In Harvey style."

"Thank you." What else could she say? Her parents would want to spend time with her, but surely they would understand the drastic circumstances. She should send a telegram and maybe they could postpone. If she could get in touch with them in time. Mother had been trying to convince Father to get a telephone since so many in their city were, even telling him they could speak to Ruth more often because they wouldn't have to leave their house to make the call. But . . . he'd refused and said it wasn't necessary. Just a new fad.

Mr. Owens left, and she went back inside with Frank and tried to get her mind back on the business of the day.

"I'm excited that your parents are coming." Frank grinned at her. "I haven't seen them since the company picnic in Kansas."

"I was going to tell you on our walk tonight. Their letter was quite a surprise." She looked over the charts and lists he handed her.

"Same time tonight?"

She laughed. "Yes. Same place?"

"Sounds good. I have a surprise for you." He looked like a little boy with his hand stuck in the cookie jar.

Tucking the papers under her arm, she quirked an eyebrow at him and narrowed her gaze. "A surprise? What's the occasion?"

"There isn't one. That's why it's a *surprise*, silly." He shook his head and wagged a finger in her face.

She couldn't help but laugh at him. "You know I love surprises."

"That I do." He pretended to straighten some bowls on a shelf.

"No hint? Nothing?" This time she put her hands on her hips.

He put his fingers to his lips and pretended to zip them shut. With the papers in her hand, she swatted at him as she left the kitchen. "Frank Henderson, you are infuriating." But she loved it. And by every indication, he knew it.

As Frank paced beside the bench where he met Ruth each evening, he hoped his plan would work. Checking his pocket watch, he rolled his eyes at himself. He'd let his excitement take over and now he would probably be waiting another ten minutes. Oh well, at least he was early and would be here when she arrived.

Ever since Ruth had been injured helping Julia and Chris search for the treasure from the 1500s, she had kept Frank at arm's length. Over time, it bugged him more and more. But he'd kept his mouth shut and a smile on his face. Most of the time.

The camaraderie they'd shared for many years was closer than friends, but not like siblings. They'd shared a passion for the work they did, a love of studying and discussing the Bible, and they could banter back and forth and make each other laugh.

It had been easy. Comfortable. Close.

Now, even though they saw each other every day and still talked, it wasn't the same. And Frank missed her. The real woman, for some reason, was locking up inside and building a substantial wall to protect herself.

The way he understood it, she couldn't get past her scars. So she didn't think anyone else could either.

Well, after two years, he was tired of waiting. He'd prayed about this more in the past few days than anything else.

It was time to start pursuing Ruth. It would probably take a good deal of time to earn her trust and convince her to let him back in, but he had to break down the wall somehow. Hopeful that his gift would do just that, he prayed it would also get her mind off her troubles. Perhaps get her back to her normal, positive, joyful self.

His timing probably wasn't the greatest since the upheaval at the hotel seemed to have everyone on edge. But when it came time, he'd speak with Mr. Owens about it. He'd wait until all this trouble was past, but he was determined to move forward. Neither he nor Ruth was getting any younger. They'd spent their lives giving to and serving other people.

He'd waited a long time for love. For God to show him the woman He had for him.

Ruth was the one. He was confident in that.

Oh, he'd had plenty of doubts creep in that she might reject him—and that was a very real possibility. But he was tired of sitting on his hands and doing nothing.

If anything, their brief walks at night had shown him that. The last two nights he'd been antsy with the knowledge.

But patience would have to win out. Just a little more.

Inside, she was hurt. And not the physical injuries. Frank was determined to see that she healed from whatever hurt festered within her. Even if it meant that she didn't accept his love. At least she would be whole again.

He wanted the best for her. Because he loved her.

There. He said it. At least in his mind. Oh, he'd loved her as a friend, and he'd loved her as a sister in Christ for a long time.

But he *loved* Ruth.

The syncopated rhythm of footsteps told him she was on her way. Frank turned and couldn't help but smile. Time to surprise her and hope that his gift would at least begin to break down the barrier between them.

"Sorry to keep you waiting. I telegrammed my parents and just received a reply." She didn't look all that happy.

"What did they say? Could they postpone their trip?"

The paper was still in her hand. It waved in the breeze as she shook her head. "They said it's been too long since they've seen me. They're still coming."

"Look, I know the timing is difficult, but this is a good thing. Your parents are lovely people. I'm looking forward to seeing them again." He wasn't sure what the correct response was at a time like this, but he could at least be positive and encouraging. Besides, he didn't want to ruin the mood for what he had planned.

Her shoulders slumped a bit. "It is a good thing. I just didn't want it to be a stressful time while they were here. We've never had to deal with anything like this while I worked for Harvey."

He patted her hand. "I know. But God will get us through this. The truth will come out. Besides, you're doing an amazing job and your parents need to see you at your finest." He wiggled his eyebrows.

Ruth rolled her eyes, but the grin that broke through her frown made him feel like he was king of the mountain. "You are such an optimist."

"I am. And I'm not ashamed to admit it." He clapped his hands together. "Ready for your surprise?"

"Of course." Still, her broad smile couldn't hide the weariness in her eyes. Well, maybe this would help.

He pointed to the bench. "Have a seat, Miss Anniston. Instead of a walk tonight, I thought this might be a better option."

She took a seat and placed her hands in her lap. "I'm intrigued."

"You should be." He stepped over to the side, where he'd covered the surprise with a blanket. At the moment, it looked like a bumpy mound, but wait until she realized what it was. "I know things are very busy right now and you're pulled in many directions all the time. I thought this might inspire you. Get you out in the fresh air a bit . . . at least to the rim." He lifted the blanket.

"Is that a camera?" She gasped as both of her hands flew up and covered her mouth.

"That it is. And it's yours. The same model that Mr. Watkins has—I have to admit I had Ray help me. And it even has a tripod stand."

Her lashes brushed her cheeks as she blinked. Over and over. All he could do was watch her. And wait.

"I don't know what to say." She seemed frozen in place.

He picked up the Century camera and handed it to her. "There's more. I've asked Ellsworth and Emery Kolb if they could give you some pointers. You know . . . like lessons on how to take pictures and develop them and such."

"You did all this for me?" She shook her head and caressed the camera. "But how did you know?"

"Know what?"

"That I've secretly wanted to learn?"

He shrugged. "Over the years, you've made a comment here or there, and I thought it sounded like you were interested."

As she turned the large box over and around in her hands, her words came out breathy. "I can't believe that you picked up on that. I *have* always wanted a camera."

"Perfect. I know how much you love the views." He held up a hand. "But I made the brothers promise that they wouldn't do any of their daredevil stuff with you."

Her laughter broke the trance she'd seemed to be in. "Thank you. I don't think I want to be jumping crevasses any time soon." Ruth set the camera down on the bench and came to her feet. "You . . . I . . ." She shook her head. "This is such an expensive gift—"

"We've been friends a long time, Ruth. You've done a million things over the years for me. Allow me to do this for you."

"I—I don't know what to say."

He shrugged. Her scrutiny made him blush. Good thing it was dusk outside. "I wanted to do something for you. To make you smile. That's all."

Why didn't he simply tell her everything right now? Pour out his heart? What was stopping him? He opened his mouth, but the words stuck in his throat.

Now wasn't the right time.

"I love it. Thank you, Frank." She stepped forward and wrapped him in a hug.

She was such a tiny thing. He placed his arms around her and hugged her back. Which might have been a mistake, because his heart kicked into high gear. He pulled back, hopefully before she noticed. "Once all this bookkeeping mess is over with, we can schedule some days off just to take pictures." He pointed to the bag on the ground. "I think I got you everything you need to get started. There are plenty of glass plates in there. Emery said Blanche can help you learn how to develop them too, in case they're not around."

"Before long, I bet little Edith will even know how to do that. I've seen Emery showing her how to use his camera already."

Emery and Blanche's two-year-old daughter was the highlight for most of them at the canyon. Filled with the same adventurous spirit as her parents and uncle, she could light up a room with her smile and giggles.

"At this rate, I bet that little girl has seen more of the canyon than I have." Frank tucked his hands into his vest pockets.

They were on neutral ground again. But Frank wished he could push for more. *Give her time. Give her time.* The chant began in his head.

The hug from Ruth would have to be enough for now. And seeing the delight on her face. All her trepidation and fear seemed to melt away. If only he could do that for her every moment of every day.

He checked his watch. "I know it's getting late. Let me carry all this back for you."

"I would appreciate that. Thank you."

He gathered up all the equipment. With his arms full, he adjusted everything and blurted out, "You really like it?" He hated being so insecure, but he needed to hear it from her lips again.

Ruth smiled the smile that he hadn't seen in more than two years. Her eyes sparkled in the moonlight. Then she put her hand on his arm. "I love it, Frank. It's the best gift I've ever been given."

He followed her back to the hotel, his feet barely touching the ground.

A long whistle signaled the approaching train.

Oliver looked at the four men he'd hired. Big. Imposing. Strong. They were perfect for the job. Of course, he paid well, with more to come, so they were eager to please. "I'll meet you at the house at ten o'clock sharp. Make sure they're alive but restrained. Understood?"

They shouldn't need the instructions, but he wanted to make sure. He'd be watching from a hidden location. He couldn't risk being seen with them. He walked briskly to the spot he'd chosen earlier. Looked at his pocket watch. Then started his countdown.

The train should be arriving in the station right about . . . now.

His men would be on the train in seconds.

Act as escorts for the Harvey Company men. Then, as soon as they had them in the coach, they would knock them out and bring them to the farmhouse miles from town.

Watching from his perch, he saw six men amiably walking toward the prepared coach. They must have been convincing. As long as they stuck to the story he'd given them, he was confident of his plan.

Time to put part two into motion.

Heading back out to the platform, he found the other two men he'd hired. He studied them from head to toe. They were dressed almost identically to the men they were to impersonate. Their briefcases and luggage were a decent fit as well.

No one at the El Tovar should suspect a thing. They knew the auditors were arriving on this morning's train. These two could play the part. And with him there to supervise, the next moves on his part would be played brilliantly.

He gave them a nod. "I'll see you this afternoon."

As he rode a horse out to the farmhouse, he checked his pocket watch again. Timed to perfection.

If he wasn't out to right a wrong done to his family, he might even consider making a life out of crime. Because he was that good at it.

The thought made him laugh to the dry, desert landscape around him.

When he reached the farmhouse, there was no sign of life there, which meant the men had done their jobs. Good.

He unlocked the door and headed toward the basement cellar, which they'd reinforced over the past few days. No windows. No exits. No light.

Should be perfect for what he needed to accomplish.

"Well now. Gentlemen. Good job." He looked at his men. "Why don't you go upstairs for a few minutes while I speak to our guests?"

The two men in the chairs were battered and bruised. One had a black eye. The gags around their mouths kept them from saying anything, but their eyes said enough.

Fear was what they felt right now. That's exactly where he wanted them.

"Let's get down to business, shall we?" He sat in a chair as the men in front of him squirmed. "You have information that I want. I have the power to set you free or to kill you. It's your choice."

He really had their attention now.

"Mr. Smithey." He used a tone smooth as silk. "I hear you have a beautiful wife with two lovely children. I have a friend watching them. In fact, this morning, as your wife bought flowers at the market, she told him how much she loves her roses."

The smaller of the two men squirmed and squawked against the gag in his mouth.

Oliver put a finger up to his lips. "Shh, now. There's no reason to get upset. As long as you do as I ask, they will stay safe."

"And, Mr. Lovett, I believe your wife had an appointment

with her doctor this morning. Because you are expecting your first child. Let me be the first to congratulate you." He clapped his hands together and smiled.

A tear slipped out of Lovett's eyes, while the other man kept his eyes closed. Whether it was rage that filled him or fear, it didn't matter. Both would work to Oliver's advantage. Until he broke them.

Eventually, he'd have what he needed and they could be disposed of. But for now, it was good to give them some hope.

Besides, *he* wasn't the one making these men suffer. Harvey was.

"Now . . . who would like to start?"

# 10

It has me worried, Miss Anniston." Gregory Owens stood in her office and paced the floor. Something that he'd become very good at of late. Every time she saw him, the man seemed to be pacing.

Which wasn't at all like the manager that she'd met five years ago—the man she'd worked with all this time. Always in control. Steady. Even if a bit somber, he could be trusted and relied upon to be a rock.

But this morning, here he was. In her office. Pacing.

"Is there anything in particular that makes you more on edge about this? I thought the Harvey Company often sent out men to audit."

He stopped pacing and stared over her head and out the window. "I haven't felt right about this whole thing. Not since the beginning." He pushed his glasses up on his nose.

"Since you found the discrepancy?"

His lips pursed. "To be honest, not since Mr. Hammond died. Before that, all I had to do was look at the big picture. The income versus the expenditures. Hammond was meticulous about everything. I never had to worry. And there were *never* any discrepancies. Ever." He blew out his cheeks and a huff of breath escaped. "As soon as the numbers didn't match, my stomach tied into a knot and has been that way ever since."

"We've been going over every single number, sir. It's a tedious process, but I'm sure we will figure it out."

"But not before the men arrive. They'll be here on the train today."

"True, but we will keep at it." The clock on her desk chimed the quarter hour. She really didn't have time for this. But he was her boss.

"I wish I knew who was behind it." The pacing started up again.

Ruth nodded and went back to the kitchen charts for today. There was a lot to do, and though he needed to vent his frustrations, there really wasn't anything she could do about it. But she could listen and respond and still get some work done.

"The El Tovar has always had the highest reputation. Why, we've never had any complaints. Not one! Who would make such comments to the papers? It's slander . . . that's what it is."

"It should be illegal to print things without proof." She checked off another list. Good thing Frank was so good at what he did and they had this process down to a science. Otherwise, Mr. Owens' presence would stress her out even further.

"Agreed. Yellow journalism. Makes a mockery of good and decent journalists."

"Umm-hmm." She took a sip of water without even looking up. Her mind slipped back to last night. Frank's gift had been more generous than anything she'd ever received. It was amazing he understood her so well that he knew what she wanted. Something deep down she had dreamed about but shoved aside after her injury. Oh, if only they weren't in the middle of this giant mess, she'd take her next day off and spend the entire time learning everything she could from the Kolbs.

For years, she'd watched and marveled at their willpower and energy, their ability to race up and down the switchbacks of the Bright Angel Trail multiple times a day just to develop the pictures for the tourists. That trek exhausted any normal person, and that was only hiking down and back up *once*! Then there were the times when the brothers put their showmanship to work and took those crazy pictures of themselves jumping from rock to rock or dangling from a cliff. She had to admit, she loved it. Even though *she'd* prefer to stay on safe ground, thank you very much.

What a joy to have a camera of her very own.

All because of Frank.

Frank.

The man who'd stuck by her through thick and thin. The man whose green eyes could see straight to her soul. Heat filled her cheeks as she thought of him.

His gift was extravagant. Quite a sacrifice for him to spend so much on her.

"I wonder if the company has thought to put an investigation into these reports? Perhaps the papers *could* be sued for printing lies against an upstanding, well-known establishment."

Oops. She hadn't been paying attention. Taking another sip of water, she hoped it would help to cool her face. "I'm sure everything will right itself in the end, Mr. Owens."

"Yes, yes. Of course, you're right." He stopped his pacing and tapped her desk, which brought her attention back up to him. "Thank you for all you have done here, Ruth. Honestly. From the bottom of my heart, I wish for you the very best and appreciate everything that you have poured into the work here at the El Tovar."

Even though it sounded like he thought their employment might be coming to an end, she offered him a smile. "You are most welcome, Mr. Owens. I look forward to many more years of working together at Harvey's Crown Jewel." Hopefully the last part wasn't too over-the-top encouraging for him to look at the positive.

The train's whistle in the distance stopped him from responding. He stood there for a moment with his mouth open, then snapped it shut. Then opened it again. "Shall we go out and greet the Harvey auditors, Miss Anniston?" He held out his arm, not really giving her any option to decline.

She stood and prayed her leg would hold her. Normally she rubbed it before she started walking, but she couldn't exactly do that right now.

As he escorted her out of her office, he took it slow, and for that she was grateful. Once they were out in the rotunda, she glanced around and saw the rest of the staff had gathered. At least, all who weren't busy serving their other customers. Everyone had been informed of the men arriving today.

Mr. Owens stepped forward and held up a hand.

A hush fell over all the employees.

"In a few minutes, we will be welcoming two men who represent the Harvey Company. We all know why they are here. I want everyone to proceed as usual. Do your very best. Answer questions when asked. Serve our guests. Now please, back to your work."

No one said a word as they scattered.

"Miss Anniston, I would appreciate you accompanying me to the front of the hotel."

"Of course, Mr. Owens." No longer holding on to his arm, she slowed her pace and did her best to hide her limp.

By the time she took her place at his side, the front doors had opened in a whoosh, and several people stepped into the welcoming Rendezvous Room.

Mr. Owens dipped his chin at each person. "Welcome to the El Tovar." The pacing man filled with anxiety over the new arrivals from moments ago was now gone and replaced with the one she knew well.

Put together. Calm. Collected. In control.

Then he stiffened.

Two men entered and headed straight for them.

"Mr. Owens, I presume?" The taller man stuck his hand out. "Tyrone Smithey." He shook the manager's hand and nodded his head to the man beside him. "And this is my associate, George Lovett."

Mr. Lovett extended his hand as well. "It's a privilege to make your acquaintance, Mr. Owens."

Her boss shook his hand. "Allow me to introduce to you Miss Anniston. She is the supervisor of the kitchen and dining room here at the El Tovar."

"Ah, Miss Anniston. Your reputation precedes you." Mr. Smithey smiled and showed a row of straight, white teeth. "But I must admit, I was expecting someone a good deal . . . older. You've been in the Harvey employ for quite a while. Longer than me." The good-natured tease set her a bit at ease.

She offered a smile to both men. "It has been my honor to be here."

"Miss Anniston started out as a Harvey Girl more than fifteen years ago, rose to the rank of headwaitress a decade ago, and has been serving diligently in a supervisory position for the past two years," Mr. Owens added. "I don't know what I would do without her."

There really was no way to respond, so she changed the subject. "Gentlemen, I will leave you to get settled into your rooms, if you will excuse me." Each man dipped his head at her and then waited.

Oh, she hadn't thought that through. No chance she was about to walk away in front of these men.

Thankfully, Mr. Owens must have sensed her dilemma and held an arm out toward the rotunda. "As you know, the hotel is booked for the summer, so our staff are quite busy. Let me personally show you to your rooms."

As he led them away, Ruth put a hand to her stomach. The Harvey men would be given the special guest quarters they kept for employees who traveled to the El Tovar. While they might not be as posh as the rooms on the upper floors, any Harvey employee should be happy with them. Because the customer always came first.

She made her way back to her office, taking her time with each step. Her leg was not happy after all that standing.

At least it was time to take the elixir again. That should see her through.

"Ouch!"

Frank didn't want to look. But he had to. Matthew held his hand in the air and raced to the sink. Another burn? That would be four already today.

Three sliced fingers. And two chefs had collided earlier and salad had flown through the air, sticking to the ceiling, the walls, their hair, chef coats, aprons, everything.

Of all days for things to go awry, it had to be the day that the Harvey auditors arrived.

Why was everyone so nervous?

Howard assured him that he'd given everyone a calming pep talk this morning while Mr. Owens had gone over the menus with Frank. But apparently it hadn't worked.

Something had the whole kitchen wound tighter than the string around the stuffed eye of round slow-roasting in the oven for dinner.

Luncheon would begin service in ten minutes, and the place was a cacophony of noise. Not the normal hum of all the gears working in perfect unison. No, this was loud. Stressful. More like the sound of a battleground.

Which was not encouraging.

Not that he had anything to prove to the Harvey auditors. He was the head chef. They weren't here to examine *him* or how well he ran his kitchen.

But . . . they could report back about the food not being top notch. Or accidents happening while they were on the premises.

Frank knew better. This worry churning in his gut had to go.

*Heavenly Father, I need help. Please. Cover this place with Your peace. Help me to do my very best and keep tempers in check. This needs to be for Your glory. Not mine. I need my perspective—my focus—to be on You.*

Frank breathed deep and let it out in a long, measured exhale. There, that was better.

He wiped his hands on a towel and went to each man and

spoke a few encouraging words. Not much. Simply, "that is perfect," "tastes great," "good job," and "the guests will love it."

Back at his own station, he lifted the saucier with his special mushroom sauce and gave it a stir. Almost thick enough. He shifted to the sauté pan, where the quartered mushrooms were browning beautifully. Tossing them lightly to turn them, he checked the clock on the wall. In a minute, he would add the mushrooms to the sauce, add a touch of salt and pepper, taste it, and it would be ready for the browned steak cutlets. A special recipe of his that had quickly become a luncheon favorite in the dining room.

He smiled to himself and stirred the sauce. He added the mushrooms, gave it all a quick swirl, and finished it off. Now he needed to transfer it to the warming station, where the men who finished the plates could add it to the orders.

Frank lifted the large saucier and headed for the station. "Coming through."

Everyone made a path as he carried the pan. It was almost like a dance. Each man knew the steps and had been in the same position hundreds of times.

Something blue out of the corner of his eye didn't fit the scene, but he kept his eyes on the pan so he wouldn't spill.

A flash of a burner on his left flamed up, then something hit him from the right and sent the pan of sauce down the front of Frank's white chef's coat, pants, and shoes.

Standing there holding an empty saucier, he bit his tongue and forced himself to count to ten as the heat of the sauce seeped into his body and made him cringe. Most of the time he was a calm, easygoing guy. But his temper could also be fiery.

And he was about to lose it.

The kitchen hum came to a complete halt. All eyes were on Frank. Would he blast everyone for the chaos of the morning?

"I'm so sorry, Chef!" Leo was on the floor, where he'd also been splayed with sauce. "I don't know what happened. All of a sudden, I just slipped." He gripped his arm, where some of his exposed skin had sauce on it. A grimace crossed his face.

Frank helped Leo off the floor. "You need to change and get your arm looked at. That might be a burn that needs treatment."

With as much calm as he could muster, he turned to Howard. "There's no time to make more of my special mushroom sauce. Please make a simple mushroom cream sauce instead and instruct all the waitresses on the menu change. I will need a few moments to change."

And with that, he headed out the side door and counted each of his steps to keep him calm.

He'd prayed for focus. Guess he needed to spend a few minutes in his room doing just that.

The day hadn't been a *complete* disaster.

Although Ruth had heard of the kitchen having one problem after another. And almost every Harvey Girl on the floor had needed to change her apron because of spills—some even had to change their dresses as well.

Guilt riddled her a bit since she admittedly hid in her office all day. Even for meals.

But it was easier that way.

More peaceful.

And she'd kept her sanity.

Which was more than she could say for Mr. Owens. The man had come to see her five times.

*Five. Times.*

Beet red each visit. Pacing her office. Ranting and raving about how things were falling apart around them.

When she'd tried to convince him that things weren't really all that bad, he'd narrowed his eyes at her, mumbled something under his breath, and slammed the door behind him.

So here she sat. Sipping tea in her room, doing her best to forget the day and stay awake because she'd promised to talk to Charlotte.

All she wanted was a good night's sleep. Actually, she wanted for this nightmare to be over and to go back to being the headwaitress. But that wasn't going to happen. So, sleep was the next best thing. The elixir helped her feel better during the day. It boosted her energy too. But she must not be sleeping well, because she felt more tired tonight than she had in a long while. Even after staying up all night last week. Which was odd.

Tap, tap.

"Come in." She didn't even have the energy to get up.

Charlotte entered, her eyes red.

"Are you all right? Have you been crying?" Ruth sat up straight on her bed and set her teacup down.

Her friend's chin lifted. "I'm fine. Louise and Tessa had to give us a talking-to." She swiped at her hair.

The headwaitresses were not prone to lashing out. "Was it about today?"

"Yes." Charlotte plopped in the chair and picked at a string on her housecoat. "There were too many mistakes. Too many spills. Too many fusses."

"Ah. So the girls have been on edge with one another?" Ruth leaned back against her headboard.

"Yes. Louise says it has to stop . . . which of course, we all know, but no one likes to be under a microscope and that's how we feel with the auditors here."

She reached for the teapot. "Would you like some?"

"Yes, please."

Ruth poured a cup, and Charlotte leaned forward to accept it. "You know, after they've been here a day or two, things will settle. Nerves will calm down. And we'll be back to normal." That's why she planned on staying holed up in her office as much as possible. Not that she would say that out loud.

"I hope so. Because Tessa also caught wind of Mr. Denton's intentions, and she gave me a strict talking-to about the rules and all." The younger woman took a sip and looked completely miserable.

"Mr. Denton? Is that who you wanted to talk about?" Time to smooth frazzled emotions over and hopefully bring back the Charlotte she knew and loved. "Tell me about him."

"He's a businessman. From California." She perked up.

"What kind of business?"

"I'm not sure. He owns two buildings . . . I know that much."

Two buildings. Great. That gave her so much information. Okay, so different tactic. "You say he's already declared his intentions?"

"Yes." A giddy nod followed.

"Well, you know the rules, Charlotte." The scolding in her tone was probably a bit stronger than she'd intended.

The younger woman wilted a bit and looked about ready to pout. "Of course I do. That's why I wanted to speak to you. No one has given me a chance to tell them anything." Tears shimmered in her eyes.

"I'm sorry." Ruth did her best to push her snippy and pessimistic thoughts aside as she patted Charlotte's hand. "I'm giving you a chance right now. So . . . what do you like about him?"

"He brings me flowers almost every day. And has one of the other girls deliver little gifts to me." She prattled on about all the little gifts but said nothing of Mr. Denton. Her smile showed she was smitten. Not with the man. But with the idea of love.

"Do you know anything about his family? What his future plans are?" She really was too tired to be dealing with an infatuation.

Charlotte shrugged. "Not yet. But I'm sure we'll talk about it."

"If he's talking about a future with you, he really should let you in on his plans." Didn't Charlotte know better?

"I know that. But we don't have much time together."

"Is he a man of faith? Does he go to church?"

The light in her friend's eyes dimmed. "Yes, he goes to church." Her words were clipped.

"I'm sorry. I don't mean to pry. Just wanted to learn about him." She took a sip of her tea. "I take that back. Yes, I'm prying. But isn't that why you came to talk to me? It seems to me that this man is leading you on. Why, you barely know anything about him."

Charlotte set the teacup down on the little table with a loud clink against the saucer. "You're as bad as Tessa." She stood. "Look, I know things have been hard for you since the accident. But there's a man who has shown genuine interest in me. And I was hoping for a little encouragement. A little joy from my friend. Just because *you're* not happy doesn't mean the rest of us can't be happy." She stomped her foot, and in a swirl of housecoat and nightgown, Charlotte left the room.

Tears burned the backs of Ruth's eyes as she blinked. What had just happened?

# 11

**MONDAY, JUNE 7, 1909**

The palpable tension in the air at the hotel the past few days made Charles want to chuckle. But he refrained. To think that a couple of auditors could create such chaos.

Of course, the guests were off in their own little world, buying baubles at the Hopi House, gushing over the views, and wondering why the *servants* were in such a dither.

Funny how the upper crust of the wealthy looked at everyone beneath them as such.

Of course, the black-and-white attire of the Harvey Girls was eerily similar to many of the maids in most of their stately mansions. It made them invisible unless needed.

Status and class were everything to these people. It made them who they were. It divided them from one another and anyone distasteful enough to have been born without money.

Charles studied the dining room. His breakfast had been exquisite. But watching the room was almost as good. Funny how these people threw scads of money at him to make them feel better about themselves.

He'd had enough business the last few days to fund a small town for a month. His sights were on something greater, but this would do for now.

Rising from his seat, he picked up his briefcase and walked out of the dining room, down the hall, and turned at the rotunda to head to Miss Anniston's office.

At her door, he straightened his shoulders and knocked.

Her usual greeting had him opening the door with a smile. With a bow and a few quick steps, he stood in front of her desk. "No need to get up. I've brought you what you requested."

A tiny gasp. She put a hand to her throat. "That was faster than I expected."

"I'm thankful for the swiftness of our railroads, Miss Anniston." He pulled out two large jars, both with gold lids and gold filigree labels. "I've taken the liberty of labeling each with a number since the medical terminology might be a bit foreign to you."

"Thank you." She looked at him expectantly.

"The first is labeled number 1. It's the one to apply first on your leg. It needs to soak into the muscles for at least an hour before you apply the second cream. You'll feel some intense cooling deep in the tissue. That's normal. Again, try to stay off your leg for as much as you can the first three or four weeks. Both need to be applied twice a day for the optimal results."

She nodded and picked up the jar, opened it, and sniffed. Her eyes widened a bit, but she didn't say a word.

"As you can guess, the jar labeled with a 2 is the cream that will help your scars to heal. The main ingredient is the very finest and most rare of the aloe vera plants that only grows up in the mountainous regions near Mount Everest."

Hopefully she wasn't a scholar in botany or geography. Rarely did he have anyone question him, and most of the time he kept it as truthful as possible, but this woman seemed to need a little . . . embellishment. And he definitely knew how to weave a tale. Especially with the tone of his voice. He was positive he could convince a woman of almost anything just by the smooth, lyrical tone that he used.

"Thank you, Mr. Goodall. I've had good results from the elixir so far, and I look forward to trying the creams as well." She tucked the jars into a satchel by her desk.

"If I may be so bold, Miss Anniston. Why is it you've never married? A woman as lovely as yourself . . . it's hard for me to imagine. Your injuries were recent, right?"

The smile on her face slipped.

"Oh, I'm sorry. Did I assume wrong? Is it Mrs. Anniston? Did you lose your husband?" He knew it wasn't true, but he had to pretend.

"No. You were correct the first time. I've never been married. I've worked for the Harvey Company for many years and loved my work."

"Surely you had many proposals. I hear that's how the West has been settled."

"I've had many, yes. But perhaps I'm a bit old-fashioned. I was waiting for love. But I believe my time has passed."

"Not at all, Miss Anniston." He gave her a sympathetic sigh. "You are lovely. And with these creams, you'll be restored and any man would be lucky to have you." The tone was his best soother, but the words hit their mark. He could see it in her eyes. "Mr. Harvey owes you a great debt for you to sacrifice your life for the company."

"Not at all. It has been an honor. The opportunities provided through this company for women are unparalleled."

He leaned an inch closer. "You are a most remarkable woman, Miss Anniston. I count it a privilege to know you. Perhaps . . . you might be willing to walk with me one evening?"

The desired effect was clear on her face as her eyes widened and she blinked several times. She put a hand to her throat. "That's very kind of you to ask, Mr. Goodall."

He dipped his chin. "Well, I must be on my way. Don't hesitate to let me know when you need more of the elixir or creams. I have plenty with me now."

The pink in her cheeks was refreshing. "Thank you, Mr. Goodall."

Charles grinned as he shut the door behind him.

Now . . . who was next on his list?

Their steps were slow as Frank walked beside Ruth along the path at the rim. They hadn't gone very far—she said she didn't want to overdo it after a long day. But she was also quieter than usual. Even more reserved.

"How's your leg feeling?" He ventured into a topic that may or may not help their conversation.

"I purchased some creams from Mr. Goodall after Doctor Newport mentioned him. I don't want to get my hopes up, but it did feel a lot better this afternoon." Something was off with her. But what? "Mr. Goodall has been very generous and kind to me. Even asked me to take a walk with him sometime."

Creams? From Goodall? What was that about? Wait. What did she say about a walk? He'd have to get more information later because she'd gone back to speaking about the creams.

How could she drop a comment like that and not explain? The man was handsome and quite the charmer. Frank collected his thoughts and cleared his throat. "I hope they help."

"Me too. Have things gotten better in the kitchen since the disasters of Friday?"

His hearty chuckle echoed around them. "I don't think I've seen so many accidents in a kitchen since I was young and first being trained. I shouldn't laugh about it, I know. But there's nothing else to do—unless I want to wallow in self-pity and relive it all."

"That's good."

Huh? Was she even listening? Time to stop this frivolous chatter. "Ruth, is there something bothering you?"

"No. I'm fine." But she kept her gaze straight ahead.

He touched her elbow, stopped her, and turned to face her. "Look . . . I know you've been hiding in your office and trying to figure out where the discrepancies came from so that the auditors can be done and leave, but you missed church yesterday—which is unlike you—and you seem . . . distant."

Her eyes shone with the glimmer of tears. But she didn't say anything for several moments.

Frank handed her his handkerchief, thankful he hadn't pushed about the other subject.

"Thank you," she whispered as she took it and dabbed at her eyes.

Rocking back and forth on his feet, he watched her. "Would you like to sit?"

With a nod, she led the way to a couple of large boulders. She sat on one and twisted the handkerchief in her hands. "I'm fine, really."

"I don't believe it. So why don't you tell me the truth?"

Her eyes snapped up to his. There. The fire was back. The Ruth Anniston he knew. If only he could get her to stay.

The seconds passed with only the sounds of the canyon around them. Every once in a while, they'd hear the screech of an owl or the wail of a coyote. And he waited. Their gazes locked. Did she think she could get him to give up so easily?

Finally, she huffed. "Charlotte and I had words the other night."

"You and Charlotte? Really?"

"I know. It shocked me too. She came to me because she wanted to talk about a man who is interested in being a suitor. But it had been a long and disastrous day for most everyone and tensions were high and we were both exhausted . . ." Ruth looked away. "She was upset when she left."

"What did she say?"

This time, a tear slipped out. And she didn't stop it. "Basically that I don't want anyone else to be happy because *I'm* not happy."

That took him aback. "It's hard to imagine Charlotte saying that."

Ruth waved it off. "I know she wanted me to be excited for her, and I guess I probably wasn't. I simply asked her questions about the man, and she didn't know anything about him. She's all caught up in the thought of being in love. I get that. But I can't seem to get her words out of my mind. Does everyone think I'm unhappy? Is that how I come across?"

"No. I can't see that at all. Yes, you've had a tough row to hoe the past couple years, but you're certainly not unhappy. A little more reserved. A little quieter, maybe . . . but not *unhappy*." Frank paused. Was he allowing his feelings for her to cloud his judgment? As much as he hated to admit it, Ruth hadn't been the same. And if he was honest, she hadn't seemed very happy. With a deep breath, he took the chance. "*Are* you happy?"

"You know, I can't say I *am* all that happy. I've done plenty of wallowing in my own pain and misery. I've done a lot of questioning God. Is that wrong?"

His heart ached for her and the pain that was written all over her face. "I don't believe it's wrong to question Him. I think He wants us to know Him."

She rubbed a hand over her injured leg. "Just last week, Charlotte and Tessa and I had an interesting discussion about grace."

He knew there was more to it . . . but understanding the complex mind of Ruth Anniston took time. He was accustomed to waiting and listening. "What about grace?"

The handkerchief was wound around her fingers now. She turned to face him more, which was always a good sign. "Well . . . I've approached life always thinking that I had to earn everything. I had to earn my job. Earn my wages by doing the work. Earn the promotions. Earn the ability to keep those promotions. I've always tried to *earn* my place."

"I think we're all guilty of that. That's how the world works, isn't it?"

"And once I became a headwaitress—gracious that was more than a decade ago—*I* was the one who everyone turned to. So I diligently stayed in the Word, went to church, gleaned everything I could from those wiser than me so that I could guide the girls in my care. I always had to be the one with the answers and wisdom. Again . . . trying to *earn* my place. Thankfully, God gave me the answers to be able to help.

"But then Tessa made a comment when we were talking about faith and works—and how we still think we have to earn our way by doing good works, but faith without works being dead—and she said we couldn't understand it because it was all about grace. Grace alone. She used the phrase 'grace plus nothing,' and I've been trying to wrap my mind around that ever since."

"Grace plus nothing." He let that sink in. "I like that."

"I do too. But that's the thing. I don't understand it. I have no idea how to live that out. Because I still feel like I have to earn everything. We talked about how we are so ingrained with good behavior equaling good results and bad behavior equaling bad results—and that's where I've struggled for two years. Because I keep questioning God. Why? Why me? Why did such a horrible thing happen?"

He could tell she wasn't done, so he sat in silence with her. Looked up at the stars and then back to her.

"The thing is . . . I stepped in front of Julia on purpose that day."

"I know." His heart swelled for her. "You sacrificed yourself for her."

"And I tell myself every day that I would do it again. And I would. At least, I'd like to *think* that I still would—even knowing what would happen. But ever since that day . . . I've been questioning God."

The misery in her expression showed him the battle inside that she'd tried to keep hidden. "That's understandable, Ruth. We all question Him when bad things happen."

"I think Charlotte is right. I'm unhappy. Because I can't seem to move past my injuries. But it's not that I *don't* want anyone else to be happy. Oh, it's all such a mess." She put her hands on the sides of her head. "And now my parents are coming for a visit and I haven't seen them in more than two years. I don't want to let them down."

"You could never let your parents d—"

"We're human, Frank. We let people down all the time."

"I've met your parents. They adore you. Exactly *how* are you going to let them down?"

"I don't look the same as I did before."

"And *I* don't look the same way I did ten years ago either. I doubt your parents are worried about how you look. You're beautiful."

The swift shake of her head back and forth and her pinched lips showed her displeasure. "No. You're saying that because you're my friend. You see me every day, so you're used to . . . *this*." She pointed to her face and then her leg. "I'm afraid it's going to be quite a shock to them. Then the auditors are here . . ." Her hands waved in the air as she abruptly changed thoughts. "And I feel like the world is spinning out of control and I don't have any good answers for anyone anymore. What use am I to anyone? Why didn't God take me that day?"

Frank's heart ached for her, but with a bold move he took her hand and squeezed it.

*I need help here, Lord. Please give me the words You would have me say.*

But his mind was blank. He looked back up at the vast expanse above them. "Have you read the book of Job lately?"

Her brow creased. "No. Can't say that I have."

"But you know the story, right?"

She nodded.

He held tight to her hand because it looked like she could bolt at any moment. "All these devastating events happen to Job—one right after another, loss after loss—and then his friends come and sit with him. They sit in silence for seven days, which is quite the sacrifice and love for their friend, right? But then they start giving their opinions about *why*

158

all of it happened. These long discourses full of what they think of as wisdom and advice. Big words and thoughts about God. These discussions go back and forth. Job questions God. Again and again. But when God finally speaks to him, He says *nothing* about the why. Instead, He poses question after question about things unfathomable to the human mind."

"I'm not sure I'm following where you're going with this." She studied him, and he could see the deep need for understanding in her eyes.

"I think that's the point. It's like God is questioning us, 'Do *you* know where the storehouse of grace is?' 'Can *you* by trying and doing and earning ever find the key to unlocking it?' And the answers are all no. Because *we* are not God—the Creator of the universe. I think Tessa hit the nail on the head. It's grace plus nothing. By His unfathomable grace, you are here, Ruth. I am here. It has nothing to do with us. Or what we do. Or how we strive to earn it. It's all Him. His grace."

She was silent for several moments, and he allowed her the space. But he couldn't help but watch her. Her other hand lifted to her cheek. The one the lion had scarred.

He covered it with his own. "You are the most beautiful woman I've ever known, Ruth Anniston. Inside *and* out."

He hated for the moment to end because everything felt . . . right.

"The mountain lion left quite a mark on me." She didn't remove her hand.

"It doesn't matter. You are still Ruth. A beautiful child of God. Saved by grace." Removing his hand that was on her cheek, he held her gaze.

Her lips tipped up in a simple smile. "Grace plus nothing."

With a squeeze to her hand, he let go. "The most unfathomable thing of all. Keep asking the questions, Ruth. It's all right. One of these days, we'll understand it better."

"Thanks, Frank. I needed that." She lifted her chin to the night sky and took a long, deep breath. "I need to make things right with Charlotte. And I probably need to spend some time reading Job."

It was getting late, so he stood up and held out a hand for her. "Remember you're not alone in this." Her mention of Goodall's invitation came back to his mind. Frank didn't have competition . . . did he?

She took his hand and allowed him to help her get to her feet. "Thanks."

"So . . ." He offered his arm to her and shook off the doubts. Ruth was with *him* at this moment, and he wouldn't take that for granted. "When are you going to try out the new camera? I could be your subject, you know." He struck a pose with his chin lifted high. "Although the canyon would probably look a lot better."

Hearing her light laughter did his heart good. She was healing. It took time, but he could wait. As long as she needed.

But hopefully it wouldn't be *too* long.

# 12

It had been almost a week since the auditors arrived and Ruth had already wished at least one hundred times that all this mess could be sorted out and over. It was only nine in the morning, and she was sick of the walls of her office.

Mr. Owens had asked her to keep going through the tedious ledgers and orders on her own in every spare moment she had. Which wasn't a lot. Because being the supervisor of the kitchen and dining room—especially when they had two Harvey men on site—was a huge job in and of itself. She missed Frank.

And not because it helped to have an extra set of eyes, which cut her work on the books in half, but because she missed *him*. His calming presence. The way he could make her smile.

Now he wouldn't have a day off until the auditors left. Because Mr. Owens insisted—and she didn't blame him— that Frank be in charge of the kitchen every day. Everything needed to be perfection while the men were here.

Mr. Owens was going through procedures and other paperwork with the men. The El Tovar wasn't a typical Harvey House, after all. His plan was to stall the auditors with other things for as long as he could, hoping she could find the issue. But it couldn't last much longer.

And she wasn't any closer to finding the discrepancies.

The manager had wanted her to check six months' worth, and she had successfully finished four and a half. So far?

Nothing.

She tried not to let all the numbers blur together, but her brain was screaming for a break from the monotony.

Leaning back in her chair, she rubbed at her eyes and turned to look out the window. A typical audit at a Harvey establishment had the auditors going over every facet of the facility. From cleanliness, to maintenance, to the food, the service, the uniforms, the linens, the tableware, everything—absolutely *everything*—was inspected. Then the staff were watched and given an assessment. Then the books were reviewed. The Harvey Company was known for its accuracy in bookkeeping. Mistakes were not allowed.

At most places she'd worked, an audit lasted at most a week. But they were much smaller than the El Tovar. And this was no ordinary audit.

Accusations had been made. The auditors had to not only inspect like usual, but they also had to get to the root of the problem—if there was one.

She turned back to the bank deposits. What if the mistakes weren't on their end? Could there be an issue at the bank?

But she dismissed that idea almost as quickly as it came.

The problem had to be here. Somewhere.

She stood, stretched, and rubbed her right hand over her leg. The creams seemed to be working wonders. Most of the time, during the day, she didn't feel the discomfort and pain that she usually felt. Mr. Goodall had been correct—the cooling effect went deep and made her feel like she was getting stronger every time she applied it.

She placed her hands on her hips and looked down at the mass of papers and books on her desk. What was she missing?

Mr. Owens hadn't noticed any problems until after the time that Frank became the head chef. But he didn't have anything to do with this.

What else had changed?

Mr. Hammond had died.

The new bookkeeper got very sick and left for California.

No one else had been sent by the company. Why was that? Something didn't set well with her. Wait a minute . . .

She shuffled through some papers. "Frank always made the orders as the assistant chef—that was part of his duties. Which meant he passed it on . . . to Howard." Saying it out loud made her thoughts come together. Could the new assistant chef have something to do with all this?

She bit the inside of her cheek. Frank trusted the man. Said he was loyal and a wonderful assistant.

She sat back down and found the stack of orders from the time since Howard took over. Flipping through the papers, she saw a familiar name. Mr. Patterson owned a farm that grew wheat. He'd been supplying the hotel with his freshly ground wheat flour ever since the El Tovar opened.

Ruth hopped out of her chair, grabbed the paper, and headed out. After she locked her door, she went to Mr. Owens' office.

The clerk at the front desk stopped her. "He's not in right now, Miss Anniston."

"Oh, all right, I just need to make a telephone call." She brushed right past the young man and went to the telephone on the manager's desk. Once she'd spoken to the operator and had the call directed to the Patterson farm, she waited and tapped her foot.

"Hello?"

"Mr. Patterson?"

"Yes?"

"This is Miss Anniston from the El Tovar."

"Ruth!" The older man's sweet voice held a hint of a smile. "How lovely to hear from you. Is everything all right with the wheat?"

She couldn't help but grin. The man was always making sure his product was of the highest quality and that his customers were happy. "It's wonderful, Mr. Patterson. Makes the best bread around."

"Glad to hear it. Glad to hear it."

"Could I ask you about our last few orders for the hotel?"

"'Course . . . what do ya need?"

"I'm double-checking the books and wanted to make sure our numbers were correct. According to what I have in front of me, we ordered less than we usually do this last month."

"No, ma'am. The kitchen ordered almost double the usual amount. In fact, that new assistant chef fella told me that he'd be needing more from now on. Said the demands were higher for baked goods. That's not a mistake, was it? You are my best customers. I would hate to lose your business." The man's voice sounded a bit strained.

"No, no. We appreciate you very much, Mr. Patterson. It must simply be a clerical mistake. What was the amount?"

As he listed off the numbers, she scribbled on another sheet of paper. That was over 1,500 pounds a day! When the last order had been around 800 pounds a day.

"Is everything all right?"

"Yes. Don't you worry. I'll get it all straightened out." The man was like a grandfather to everyone at the canyon. She hated to upset him.

"Oh, good."

"Thank you, Mr. Patterson. I better go get this fixed."

"Glad I could help. I'll see you next week when I bring the next order."

"I'll look forward to it. Bye now." She hung up the mouthpiece and tapped the paper against her palm.

Had Howard given Frank the wrong order? Or had he forged this?

Twice as much wheat as usual. That was a hefty order indeed. It certainly would make sense and would help to balance the books.

And what on earth was he doing with all that flour?

It gave her a spring in her step to at least have somewhere to start.

She waved at the clerk as she headed back to her office. What if Howard had done that with other orders? Ordering more . . . and the hotel paying for it. So where was it going? Where was the surplus?

It didn't make sense.

When she rounded the corner, her door was open.

Funny. She'd made sure to lock it.

"Ah, Miss Anniston." Mr. Owens greeted her. "I was just letting the auditors in. They are anxious to get working on the books." The expression he sent her was filled with questions.

Mr. Smithey and Mr. Lovett both sent her large smiles.

Mr. Smithey tipped his head at her. "You do a fine job here, Miss Anniston."

"Thank you, sir." She made her way back around her desk and took her chair. She didn't need this interruption right now, not when she might be on the cusp of figuring it all out.

"Owens here was telling us that you haven't taken a day off in a while."

She didn't even look up at him, just glanced at all the other orders Howard had made. "There's been a good deal of work to do."

"Well, we think that you need some time off—with pay, of course." Mr. Lovett was the one speaking this time. "Mr. Owens here has offered us your office to use for a couple of days."

That brought her attention up. She glared at her boss. "Oh, he has?"

Her boss's expression was full of regret. "My apologies, Miss Anniston, but we have several important parties that must use the private dining room. By Saturday, it will be available to them."

"They can't work in their own quarters?" It sounded insubordinate and defiant, but the thought of these men in her private space unnerved her.

"We need a large space to spread out the documents."

"We are very sorry to inconvenience you, Miss Anniston. We will make sure that everything is *exactly* as it is now." Both of the auditors looked apologetic. Too apologetic. And too smiley.

She didn't like it.

But she didn't have a choice.

"I need a few minutes to gather my personal possessions that I have need of for the next couple of days."

"Of course." Mr. Smithey's smile kept getting wider.

She wanted to yell, *stop that!* But it would be rude. And probably get her fired. What was going on with her?

"Leave all the ledgers and accounting paperwork on the desk. We'll get through it."

"Yes, sir." She couldn't look at any of the men in front of her.

They left and shut the door.

Before she did anything else, she scribbled down all the numbers and items from the order she'd spoken to Mr. Patterson about. She'd have to ask Frank about it later. Then she gathered up her things, shoved them in her satchel, and made sure the elixir was out of her desk as well.

Straightening the papers and orders, she shifted everything that Howard had done to the middle of the pile. Something didn't feel right.

She didn't trust the Harvey men at first glance, but she couldn't say why. Was it because she was uneasy about them using her office? She had become quite the hermit, loving her private space. Was it because she didn't know them? Or maybe because something in Mr. Smithey's smile and Mr. Lovett's voice seemed a bit too . . . smooth. Of course, she and Mr. Owens and Frank had their suspicions up about everything right now. Perhaps that was why she was on edge. Maybe she should talk to Mr. Owens first and tell him her suspicions. He was in charge, after all.

When she was sure she had everything, she left her office and shut the door.

"You do realize that the only way you get to go home is if you tell me everything you know." Oliver towered over the slouched man in the chair.

Bloody and bruised, the real Mr. Smithey lifted his face. "I don't understand. . . . We've already given you every single detail about our procedures as auditors. What are you after? We run restaurants and hotels. We serve people along the railroad." The man sounded on the brink of giving up. Which was perfect.

Oliver nodded to his hired brute.

The guy delivered another blow to Smithey.

Smithey groaned.

"I'm the one asking questions here." Oliver stepped over to Lovett. "Are *you* ready to talk?"

"You haven't given us food in days. We can't sleep tied up in these chairs." The man's voice was weak. "We gave you everything about our jobs. Isn't that enough?"

"No. It isn't. There's plenty more I need to know about the Harvey Company. Tell me what I want to know and you can have food and a bed." He straightened his shoulders. "I'm not an unreasonable man." But he had left them alone with his thugs for several days so they could get good and scared. Worn out. Roughed up a little.

The two men sent each other weak glances. Lovett lifted his chin. "What do you want to know?"

With a smile, Oliver pulled up a chair and sat in front of them. "That's more like it." He waved Ronald over. "Take notes."

"Sure thing, boss." Ronald pulled out a pencil and notepad.

"Now, it might seem trivial, but we're going to start at the very beginning. I need every detail, every function, every minute piece of information. When I ask a question—keep that in mind."

After he took down the El Tovar, he had plans to do the same to the rest of the empire, which would easily fall with a little help from him and once everyone heard what had happened at the best of the Harvey Houses. He simply needed some insider information.

This was going to be fun.

# 13

**THURSDAY, JUNE 10, 1909**

Ruth walked straight into Mr. Owens' office and shut the door. "I need to talk to you about something."

"Go ahead." He offered her a seat.

"Why is it that we don't have a new bookkeeper yet?"

The man rubbed his jaw. "I have to admit, I've had the same question. Especially after Hammond passed and then the new man left suddenly. It has made me a bit wary."

"Have you spoken with the company about it?" She bit her lip.

"At this point, I'm afraid to say anything negative. Especially since the auditors arrived. Maybe they are planning to send us someone new after all of this is resolved." His brow deepened its crease. "I wish I had an easy answer to this mess."

"Well, this morning, I was thinking . . ." She took a long breath. "I have made it through four-and-a-half months' worth of the books and orders, which made me think back to when you first told me and Frank what you had found. The discrepancies started soon after Frank was named head chef."

"You don't think that Frank has anything to do with this?" The man looked incredulous.

"No. Not at all. But I *am* wondering if it has anything to do with the new assistant chef, Howard."

The manager leaned forward. "What makes you think that?"

"Look." She put the scribbled piece of paper in front of him. "When I thought of it this morning, I went through the orders and thought I'd call Mr. Patterson, since we've worked with him for many years. And he told me that last month, our order was almost double the normal. But on the order sheet? It didn't say that. Neither did the receipt. But I don't think Mr. Patterson would lie to me."

"Where are the papers now?"

"On my desk. With the auditors." Her tone was a bit snippy on the last words. "Sorry, Mr. Owens. I'm not trying to be disrespectful."

"No apology needed." He perched his glasses on the end of his nose and took another look at the paper. His jaw worked while he squinted. "Could there be a reason for doubling our order?"

"Not that I can see, sir. But I haven't asked Frank yet."

"It wasn't a mistake?"

"Apparently not. Mr. Patterson told me the next order is the same." She bit her lip and watched him mull it over. "He seemed pretty concerned and wanted to make sure he hadn't made a mistake because we are his best customer."

He laid the paper down and looked up at her. "So what . . . ? What could he be doing with all the extra wheat?"

"My question is, has he done this with other orders? Were all the orders and receipts all forged in some way? That *would* help to explain the money we can't account for that seems to be missing."

Mr. Owens tapped his desk. "Did you show this to Smithey and Lovett?"

"No, sir."

"Hmmm. Let's keep this between us for now. I don't want to cast blame on an innocent man if we're wrong. It might make them think we're trying to cover something. Why don't you discuss it with Frank and compare notes with him? Once we hear from him, we should speak to the auditors about what we've found."

While she didn't like having to wait for a moment longer, she had to agree. Owens was her boss, after all. And Frank should know the truth. "Yes, sir."

"Now go. Take the rest of the day off. I'm sorry I have been driving you so hard these past few weeks. It's not your problem, but you've been gracious enough to help." He removed his glasses and wiped a hand down his face. "This job has been quite strenuous of late."

Ruth studied him. Weariness stretched over his features. "Maybe you should consider taking some time off too."

Owens put his glasses back on. "All in good time, Miss Anniston. Once the audit is over and this mess is behind us, I will be able to relax."

"Very good, sir." She picked up the paper she'd shown him. "Do you mind if I take this? When I speak to Frank about it, I want to have the numbers correct."

"Of course." His attention was already back on something else on his desk.

"Have a good day."

"You too, Ruth." This time he lifted his face and sent her a warm smile.

The man was tough as nails and an incredible manager. But inside, there was a heart of gold that cared for people.

As she headed down the stairs to her room, she looked at the watch pinned to her shirtwaist. Not quite eleven in the morning. Perhaps she could change and then sneak in the side door of the kitchen to grab a sandwich and some fruit. Maybe see if Frank had a second to spare.

Time off sounded good. She could break out her new camera and try to forget about all this financial nonsense at the hotel and the men invading her office—*if* she could.

Back at her room, she unpacked her satchel and took a couple teaspoons of the elixir. That should keep her going for the next few hours. Within minutes, she felt better.

Ruth changed her clothes and packed up her new camera equipment so that she could carry it.

Now where was that hiking stick?

Julia had left it with her for when she came back to the canyon, saying it helped her while hiking and that Ruth could use it whenever she needed. It might be handy to help her keep her balance as she walked along the rim to the Kolbs' studio. It wasn't that far, but it was a distance farther than she usually walked on her leg.

Aha! There it was, next to the wardrobe.

Maybe she should try putting on an extra bit of that cream.

Without giving it another thought, she pulled out the jar and lifted her skirt. Massaging the cream into her leg, she immediately felt a difference. It felt cool and warm almost all at the same time.

Feeling more energized than she had in a long time, she got herself adjusted and balanced with what she had to carry and headed out the door.

She left out the basement exit and headed toward the kitchen. She deposited her things outside the side door and stood just inside so she wouldn't mess up the rhythm and movement of the men. She'd learned early on not to take up space or stand in the middle of the flow. The men were always quick and on the move with something hot and bubbly.

Frank spotted her, and she waved him over.

He set down what he was working on and wiped his hands on the towel over his shoulder. "It's so nice to see you." Scanning her attire, he raised an eyebrow.

"The auditors have taken over my office and told me to take the day off. So, I'm going to use my camera." Just saying it out loud made her smile. But then she spotted Howard. For some reason, he had stepped very close to where they were. Was he listening? She narrowed her eyes. "Could you step outside with me for a moment?"

"I'm sorry, Ruth." Frank moved closer to her, and his voice was a hushed whisper. "We're in the middle of the lunch rush, and I can't afford any mistakes."

"It's of great importance." But with Howard a couple of feet away, she couldn't risk saying anything to Frank about her suspicions. "But it can wait." She tried not to stare at the assistant chef and wonder about his motives. When did she become such a cynic? "On our walk this evening?"

"I'll be there."

She nodded, and he went back to work.

Howard glanced at her with what looked like a fake smile. "Miss Anniston." He dipped his chin and then followed Frank.

She had no intention of letting the man know that she suspected anything, so she smiled back at him. Then, she walked to the back, grabbed a couple of rolls and an apple, and headed back out the door. The food should tide her over for the time she was out and about.

Working the pack over her shoulders, she balanced herself and closed her eyes for a moment. The only way to enjoy this time was to refocus her thoughts. There was nothing she could do about their investigation into the inconsistencies of the numbers right now. With a deep breath, she planted the walking stick in front of her and headed toward the Kolb brothers' studio.

Taking slow steps since there was quite a decline on the path, she forced her mind to still and simply focus on the beauty around her. The views were spectacular. Every few yards, she stopped and took in the amazing scene before her. Never would she tire of this. The changing colors in the walls of the canyon. The ridges and ripples of granite stone walls. The vast expanse. The depth down to the river. It was simply . . . glorious.

As the tension eased a bit from her shoulders, she lifted her gaze to the sky and watched as long white wisps of clouds moved across the vivid blue.

What an amazing creation. Which pointed to the amazing Creator. As the thoughts meandered through her mind, she longed to lift up her heart and cry out to Him. But something held her back.

She couldn't come to Him right now. She wasn't ready. Hadn't figured out the problem before her. Hadn't figured out how to make herself feel whole again. Once she had this all straight, she could work on her relationship with her heavenly Father.

Wasn't that thinking a little backward? Like telling someone to clean up their life before they could come to Jesus. If anyone could actually do that. The thought was ludicrous.

And yet . . . this distance between her and God had become commonplace. She'd gotten used to it and used to ignoring it.

Ruth shook her head and started down the trail again. Something else to think about later.

The two-story house Emery and Ellsworth had built was on the very edge of the canyon. Ralph Cameron had given them permission to build it there as long as they collected the tolls for the Bright Angel Trail.

A lot of contention had brewed between Cameron and government officials about ownership of lands, trails, mines, and such. That had created trouble for the Kolb brothers, but they stuck with it.

It was brilliant what they did. All the pictures they took. One brother or the other would run up and down the trail to get to the water down at Indian Creek, develop the pictures in a cave, and then clean the slides and bring the pictures up before the guests made it back. And they'd created quite a business for themselves.

They sold picture books with photos they'd taken of the gorgeous views. They also had lots of pictures of themselves *taking* pictures so people could see what lengths they went to in order to get the perfect shot.

Ruth had never met more adventurous souls. It was nothing to them to jump across a crevasse or to hang by a rope, just to get a picture.

When Blanche had come to the canyon as a Harvey Girl, it wasn't long before Emery Kolb snatched her up. They were married, and two years later, their little girl, Edith, was born. That baby had trekked all over the canyon and rim on the back of a burro, where Emery had built a little side-basket apparatus. On one side, she sat snug in her basket. On the other, the family dog had his own basket.

Little Edith was as adventurous as her parents. More than once, Ruth had seen her standing on the back porch of the

Kolb house—one that hung out over the canyon—and her heart had dropped thinking of that little girl falling. But Edith was a Kolb. They seemed incapable of falling.

The farther down the path she went, Ruth was even more thankful for the tall walking stick. But it felt good to take longer strides and stretch out her injured leg. That cream seemed like a miracle, because she couldn't even feel any pain right now—which was amazing.

Oh, the limp was still there, but it gave her hope that she could truly recover. Even after all this time.

Maybe she should go see Dr. Collins and tell him what she'd found out from Dr. Newport and Mr. Goodall. He'd taken such good care of her . . . he wouldn't be offended, would he? Seemed like he might even have some advice to go along with what she was doing now.

Blanche must have spotted her because she came out of the house and waved at her. "Ruth! You're not going down the trail, are ya?"

"Heavens no." Ruth stopped and leaned on the stick. "Not with this leg. But I am here to see your husband and his brother."

Blanche grinned. "I heard about the lessons Frank paid for. Such a generous gift." She waved at her. "Come on in, and I'll get Emery. Ellsworth is down the trail taking pictures and the little one is down for her nap."

Once she was inside the house, Ruth felt a bit more secure than if she were standing on the rim. The view out the windows was incredible. "You've made this a lovely home, Blanche."

"Thank you. It was quite the mess with those two bachelors living here on their own, but I've whipped them into shape."

"I have no doubt." If anyone could tame a wild horse, it was Blanche.

"I'll be right back." Blanche left the room, and the pitter-patter of feet greeted Ruth.

She looked down into the big brown eyes of Edith. The little girl waved a hand, the thumb of the other one in her mouth.

"Hello, Edith. Are you supposed to be sleeping?"

Her curls bobbed as she shook her head. But her eyes were still glazed over with the remnants of sleep.

"Ruth, it's good to see ya." Emery walked toward her and swooped up Edith. "Aren't you supposed to be taking a nap?" He tickled the toddler's belly.

"I'm sorry. My arrival must have woken her up."

"It's not a problem." Blanche took the child. "I was about to wake her for lunch, anyway."

"Would you like that first lesson?" Emery wiggled his eyebrows.

"As long as I don't have to hang from any ropes or jump off any rocks, I'm ready." Ruth's excitement built.

"Then let's head out on the porch. That'll give you a great view."

Out on their bench, Frank sat down and smiled at the satisfaction on Ruth's face. "You look positively radiant. I take it you had a good day?"

"Wonderful. Now close your eyes."

She'd gone from looking worried and stressed when she'd come to see him to looking refreshed and at ease. He loved it. "Why do I need to keep my eyes closed?"

"Humor me, Mr. Henderson. You're not peeking?" Ruth's voice sounded young and girlish. It was good to hear her spirits up.

"No, I'm not peeking." He put his hands over his eyes. "See? There's no way I can peek."

She pulled one of his hands down and placed something in it. "Okay. Open."

He glanced to his hand and saw a beautiful picture of the canyon. "Did you take this?"

"I did." Her chin and shoulders lifted. "All by myself. And I even developed it myself."

"It's lovely. Not even blurry."

She swatted at his arm. "Did you expect it to be blurry?"

"Maybe." He shrugged. "Seems like the first few might be kinda hard. And here you've mastered it already."

She took the picture back and stared at it. "I wouldn't say I've mastered it, but I do love it. Thank you again for the camera, Frank. It means a lot to me."

"You're welcome. I'm glad you are enjoying it."

"I am." With a tug to his arm, she nodded toward the rim. "Let's walk a little."

"Is your leg feeling all right?"

"Better than all right." The sigh that left her sounded relieved and happy. "I've been using the cream an extra time each day, and it's done wonders."

The limp was still there, but he didn't care. As long as she was feeling better. "How expensive are these treatments from Mr. Goodall?"

"You don't want to know. But he has been giving me a discount. He's such a nice man."

Frank nodded and tried to hide his discomfort—and the hint of jealousy that kept creeping up whenever Mr. Goodall's name was mentioned. But at least Ruth hadn't mentioned another invitation. Yet. "I've heard he's extremely wealthy."

"I guess so. If he has the funds to vacation all summer here." Ruth's steps were slow but steady.

"Do you think his money comes from selling the treatments?"

"What?" Ruth frowned. "No. I think he does this out of the goodness of his heart. He sincerely wants to help people heal. The ingredients are very rare."

He bet they were. Why was he second-guessing her? If the treatments were helping, he should keep his mouth shut. "Well, I'm glad that you are feeling better."

"I am. It's been a while. But I feel like I have more energy. Taking pictures today made me feel like I was on top of the world, and Mr. Owens and the Harvey men gave me two days off. I'm going to spend the entire day tomorrow taking pictures. As long as the weather cooperates."

He chuckled. "That would make me feel pretty good too. I'm sorry they took over your office. I bet that didn't sit well."

She gave him a look and smirked. "You know me well, Frank Henderson. I was not happy about that. Not one bit. But . . ." Glancing around, she released a long breath and lifted her shoulders. "As much as I hate to dampen our conversation"—she pulled a piece of paper out of her pocket—"there is something of some urgency I want to ask you."

"Go ahead."

She stopped and unfolded the paper. "Right before Smithey and Lovett came in to take over, I thought about the first time Mr. Owens found that the numbers in the books didn't match. It was right after you became the head chef."

His heart sank. But it was inevitable that she'd come to

this conclusion. He'd had the thought himself. "You don't think I have anything to do—"

She put a hand to his chest, and it stopped him. "No. Not one bit. But I thought about the fact that it was your job to make all the orders for the kitchen as assistant chef. So, when you became the head chef, then your new assistant would have that job."

"Right." At least she didn't think he was the culprit. Although deep down, he'd held on to the fear that it could've been his mistake somehow.

"Everything I've been through so far showed no signs of anything being off. But I'd checked all the books up until the point when you took over. So, I pulled out all the orders and receipts that Howard gave to you. I looked through the first few and something caught my eye, so I thought I'd give Mr. Patterson a call since I know him pretty well."

"What did you think you'd find?" He crossed his arms over his chest. Now he was intrigued. Where was she going with this?

"I spoke with him and asked about the last order being less, like what the order sheet from Howard showed. But no, he corrected me and told me that our order for his ground wheat was almost double."

"Wait, double?" His eyebrows shot up, and he straightened.

Ruth nodded. "Mr. Patterson was very grateful for the order, but he was so concerned about my questioning him that he thought it was a mistake. I thought he might cry right there on the phone. I told him not to worry about it, that we would figure it out. But he said the order coming this week is the same almost-doubled order as well."

"I did *not* ask Howard to order that much wheat flour.

Unless the bakers needed more, but they would have come to me." Frank couldn't help it. He stood and started to pace back and forth. "What do you think this means?"

"What I think is that Howard might be padding the orders for the kitchen and the hotel is paying for it. But why? And what is happening to all the extra?"

They'd gone over enough numbers that he knew it made sense. Multiple orders increasing would mean the expenditures would increase. Not the profits. Which might make the discrepancies. But he couldn't believe that Howard would intentionally do such a thing. "I don't know, Ruth. Howard would have had to rewrite all those orders and receipts to cover it up, right?"

"The order he gave us for Mr. Patterson wasn't correct."

"Okay. But Howard has been extremely supportive and loyal through all this. He hasn't caused any arguments in the kitchen or tried to take over. He's been an excellent assistant chef. I can't see him doing it."

Ruth's mouth twisted as she tapped her chin. "What other explanation could there be? Does anyone else have anything to do with the ordering, the receiving, or the receipts?"

His heart fell. "No. It's just him. And me." He swallowed hard. "Do you think that I could have made some kind of mistake along the way?"

"Frank." She reached for his hand, pulled him back to sit on the bench, and squeezed it with an emphatic shake of her head. "You are meticulous. When you were doing the ordering, nothing of this sort ever happened. I know how much you like Howard and have come to trust him, but my instincts are telling me that he's got something to do with this."

"But I was so busy with taking on head chef. I don't want

to discount the fact that I could have contributed to the problem."

With a roll of her eyes, she released his hand and tapped her finger on her knee. "While it's very noble of you to admit that you're not perfect, I have my doubts that you could have done anything like this. This is way too much money for a simple mistake on your part."

"So how do you propose we figure this out?"

Her lips pinched together as she folded her hands in her lap. "I don't know. But I think it's better if we figure it out before the auditors do. I don't want to throw Howard to the wolves, so to speak, until we know for sure. And how do we know for sure? I mean, we have Mr. Patterson's word, but we need to find all the extra flour, right?"

"Yes, that's probably best. And I should casually make an appearance when Patterson's order delivers. See it with my own eyes. I'll also be on the lookout for whatever else Howard might be padding in orders. As long as he doesn't think we suspect him, he'll continue on with his theft . . ." He hated to even think of it. "*If* he's the culprit."

———— | ————

**FRIDAY, JUNE 11, 1909**

"I have an idea." Howard twisted his chef's hat in his hands.

Oliver crossed his arms over his chest. He'd called the kid out here for *his* purpose, but he might as well hear him out. "I'm listening."

"I've come up with a way to give another blow to the business here."

"And? What is it?"

"Mr. Cameron has a friend who is opening up a restaurant in California. He offered to pay—and pay handsomely—for secret recipes out of the El Tovar kitchen for his new restaurant."

"Exactly *how* is that going to hurt the business here?" Thankful for the cover of dark, Oliver rolled his eyes at the lanky young guy.

Howard held his hands out in front of him. "Don't you see? The El Tovar prides itself on secret recipes that no one else has. If other restaurants have them, it won't be secret or special only to the El Tovar anymore. See? It's brilliant."

Oliver wouldn't call it brilliant. No. But he needed the kid around for a little bit longer. "And how is this going to help *you*? Because I'm sure you wouldn't bring the idea to me unless this was to your advantage as well."

Howard had the good sense to look a bit sheepish. "If I do this, Cameron said he'll make me head chef at his new restaurant."

"You'd prefer this rather than my restaurant?" Not that he ever planned to follow through with that.

"Well . . ." Howard toed the dirt with his shoe. "You said it might take a while, and I have a feeling I'm going to need to get out of here before they find me out."

Oliver clapped a hand on the younger man's shoulder. This couldn't be working out better if he'd maneuvered it himself. "Good for you, then. It sounds like a great opportunity." He didn't remove his hand. "As long as you don't mind finishing the job here."

"Yes, sir. I promised you I would. And you like my idea?"

"You go right ahead." He tightened his grip. "Just remember, you can't leave yet. I have one more thing for you to do."

Even in the dark, he could see the man pale. "And you'll pay me the extra?"

"Yep. You can start that new life in style."

He felt the man's breath shudder through him. But then Howard lifted his chin. "Tell me when. I know what to do."

# 14

It was here. The day Ruth's parents were supposed to arrive.

The weather had been glorious, even though it was quite warm.

Her morning passed in a flurry. Since the Harvey men had given her back the use of her office, she'd been holed up, trying to catch up on all the paperwork she needed to do for the daily workings of the dining room and kitchen. Just the scheduling of the Harvey Girls could be an intricate process that took full brain power and hours of her time.

But the mystery around Howard's order with Mr. Patterson was driving her batty. Especially since she and Frank found no sign of the missing excess.

The auditors had taken all the books and papers with them. She couldn't remember that being standard protocol. If she could only get a glimpse of all the orders Howard had made—just one more time—maybe she could see if she'd missed anything.

But the men hadn't said a word about it, and she'd begun to doubt herself. Had she written the numbers down correctly?

Ruth shook her head. She needed to let that go or she'd be all stressed when her parents arrived.

Mr. Owens had given her the rest of the day off. So, she stood at the rim with her camera on its tripod, hoping for the right shot to get her mind off all the troubles when the sun's rays cut through the clouds and the canyon lit up. After taking several pictures, she allowed her thoughts to turn to her parents while she waited for another dazzling display that was sure to come as the clouds rolled past.

Mom and Dad said they wanted to actually have a vacation. Be tourists and do all the crazy things that visiting people did.

Ruth had laughed when she read the letter. But it sounded like they were content with being there and knowing that she had a job to do. They understood that Ruth would be very busy, since the hotel was packed and there were several groups of important guests staying at the El Tovar at the same time. It was very special that Mr. Owens wanted to give her this first afternoon and evening with her parents. Now if she could tame her thoughts and stop thinking about all there was to do . . .

Thankfully, the nerves of the staff had been settled for a few days now. The auditors even appeared more relaxed. Or maybe it was that the newness and scariness had worn off.

They seemed to convey warmth to everyone. Were they trying to ease their stress? Or maybe they were just nice men. Doing their job like everyone else.

The more she thought about it, the more she'd hate to be

in their shoes. To have the job in which the sole purpose was to check up on people? Inspect them in every way imaginable?

No thank you. She imagined they weren't liked very often. Which was a shame.

Even so, Mr. Owens had been delighted with how smoothly things had run for a week now. He had relaxed, and as long as the Harvey men were happy, he was happy.

Which meant Ruth, for the most part, was happy too. At least she *should* be.

She'd taken to drinking an extra teaspoon of the elixir each day. Mr. Goodall had recommended five times a day and she'd upped it to six. Couldn't hurt. Especially with all the stress she'd been dealing with. The elixir really was a miracle, like he said. She always felt amazing after she took it.

But she'd been so tired the past few days that she needed a bit more zip to help her. Sure, she should have asked him about it, but he said it was natural and healthy. What could a little more hurt?

"Oh!" she gasped. The clouds moved just enough. The picture was almost perfect. Getting herself ready, she peered through the viewfinder and held her breath as she waited. There! The rays fanned through the sky.

Counting to twenty, she got the perfect shot. At least she hoped it was. The scene before her was breathtaking. She took another and couldn't help but smile. Now if she could get this picture developed before Mom and Dad arrived. Wouldn't they love it?

"Mama . . ." A little voice beside Ruth drew her attention.

"Yes, my love." The elaborately dressed woman had another woman beside her, holding an umbrella over her head to shield her from the sun.

"What happened to that lady's face?"

Ruth stared at the canyon and blinked at the tears.

"Hush. We don't ask questions like that," the mother whispered.

But Ruth looked at the little girl and smiled. Her heart might be breaking on the inside, but it wasn't the child's fault. She leaned over. "A mountain lion scratched me. But it's been a while now."

"Gracious, you don't have to make up fantastic stories." The mother's haughty tone stayed with Ruth as the woman dragged her child away.

She couldn't win. No matter what. It had taken all her willpower to smile at the child and answer. But the answer was too horrific. Just like her face.

Wiping at the sweat on her forehead, Ruth wished she could crawl in a hole. Of course the scar had been more prominent because it was hot. She was sure to be red-faced. And with the heat, she'd sweat quite a lot, which had probably made all of her makeup fade away.

To think that she'd come out here—for the first time in a long time—not even worried about anyone seeing her scar. She had been focused on the beauty before her and taking some pictures.

The beauty *before* her.

There was the crux of the matter. The beauty would always be in front of her. In front of her camera. It would never be *her* anymore.

As that thought settled into place, her stomach twisted into knots.

No. Stop it. What arrogant thoughts. That's what happened when she'd heard all her life what a pretty face she had. She shook her head. She'd come out here to get a picture for her parents and she had.

It was still a beautiful day.

She should go develop the pictures and get cleaned up. Her parents would be here soon.

But on her way back to her room, she couldn't stay as strong as she told herself to be.

Words. They could cut like a knife.

Even from an innocent child.

Maybe after the creams had done their work, she'd be able to hold her head up high again.

Maybe one day.

As the train pulled in at the El Tovar, Ruth kept her hands clasped tightly around the long walking stick. She hadn't *walked* down to the train in two years because it was steep. There were a lot of stairs. And the ground was uneven in many places.

Today, determined to meet her parents in person, she'd brought Julia's hiking stick to steady herself and to help hide her limp.

When Dr. Collins had wanted her to use crutches the first few weeks, that hadn't been so bad. But then he'd instructed her to use a cane. She'd lasted all of one week with that because it only made people stare more. At least that's what she told herself.

So she'd determined to walk without it.

Granted, she had a limp. She walked slowly. But she could hide it pretty well with her skirts most of the time.

After using the hiking stick a few times as she'd headed out with her camera, she had to admit what an amazing help it was. It took a good deal of pressure off her bad leg and helped her walk with even less of a limp.

What would have happened had she used the cane like she

was supposed to from the beginning? Her stubborn pride had gotten in the way again.

Not wanting to look like an old lady or a cripple, she'd tossed aside the one thing that probably could have made life a lot easier. If only she could learn without making all the mistakes along the way. Perhaps her atrophy wouldn't be as bad . . . and she wouldn't spend so much time hiding in her office.

A sobering thought.

The engines hissed and released their steam as the first few passengers began to disembark.

Although she was nervous about seeing her parents, Ruth found herself excited too. She loved her family. Missed them.

Just didn't want them to have to see what she'd become.

"Ruthie!" The squeal was her mother, even though she couldn't see her through the crowd yet. Mom had obviously spotted her.

"There's my girl!" Dad reached her first with open arms and almost knocked her over. "Look at you! You look wonderful."

"Thanks, Dad. It's good to see you too."

"Oh, my dear." Tears filled her mother's eyes. She put her gloved hands on either side of Ruth's face. "How I have missed you."

After they hugged several times, Dad's eyes widened. "Oh, I almost forgot about the luggage."

"Your checked bags will be taken straight to your room. Do you have whatever personal items you had with you in the railcar?"

He patted his pockets and then looked down at his feet, where he'd dropped his case. "Ah yes. We're right as rain."

Hearing her parents' voices and seeing their faces in person made her smile even wider. "Let's head on up to the hotel, and I will help you get settled."

"I don't move as fast as I used to, so take your time." Dad's voice was a bit louder than necessary. Was that for his benefit or hers? As far as she could tell, he was as spry as always.

The trek up the stairs and up the hill wasn't a long one, but it did put a strain on her bad leg. She should have thought about putting the deep cream on again before this. It always helped to numb it, or at least feel that way. But she made it to the front of the hotel, where her parents oohed and aahed over the canyon.

"Do you want to see the canyon more now or get settled in your room?" Ruth smiled at her parents.

"Why don't we at least get all this in our rooms? It's awfully warm. That way we don't have to carry anything else around. I'm actually famished. How about you, dear?" Dad looked at Mom.

"That sounds lovely. Room. Dinner. Canyon. Is that all right with you, Ruth?"

"Perfect." She took them to the front desk and got them all checked in. "Why don't we meet back here in fifteen minutes and we'll go to dinner?"

They went their separate ways, and Ruth winced on every stair down to her room. What had she done that made it hurt so much?

In her room, she applied more of the first cream, and the cooling effect was wonderful. She took a swig out of the elixir bottle and headed back up to the dining room. That should get her through the rest of the evening.

After a sumptuous dinner where Frank spoiled them with every one of his specials, Dad patted his stomach. "I don't think I will need to eat for days. I'd say a lovely walk out to the rim should help." He stood and held out his arm for Mom.

They were so cute together. Exactly what Ruth had always wanted. That beautiful kind of love.

They hadn't married for convenience. Neither were they *just* companions. They were best friends.

She followed her parents out of the dining room and out of the hotel.

"Where's the best view?" Her father held on to Mom with a glimmer in his eye.

"Almost every view is the best, depending on the time of day and the lighting. But I can take you to my favorite tonight and tell you about the others that are farther away. While I'm working, Mom said you wanted to explore, and there are plenty of miles to do just that." She couldn't walk at a decent pace and hide her limp, so she did her best to move steadily. Her parents didn't seem in any big hurry as they strolled along beside her arm in arm.

"Oh my. It's absolutely breathtaking." Mother put a gloved hand to her throat. "I . . . I simply don't know what to say."

For almost five years, she'd been begging her parents to come out to the canyon so they could see this for themselves. Another reason she didn't want them coming when she was first injured—they needed to see this for themselves and not be worried about her. "It's worth the long trip, isn't it?"

Dad looked at her, and tears shimmered in his eyes. "I never thought I'd see anything as magnificent as this." He came beside her and wrapped an arm around her shoulders. "But nothing can compare to seeing you, daughter." He kissed her cheek.

A tinge of guilt filled her for keeping them at such a distance. Ruth stepped away and let them soak it in. She found a rock to sit on and watched as they whispered together and held each other's hands.

She'd always been grateful to God for the amazing parents He'd given her. This beautiful couple had chosen her. When they couldn't have children of their own and had been devastated by it, they'd been overjoyed to welcome a baby into their home.

They'd picked her.

Raised her. Loved her. Shown her the love of Christ.

Mom came and sat next to her. "Your dad is going to go for a little walk. He likes his evening walks, you know."

It was one of her most prized memories. Dad on his walks. Sometimes she got to accompany him. "You both seem very happy and relaxed. The trip has been good for you, hasn't it?"

"Oh yes. Your father is ready to stop teaching at the college. I'm sure he'll still teach Sunday school, but he isn't getting any younger."

He had been almost her age now when they'd adopted her. Which meant he was getting close to seventy years old. Hard to fathom. "None of us are. Will you continue to teach your piano students?"

"Not as many. But yes . . . as long as these fingers can still play, I'll teach. I do love it so."

"I had a feeling you would say that." Ruth leaned against her mother. The woman she'd leaned on for everything until she left home.

"Ruth dear . . ."

"Yes?" She turned and stared at her mom.

"I don't mean to pry, but why do you feel the need to cover up your wounds with makeup? So you have a little scar. What does it matter? You're such a pretty woman."

A sad laugh escaped. "Oh, Mom. You wouldn't understand. You're my mother. You'd think I was pretty whether I'm covered in cow manure or dressed up to see the president."

"But you *are* pretty. You've always been pretty."

"Mom, if you saw it without the makeup, you would know how bad it is. I scared little children here at the hotel after it first happened. And one this afternoon, to be honest."

"Surely you exaggerate." Mom clucked her tongue. "It doesn't matter anyway. We are so thankful you are alive and well."

"I'm used to it now. But I'm fine, Mom. Thank you." Pasting on her best smile, she patted her mom's arm.

Several moments passed as her mother seemed to digest the words. Out of the corner of her eye, Ruth saw her mother open her mouth a few times. Then she clamped it shut, probably not knowing what to say. No one really did. And Ruth had accepted that. At least she tried to convince herself that was true.

Her mother kissed her on the cheek and stood up. "I'm going to go find your father and we'll come see you before we head to bed."

"That sounds nice." Ruth smiled up at her mom. "Do you have lots of fun things planned the next few days?"

Her mother giggled and lifted her shoulders until they almost touched her ears. "We do! I can't wait to see the Hopi House and learn how to weave. I hear that's a lot of fun to learn."

"Oh it is. And they are the best. Just don't get discouraged if a four-year-old can weave better than you." Thoughts of Sunki ran through her mind. The little girl was growing so fast. She must be at least eight years old now. Ruth had promised to come back and let her teach her how to make jewelry. But would she do it?

Mom's voice made her realize she hadn't been listening. "Anyway, I better run. . . . We're like a couple of young kids again." She scurried off down the trail.

It was wonderful that her parents were taking a break and having fun for themselves. They'd sacrificed so much for her over the years. And for their students. It made her heart happy.

It had done her more good than she could have ever imagined to have her parents here. Why had she been so scared to let them see her like this?

She eased herself to her feet and stretched. It had been a long day. Her parents were here. The hotel seemed to be running smoothly even in the midst of their financial crisis. The only thing left was her walk with Frank, and then she could get some sleep and start over again tomorrow.

No one was around, so she rubbed her right leg and then stretched it a bit more. Perhaps it was time to get back to those exercises. If the creams were working, it shouldn't hurt to get her leg moving more.

"Ruth!" Frank's voice made her turn. His copper hair caught the sun's rays and made him look like a lion for a moment.

She put her hand to her mouth to cover her giggle.

"What is it?" His eyes were full of merriment.

"You looked like a lion there in the sunlight."

"Oooh, the king of the beasts. I'll take that." He ran his hands through his hair and patted it down. "There. Is that better?"

The green of his eyes did something to her heart at that moment. Whether it was their laughter, the sunlight, or just his genuine delight at life . . . suddenly, Ruth found it hard to swallow.

Ducking her head, she pointed to the path. "Ready for our walk?"

"Always."

But as soon as she took the first step, her leg buckled and down she went.

———⊣ ⊢———

Horrified as Ruth collapsed beside him, Frank tried to catch her but wasn't fast enough. "Ruth! I'm so sorry. Are you hurt?"

For several seconds, she didn't move or respond.

"Ruth!" The panic he heard in his own voice made him want to fall apart right there. He couldn't stand the thought of anything else happening to her.

He reached for her, but she shoved his hands away.

The action pricked his heart. What should he do?

Helplessness flooded him as he watched her lie on the ground.

Another few seconds that felt like forever passed. He held his breath.

Without a word, she moved from her sprawled position to sit. With her head down, she wrapped her arms around her bent knees. Her shoulders shook.

At a loss, Frank got on the ground with her and sat. "Tell me what I can do."

"Nothing." The strangled reply was muffled against her skirt. "Go away, Frank. All right? I need you to go away." The fierce anger in her tone startled him a bit. "Did you hear me? Go. Away!"

Everything inside him hurt to see her like this, and the wound from her words felt like he'd been sliced in two with a dull butter knife. For a moment, he considered telling her "Fine!" and walking away. That was what she wanted.

He *almost* gave in to her demand. But a fraction of a second later, he calmed his temper. She was simply lashing out at him because he was there. He imagined if he were in her shoes, he'd be feeling embarrassed. Humiliated. Afraid.

Alone.

Well, he wasn't going to leave her. Not ever, if he could help it. "Can't do that, Ruth."

She smacked him with her right arm, keeping her head buried in her skirt. "Stop being so stubborn and leave me be. I'm fine."

"No." He scooted closer. "You're not fine. And I'm not leaving. If anyone is being stubborn, it's you."

She growled and lifted her face. Tears streaked through her makeup, and her eyes were rimmed with red. "You can be so infuriating."

"You too." He refused to let her best him. "I. Am. Not. Leaving. Not without you."

"Stop feeling sorry for me, Frank Henderson."

His temper began to flare again. When was she going to open her eyes and see his feelings for her? "I'm doing no such thing, you exasperating woman! I haven't felt sorry for you for one day in my life. Now stop acting like a child and realize that I love you and care about you!"

# 15

Frank stretched his legs out in front of him and looked at the sky. It had been a while since he'd had a day off because Mr. Owens wanted him in the kitchen the whole time the auditors were there. But things had finally eased up, and he was glad to have a few moments to himself. For some reason, the auditors were very relaxed about everything, which was unlike any of the other audits he'd ever been through at a Harvey House.

But they'd given him the day, and he wasn't about to refuse it.

Tensions had eased, and even Owens had looked a bit more relaxed. But when they'd spoken yesterday, nothing had been found. About anything. Which made Frank a bit suspicious.

Add to that, the order that arrived at the hotel on the train from Mr. Patterson was the amount of flour Howard *should* have ordered. Not the amount Mr. Patterson sent. Even after a phone call to the older gentleman, Frank was more confused than ever. Their longtime business associate would never make up an outlandish story like that. So what happened to all the flour that was delivered to the train station in Williams?

Patterson was so disturbed by the discrepancy that he demanded no payment be made until they sorted it out. He wanted to go to the sheriff right away, but Mr. Owens had put his foot down and said no. If the sheriff came out while the auditors were there, the press would surely get wind of it. The manager wanted to see if they could figure it all out without ruining the reputation of the hotel, which at this point could easily take a plummet off the rim of the canyon.

Mr. Owens had done everything to assuage the guests and convince people not to cancel their reservations. But would it all blow up in his face?

Frank's mind spun in circles. At this juncture, he didn't know how to figure it out. Not without going down to Williams next time Patterson delivered to the train. Which at this point, he was going to have to do. Without proof, how could they accuse Howard?

He lowered his head. *God, I'm at a loss. I want to fix this right now, and You know I am not a patient man.*

And yet, he'd waited years for Ruth. Frank chuckled. *All right, God. I get Your point. I can be patient if I have to.*

So he'd take his day off. Calm his heart and mind. Focus on the Lord and all the things for which he was grateful. An entire day to himself. It *should* sound wonderful.

Only problem was, the person he wanted to spend time with the most was working. Holed up in her office once again. So here he sat. Gazing out into the enormous canyon. All by himself.

Ever since her fall two nights ago, she'd been withdrawn. Stiff. Was it from embarrassment? Or had his declaration put a rift between them? Had it been too soon? She hadn't responded. In fact, she hadn't said another word, even as she got up and headed back to the hotel. With him silent at her side the whole time.

Could there be something else to it? Her parents?

If only he knew.

No. He knew. It was probably him. And the fact that he blurted out—in anger, no less—that he loved her.

"Chef Henderson. It's good to see you." A familiar voice called out from beside him.

Frank shifted his gaze and saw Ruth's parents headed toward him. "Mr. and Mrs. Anniston, how lovely to see you. Are you enjoying your stay at the El Tovar?"

"Very much so." Mrs. Anniston beamed. "We should have done this years ago, but I'm glad we're here now."

Ruth's father patted him on the shoulder. "It's been what . . . five, maybe six years since we last saw you?"

"Yes, sir. At least that. That was before I came here."

"And look at you now. Head chef. At Harvey's grandest hotel, on top of that." The man gripped his shoulder. "Couldn't be prouder of you, son. Good job. And wonderful food, by the way."

"I was telling him last night that it's the best food I've had anywhere." Mrs. Anniston's eyes crinkled at the corners when she smiled.

Frank bowed at her. "Thank you, ma'am. That is indeed a compliment. Have you found the grand piano in the Music Room to your liking? I have to admit, I've been hoping to hear you play again."

"We haven't ventured around the hotel much yet, I'm afraid. Mr. Anniston has wanted to explore the great outdoors as much as possible." She fanned her face. "Gracious, it's been warm, though. My fingers have been itching to play. I normally don't go a day without playing."

"Maybe this afternoon, in the heat of the day, you can relax at the piano," Frank offered. Then he turned to Mr. Anniston. "I hear you're looking to hike down into the canyon. Will you be riding the burros or actually walking?"

"I'd like to walk it, but my sweet wife might melt in this heat. Perhaps the burro is a better way to go?"

"It's even warmer at the bottom." Frank winced. "That might be the best way. Especially for the trek back up. Although lots of people do it. You need to have plenty of water and take time to rest."

"Is it true that you can camp down by the river?" Mrs. Anniston lifted one eyebrow. No wonder Ruth had perfected that look.

"Yes. You can."

"Oh, that sounds exciting, dear. Maybe we could try that?" She patted her husband's arm.

"Really? You want to camp? By the river?" Mr. Anniston looked taken aback.

"Well, I know that *you* do, and I want to be with you, so why not? This old gal can try new things."

Mr. Anniston's laughter filled the air.

Frank joined in. "You two are a joy to be around. I hope that one day I can be married to my best friend." Uh-oh. Had he said too much? "Just like you two."

Mrs. Anniston patted his arm. "We've been praying the same for you, dear boy."

It made him smile, she'd called him a boy. His fortieth birthday wasn't more than a couple years away. But he'd take it. "Thank you."

Ruth's mother took his arm. "Frank . . . we have to confess

202

that we sought you out because we were hoping to speak in private about our daughter. Do you have a few minutes?"

"Of course. Would you like to sit or walk as we talk?"

"Is there a quiet place where we won't be overheard?" Mr. Anniston stepped closer.

Frank weighed his options. "If you don't mind walking for a piece, there's a good place that is a bit off the beaten path."

"Sounds perfect." The older man took his wife's hand. "Lead the way."

They chatted about the weather and seasons at the canyon, their favorite foods, and Mrs. Anniston's favorite piano pieces as they made their way to a lovely little overlook. No one else was around, so Frank took the opportunity to wipe off a few of the rocks for them to sit on.

He held out his arms toward the canyon. "How's this for a view while we chat?"

"It's lovely." Mrs. Anniston took a seat. "Thank you, Frank." She held a parasol over her head.

"Let me be honest with you, young man." Ruth's father took a seat, placed his elbows on his knees, and clasped his hands together. "We are quite concerned for our daughter."

"Oh?" Was there something he didn't know about?

The older man continued. "Ever since that horrible mauling, she hasn't been herself. Before it happened, we actually had been hoping and praying that something would develop between you two. I hope that's not too forward of me to say, but I'm not getting any younger. I find it's best to speak my mind. It's faster." He chuckled.

Frank thought his eyebrows might be touching his scalp. He couldn't hide his surprise.

"Sorry to put you on the spot. But do you care for our daughter? Because the way she's written about you in her letters, we feel like the two of you would be perfect for each other."

"Honey, please. You're making him uncomfortable." Mrs. Anniston fanned her face. "He's turning red."

At the moment, it would be nice to have a fan for himself. Certainly he was indeed red enough to match his hair. Frank swallowed and then allowed himself to laugh. This couple clearly cared about their daughter. He did too. If he couldn't be honest with them, he might as well give up now. "I'm not getting any younger either, Mr. and Mrs. Anniston, so I will take my cue from you, sir, and lay it all out on the table, as it were."

The older couple appeared shocked, but they both leaned in.

"You see, I've cared for Ruth for many years. We've worked together a long time. I've admired her. We've shared a wonderful camaraderie and friendship. But I've been praying for the Lord to show me the right time. In fact, right before her accident, I was about to approach Mr. Owens about courting Ruth, even though there's a Harvey House rule about employees doing that. And after the accident? Well, you are correct. She hasn't been herself. I feel like I've had to work a good deal these last two years just to hold on to her friendship. She's got some sort of a wall built up around her. And I don't know why."

Ruth's mother stood and came to sit next to him. She laid a hand on his shoulder. "We couldn't ask for a more wonderful man, Frank. We've been praying for the two of you for years. Ever since we saw you at that company picnic back in Kansas."

Wow. That took him back. He'd been barely thirty at that point. Thought he'd had all the time in the world to woo Miss Ruth Anniston.

"We know our daughter has gone through a rough patch," she continued. "Frankly, that's why we stayed away. Well, she also asked us to—demanded, if we're honest—that first year, but we wanted her to feel like she could still stand on her own two feet and heal. She's always been incredibly independent. But I'm afraid we're losing her." Pulling a hankie out of her sleeve, she sniffed and then wiped at her eyes.

"What do you mean . . . losing her?" Frank's voice cracked.

"We can't allow her to continue down this road. Tell him, dear."

Ruth's father cleared his throat. "I'm dying, Frank. The doctors have told me that I could have several years left. But it may only be months. Only God knows. I don't want to spend what little time I have left away from my family. So, we are going to move here. Ruth doesn't know anything about my sickness. We want to see her at a better place before we tell her. And I don't want to do anything that might depress her further. We've already spoken to Mr. Owens and have made some arrangements of our own. I'm going to offer some lectures on geology to the guests, since that is my expertise. My lovely wife here will give concerts in the Music Room for the guests' pleasure. In exchange, we were granted permission to build a modest home close by. I'd like to see my daughter married, if that's in His plan. And maybe a grandchild before I'm gone."

"Sir. I'm so sorry."

"Don't be sorry for me, son. I know where I'm going."

"Yes, sir." All this baring of souls made Frank bold. "I . . . That is . . ." He coughed into his hand. "Does this mean that you would approve of me pursuing your daughter?"

Mrs. Anniston clasped her hands together over her mouth.

"Nothing would make me happier." Tears glistened in the man's eyes. "But it's time for you to be brutally honest with us. Is Ruth healing all right?"

Frank straightened and looked from one to the other. "Physically, I think she has healed beautifully. But I do think there's something deep down that she's waging a war against inside."

"Well then . . ." Mr. Anniston stood. "We will pray that you can get to the root of the problem, Frank. We will be here to help. Remember, only love can drive out fear."

### MONDAY, JUNE 21, 1909

Ruth took her father's hand and climbed into the horse-drawn carriage. Had it already been almost a week since her parents arrived? Yes. Hard to believe, but they were already three weeks into June.

Things at the hotel had kept her busy, especially since Mr. Owens had hired a retired Pinkerton named Mr. Asbury to come and spend a few weeks at the El Tovar. The man posed as a guest but was really there to help them figure out what was going on. For some reason, their manager wasn't willing to leave it in the hands of the auditors. So Ruth had spent a good portion of her time answering all of the man's questions behind the closed door of her office.

Frank had too, after his long shift in the kitchen was over.

Huddled in her office when it had been so late had made her very conscious of his nearness.

Ever since her fall and his words that fateful night, she

hadn't known how to speak to him. Unless it was about the hotel or business. What did that say about her?

"We have a surprise to show you." Mom's words brought her out of her thoughts as she took the seat beside her and linked their arms together. "I can't wait for you to see it!"

It was probably some rock formation Dad had found. But they'd been traipsing all over the canyon, having the time of their lives. She couldn't deny them that.

Each day at dinner, they'd regale her with their stories. From the Hopi House, to their camping trip all the way down into the canyon, to visiting Williams and having lunch with Chris and Julia. Why, her father had even splurged and bought a gorgeous piece of jewelry from their shop for her mother. Ruth had never seen them happier. It filled her with warmth. So wonderful to see two people she loved enjoying themselves so much.

The carriage surged into movement, and Ruth watched her father's face. She hadn't seen him this relaxed and at peace . . . well, probably ever.

He stared across at her. "What's put that sweet smile on your face, Ruth?"

"Just seeing you so happy, Dad. Relaxed."

He winked at her. "Wait until you see what we've got up our sleeve."

"I do hope you will be happy, dear. We know you love surprises."

Now her curiosity was piqued. What were her parents up to? She *did* love surprises. Always had.

The carriage drove to the little area where several homes had been built. Some were for permanent staff, one was the Watkinses', one was for the ranger. A few more homes had been under construction since this spring, but she hadn't asked who they were for.

The carriage stopped.

Her brow dipped. "What's going on?"

"Come with us, dear." Mom took Dad's hand as she stepped down, and then her dad reached up and put his hands around Ruth's waist, like when she was a little girl, and set her on the ground.

Ruth hugged her father and looked between the two. "Where are we going?"

"Right here." Mom pointed to a sweet little cottage and then took both of Ruth's hands. "We want to be closer to you, our precious daughter. As we've gotten older, we thought it would be perfect to settle near you. And so here we are."

Her jaw dropped. And a fountain of emotions erupted inside her. She didn't know whether she should laugh or cry or collapse onto the ground then and there.

"Let me fill in the blanks for you." Dad chuckled. "I'm retiring. But I'll give lectures to the guests here on geology. Mother will play the piano for the guests. And we will live out our last years with our darling daughter."

Tears sprang to her eyes. They loved her so much they were willing to move across the country. She didn't deserve them. But oh, how she loved them!

"Let me show you the inside. Mr. Owens told us just today that it was completed." Mom grabbed her hand and pulled her toward the door.

As Ruth limped her way through her parents' new home, her spirits lifted. It would be so wonderful to have them close.

But after the excitement of seeing the new home, Ruth couldn't help but feel guilty that she'd kept her parents away. And as the carriage drove them all back to the El Tovar, she felt unworthy of their love. It was true, they weren't getting any younger. And in the coming years, she would need to take care of them.

Lifting her chin, she inhaled the warm summer air. All the more reason to do whatever she could to walk better. To heal completely.

As she made her way through the rotunda, Mr. Owens waved her down. "Miss Anniston, might we have a word?"

"Of course, sir." She changed directions and went into his office. The two auditors stood as she entered.

"Mr. Smithey, Mr. Lovett. How are you this evening?"

"Lovely."

"Quite well, thank you."

Both men smiled with their responses as she stepped to a chair.

She took the seat offered to her and sat ramrod straight with her hands folded in her lap.

The manager remained standing behind his desk. A grin on his face. "The auditors have completed going through the books and determined that it was a simple error on my part. We haven't had any more discrepancies, and everything is in order."

She wanted to be relieved, but a part of her wondered if it were true. "But what about—"

"It's all taken care of, Miss Anniston. Rest assured, we've done our jobs." Mr. Smithey nodded at her.

Her mouth still open, she turned to Mr. Owens, but he shook his head. "Nothing to worry about."

Ruth let out a breath. "Good, then. I'm glad to hear it." She looked back at the two other men. "I hope you have enjoyed your stay at the El Tovar, gentlemen."

"Indeed we have." Lovett stood. "And we will remain here a few more weeks to make sure nothing goes awry."

Ruth tried to hide her confusion. The auditors normally left after the audit was complete. But then again, she'd never been in a situation like this one. "Oh. Well, thank you for all your hard work." Ruth stood as well, and the two auditors exited.

She waited a moment and then went to the door and shut it. "They're staying? I've never heard of auditors staying after they were finished." Why did all of this feel . . . wrong?

"They said the company has asked for them to observe for a while longer to make sure no more scathing news reports come out." But his face betrayed his doubts. What wasn't he saying to her?

"That seems odd." She crossed her arms over her chest.

"If you frown any harder at me, I might take offense, Miss Anniston." He quirked one eyebrow up.

"Tell me this isn't far-fetched to you. They're saying it was a simple error on *your* part?"

Mr. Owens took off his glasses and pinched the bridge of his nose. "It's out of my hands, Ruth. They took the books, said that the company needs to have them for records and will have them checked again. Besides, we turn over the books every year anyway. We've started new ones. Why, I don't know. It's never been done this way before, but they say it's the new policy whenever there has been an error—or *supposed* error—so the accountants at the main office can go over them."

"But—"

Owens held up a hand. "Let's take it as a clean slate and go from here. None of us need the headache of trying to track down a problem that isn't there." He reached forward and patted her shoulder. "You've done a wonderful job, Ruth. Thank you for helping."

How could that man change his tune like that? She'd spoken to the private investigator he'd hired for the past couple days. It didn't make sense. "But it *is* there, Mr. Owens. What about the orders? Even if it's just the one with Mr. Patterson. It shows that something is seriously wrong."

He put a finger over his lips and then wiggled the fingers of his other hand to wave her closer. When she stepped to the desk, he leaned over it and waved her to lean over as well.

"I don't know what's going on," he whispered in her ear. "But we have to act like we agree with the auditors for now. They could be outside the door right now, I don't know. Mr. Asbury told me to act as if someone was always listening."

She covered her mouth with her hand as she took in a sharp intake of breath at his words.

"You and Frank need to be careful. Act as if you're relieved this isn't a problem, all right?"

With a nod, she moved back to the chair and sat for a moment. How good was she at keeping her feelings from showing on her face? Guess she had done it plenty as a waitress when she had to smile and greet even the foulest of customers. It was all a bit surreal.

Mr. Owens straightened and sat back down. "So good to have this behind us, Miss Anniston. Now, keep doing the splendid job you are doing." His voice was a little louder than normal. But his attempt to put on a good show for whomever might be listening wasn't half bad.

"Thank you, sir." She could do it too.

Her thoughts went back to her mom and dad. "Thank you for what you've done for my parents. They are thrilled."

A smile filled his face. "I'm glad I was able to keep the secret."

"Thank you, sir."

"Good night, Miss Anniston."

She opened the office door and ran right into Frank. "Oh! I'm so sorry. I didn't realize you were there."

"I was looking for you." Frank grinned at her. "Care to take a walk?"

"I would enjoy that." Funny, she couldn't wait to tell him everything that had happened today. The weird thing with the auditors and then the excitement with her parents. It made her heart swell and dissipated any of the previous awkwardness. "You're a really good friend, Frank. I don't thank you enough for that."

He shoved his hands into his pockets. "Aw shucks." He shrugged.

"You're such a goof." She held on to the railing as they exited down the stairs and she headed toward the Hopi House. "Our favorite bench?"

"Sounds perfect to me."

She took his arm for stability and hobbled beside him. It would be nice to stroll like a normal person again. Maybe if she used the creams enough, that could happen.

As they approached the bench, a wave of exhaustion washed over her out of the blue. It seemed every night this was happening. Was she pushing herself too hard during the day? Maybe she wasn't sleeping well.

Before she knew it, she swayed and felt light-headed.

Frank caught her before she fell and got her to the bench. "Whoa. What was that? You feeling okay?"

With a hand to her forehead, she tried to clear away the

fog. "I don't know. All of a sudden, I felt like I could just go to sleep. Right then and there."

"You haven't been getting enough rest, have you?"

She shrugged. "I don't know. . . . Maybe not? There's been a lot going on."

"Well, I think we should sit here a few minutes and make sure you're up for the walk back." His face was serious. Protective.

"I'm fine, Frank. Really." She took a deep breath and plastered on the biggest smile she could. "I have so much to tell you."

"I can't wait." But his face still seemed wary.

She started with the news from Mr. Owens about the audit. The books. The supposed error. And that the men would be around for a few more weeks.

"And that's it?" The fire in his voice showed that he was on the cusp of anger.

She put her hand on his arm and raised her brows.

He calmed a touch.

Glancing around to make sure they were alone, she whispered the rest to him. The part about the role they needed to play. Pretending they were relieved that it was all over. Footsteps sounded down the path. She raised her voice to her normal volume. "I'm still a bit shocked, but if Mr. Owens is all right with this, then I guess we should be too." She shrugged and watched two couples meander by.

"I don't understand it. But you can count on me." He shook his head though and fidgeted with the knees of his pants. "I don't like it."

"Lower your voice. I don't either. But this is the way it is for now."

More footsteps. Ruth pasted on a smile for the group of

guests that walked past. If she didn't change the subject and soon, Frank would want to keep talking about the topic that seemed to wind him up a bit too much. "Now, would you like to hear my exciting news?"

"Oh? Of course, I would."

"You have to promise to quench that temper of yours."

"I haven't lost my temper—"

"Frank Henderson. You looked like you were about to boil." She giggled.

His face softened at that. "I'm sorry. It's not your fault that this mess seems to be getting deeper and smellier as time goes on."

She put her hands back in her lap. "You're forgiven." She couldn't keep the grin from her face. "My parents are moving here!" It made her so giddy, she wanted to jump up and down.

His eyes widened. "That's *wonderful* news."

She told him all about the house, her dad's lectures, Mom playing the piano. The more she said out loud, the more she liked the idea. But it also weighed her down. She bit her lip again and stared at the stars.

"What's wrong?"

"What do you mean?" She swung her head back to him.

"Well, your face. Your smile dimmed. And then you bit your lip. A sure sign that something is worrying you." He tilted his head and shrugged. "I know you."

With a huff, she glared at him and then looked away. "I guess it's made me more determined to get better. I need to be capable of taking care of them in case they need me."

"You're completely capable. What are you talking about?"

"Don't play dumb with me, Frank. I have a bad leg. A scarred face."

"And what does that have to do with anything?"

She lifted her hands and waved them at him. "You don't understand."

"I think I *do* understand. Way better than anyone else." There was a hint of irritation in his voice. Was it at her? Or was he still upset about the business at the hotel?

Ruth jumped to her feet, which she realized was a mistake about a second after she did it, because she tumbled back down, but he was there to catch her. Now the tears burned her eyes. She clamped her teeth as she forced her words up at him. "See?" Their faces were inches apart, and his closeness unnerved her.

"See what? That you fell down?" His arms held her tight. "That doesn't make you incapable of taking care of your parents or unworthy of someone's love."

The words stabbed her like a knife. She pushed out of his grasp, got back on the bench, and dusted her skirt. "What did you say?"

Frank sighed. "I'm making a mess of this, Ruth, but you've got to stop hiding behind your scars and your injuries."

"I'm not hiding . . ." But the words weren't even convincing to herself.

Frank grabbed both of her hands. "Yes, Ruth, you are. You're hiding. You've *been* hiding. Almost like you enjoy it. Well, it's time you accepted the fact that you are loved exactly the way you are. You were loved before. You are loved now. You are a beautiful woman of God who needs to stand up on the two wobbly legs that she has and let Him take control."

That fire was back in his eyes. And she heard the truth in his words but couldn't swallow it. Ruth yanked her hands out of his and got to her feet. Determined to gain her own balance, she gritted her teeth and closed her eyes. Once she felt stable, she took a step away from Frank. Let him be irritated with her. She could be irritated right back.

This was what happened when she let someone get too close. They didn't understand the weight these scars held. They had no idea what torment she had to endure. Well, maybe it was time to cut ties.

"I don't think we need to continue our evening walks, Frank." Even as she said the words, her heart wanted to yank them back.

His shoulders slumped. "Come on, Ruth. Just because you had a little trouble tonight doesn't mean you shouldn't try anymore."

"No. It has nothing to do with my falling down or my leg. I think I need to stand on my own two feet. Just like you said. There are a lot of responsibilities right now. My parents will be heading home and then be back here in a few weeks. I have a lot to do." She stepped another pace away. Couldn't bear the sadness on his face as she spoke.

Then his eyes turned fierce again. His hands clenched at his sides, and as she watched, she could see a number of emotions play across his face. Hurt, then anger, then a deep sadness. After several seconds, his hands relaxed, and a look of resignation took up residence. "All right. Fine. If that's what you want." He held up his hands and then stood up, shaking his head. "Good night, Ruth."

Then he walked away.

# 16

Maybe it hadn't been Frank's finest hour. Okay. It definitely *wasn't* his finest hour.

When Ruth's parents had talked to him about his feelings for Ruth, he'd been inspired, encouraged, and ready to take the bull by the horns. Finally, someone understood. Someone saw that he and Ruth were meant to be together.

What he'd *wanted* to do was go straight to Ruth, tell her that he'd loved her for years, and he was tired of waiting and wanted to marry her. There. Just like that.

But Ruth wasn't ready. She'd picked up on the fact that he'd said, *"unworthy of someone's love,"* and he was most certain that he almost scared her away.

Maybe it was time to do things differently. Maybe her parents' coming and their intuition into how Frank felt about Ruth was a sign that he needed to stop walking on eggshells around her.

It wasn't his normal style. He usually didn't mince words with her. But she'd been like an injured animal, and he hadn't wanted to spook her.

Well, too late for that. He'd probably accomplished enough spooking for a lifetime this evening.

Frank stared at the ceiling. So much for sleep tonight. He'd been tossing and turning for hours but couldn't get Ruth off his mind.

He'd get to see her every day during normal working conditions. But no more walks. At least for now. And he wasn't going to try to force her back into it.

Ruth was an amazing woman. But it wasn't his job to try and make her see that. God was going to have to work on her heart. Frank would love her no matter what.

That didn't mean he would allow her to take his heart and stomp all over it. Last night, he'd been pretty crushed. But one look at her face told him she was hurting and to be patient.

That's what unconditional love did. Not that he was any good at it. But maybe one day, he'd learn from the Father, who showed him unconditional love each and every day.

Oh no. He sat up in bed. What date was it? The twenty-second of June? He'd totally forgotten about Julia and Emma Grace wanting to throw a surprise party for Ruth's thirty-fifth birthday. That was July the eighteenth.

The two Harvey Girls—now married—had come to him back in April, wanting to get his input on what they should do. Since her birthday landed on a Sunday, that would be a good day for all the staff to have the time and be a part. The dining room only offered brunch and a light dinner on Sundays, which meant they had the afternoon to celebrate.

They'd talked about a picnic, but he hadn't spoken to them about it since. Just knew he was responsible for the food.

Maybe he should touch base with Mrs. Watkins soon.

Might help him get his mind off the fact that he'd be spending *less* time with Miss Ruth Anniston.

Perhaps a surprise party was just what she needed to prod her out of this shell she'd wrapped around herself. Ruth did love surprises. Now if they could pull it off . . .

---

The usual charade was boring him.

Probably because there were so many bigger things on the horizon. Normally, he could keep himself occupied. Be content to make money, enjoy the luxury surroundings, and hobnob with the socialites.

But now that he'd made a decision to do something bigger, he couldn't wait to get started.

Miss Anniston had sent him a note asking for more of not only the elixir but also the creams. Somebody was using them more than they should.

At first, he'd thought of using her in his scheme. To get her to help spread the word. Quietly, of course. A woman in her position could be used all kinds of ways. He'd even toyed with her a bit and flirted. Not that she was his type, but women who were smitten would do just about anything.

Then he'd heard about her strict policies as headwaitress. Her demand for honesty. She was one of those churchgoing people too. He'd abandoned that idea.

But things were going better than planned, and he really had no use for her. Again, he was bored waiting for things to play out. Simplicity was best. Elaborate as his plan had been, it didn't need all the extra bells and whistles.

Oh well. He might need her help with something later on, where access to her office would be handy. He'd supply her once more. It might get her through until he was gone. Then she could deal with her own problems.

He—on the other hand—couldn't wait until the end of his time here. It would mean that he had won.

Finally.

---

**WEDNESDAY, JUNE 23, 1909**

It was a typical Wednesday, things were moving like clockwork, and Ruth was thankful for the steady monotony that was her job.

She knew what to expect. Liked it when things stayed in that rhythm.

But she'd forgotten to write the amount of receipts from the dining room in her personal ledger last night, and it kept bugging her. Ever since they had the discrepancies—or the supposed discrepancies—she'd been keeping a journal on the side so they would have something to go back to. To double-check. Just in case. Especially since the Harvey men had taken the old books.

Not that she was suspicious or anything.

Well, she was. But she wasn't about to let the Harvey men know that. At least not yet. Not until she knew more.

Besides, it was much easier for her to worry about all the ins and the outs of the hotel than to have to face her own feelings. Which, ever since she'd told Frank she didn't want to walk with him anymore, she'd been filled with regret, guilt, self-deprecation, and loathing. Add to that the fact that she wanted to prove herself fully functioning and capable by the time her parents moved here.

She was a mess.

The way to ignore that mess was to stay busy.

Might as well go to the office and get the ledger from Mr. Owens. She could get the exact number and write it in her own.

She pulled the small notebook out of her desk and headed to the main office.

Thomas was behind the check-in desk this morning, and he nodded at Ruth. "Good morning, Miss Anniston."

"Good morning to you, Thomas." She smiled and pointed to Mr. Owens' office. "Is he in?"

"Yes, miss."

She tapped on the open door and waited for him to look up from what he was reading.

"Miss Anniston. How are your parents doing? Are they enjoying their visit?"

"Yes, sir. They're leaving this afternoon and will be back in a couple of weeks."

"Splendid." He looked back down at his desk. "They will be a lovely addition to our hotel family."

"Sir, I need to look at one of the ledgers."

He looked up at her over the top of his glasses. "Didn't you finish counting last night? I thought for sure I saw it entered in there. Mr. Lovett has already headed to Williams with the deposit for the bank."

"I did. But . . ." She looked over her shoulder, stepped forward, and lowered her voice. "I've been writing everything down in my own ledger. Just so . . . we don't have any discrepancies."

"I see." He took off his glasses and set them on his desk. "Close the door, Miss Anniston."

"Yes, sir." She closed the door and stood in front of him. Was she in trouble?

"Have you discovered anything else?"

"No, sir. Not yet. But I still don't see how they could say that the audit went well." She bit her lip. "I've tried to think of every way I could to needle through the mess."

"You know I've had my concerns as well, and I appreciate your diligence. But my hands are tied. Everything has been running smoothly, so I really don't think we should worry." He unlocked the drawer in his desk and pulled out the ledger. "The Pinkerton I hired said it might take him some time, but he's got a lead."

"Oh, that's encouraging." Ruth opened it up to the entry from last night and did a double-take at the number. "Um . . . sir?"

"Hm?"

"This isn't the number I wrote last night."

He walked over and looked over her shoulder. "Are you certain?"

She pointed. "The first number was a nine. Not a six. I'm positive. I simply couldn't remember the change, sir. I remembered the dollar amount."

With a deep huff that was almost a growl, Mr. Owens wiped a hand down his face. "The only ones who have seen that book other than you and me are the auditors."

She tried to cover her gasp. "The company men are changing the books? Sir, we have to do something about this. Right away."

"Write down the number you were sure was there last night in your journal. And then every night, I want you to double-check my counting and write it down. There's nothing we can do about this deposit, but we can try to stop it before the next one."

"But, sir—"

"Ruth. Please. You have to let me figure this out. Somehow

I have to alert the Harveys without Lovett and Smithey finding out. But we need proof. Solid proof."

"Isn't that proof enough?"

"Not when it's our word against theirs."

An idea burst forth. "I can take pictures."

"What?"

"I can bring my camera in here and take pictures of the money and the amounts. If someone is changing them, we'll be able to prove it."

"Brilliant idea." Her boss nodded. "Just remember to make sure no one sees you."

"What if I keep my camera in my office and we do the counting there? If anyone asks, you can say it's because my leg is bothering me." For the first time, she didn't mind using it as an excuse.

He sat back down at his desk. "I think this will work. I didn't want to say anything, but for some reason, I haven't trusted those two. I've never had that problem before with company auditors. I hated to believe that it *could* be true."

Ruth glanced at the clock. It was almost time for her meeting with Frank in the kitchen. "I need to go, but I'm glad we at least have a plan." She held her notebook up in the air. "We will figure this out, sir."

As she limped her way to the kitchen, Ruth's stomach did a little flip. She hadn't left things on the best of terms with Frank. In fact, she'd been quite mean to him. Shut him out. For two days, they'd seen each other and talked business, but she'd avoided eye contact. Two. Brutal. Days.

Probably because she felt like a heel.

The Harvey Girls were all lined up, listening to the headwaitress. The sea of black and white always made her feel at home. Nostalgic. Comfortable.

In a quarter of an hour, the dining room would be filled with the bustling of guests and the warm sounds of conversations and silver on china.

She entered the kitchen, and the scent of garlic and onions and fresh-baked bread made her mouth water. What she wouldn't give for a bowl of Frank's French onion soup right now.

"Miss Anniston." He welcomed her with a smile. But it didn't quite meet his eyes. Because hesitation had taken up residence.

She hated that she'd done that. "Chef Henderson. How is your morning going?"

"Quite well, thank you." He handed her the charts and lists for the day.

"Everything smells delightful."

"Thank you." He clasped his hands behind him.

"Anything that needs attention today?"

"Not that I can think of." He glanced over his shoulder. "It's shipshape in here." Another weak smile.

This wouldn't do. She couldn't deal with it. "Frank, could we step outside, please?"

"Yes, Miss Anniston." He walked to the side door and opened it for her.

She walked outside and turned to face him. "I can't stand for us to be like this."

He crossed his arms over his chest. "What do you propose we do?"

Her shoulders slumped as she grunted at him. "I don't know. I just know that I don't like it."

"I don't like it either. But you were pretty clear the other night."

"No, I wasn't. You know that better than anyone. I'm a mess.

I admit that. But I don't want to lose my best friend because I've been too stubborn to admit I have no idea what I'm feeling."

He studied her and stayed quiet for several seconds. "That's honest."

"It's the best I can do for right now."

"Honest is good. That's all I've ever asked of you."

With a glance down at her shoes, she felt the heat rising to her cheeks. "I'm sorry, Frank. Please forgive me."

"You're forgiven." One side of his mouth tipped up. "Please don't shut me out again."

Then she saw it. The heartbreak in his eyes. Was that because of her? Or was he feeling sorry for her again?

"You asked for honesty . . . Well, I need it in return. I need to know . . ." Ruth began.

"What? Ask me anything and I'll be honest."

"Could you please stop feeling sorry for me?"

His head jerked back like he'd been slapped. "What? I don't feel sorry for you!"

"Yes, you do. It's the only reason you would look at me like that and I can't handle it."

"I do *not* feel sorry for you."

Infuriating man. Why wouldn't he just admit it? "You said you'd be honest."

"I *am*."

"Chef—" Howard interrupted from the doorway. "Oh, I'm sorry. I don't wish to intrude."

"It's quite all right, Chef Monroe." She let out a breath.

Howard leaned toward Frank. "We need some assistance with your cherry sauce, sir."

"I'll be right there." Frank nodded at the younger man but then pointed his glare back at her. After the door closed again, he raised his eyebrows at her. Waiting.

225

She held up her hands in surrender. "Shall we call a truce?"

"I didn't realize we were in a battle." He wasn't backing down. So like him. She should have known.

"You are needed in there, and I need to get back to work as well. We can discuss this later."

"When?" He hadn't budged.

"Look. Can we let it go? I have enough on my plate today."

"Fine. I'll let it go . . . for now. But mark my words, Ruth. We *will* come back to this discussion." He pointed at the ground emphatically.

Her feet wouldn't budge, and he wasn't leaving. She had to do something to steer them back to neutral ground. "My parents are leaving this afternoon."

"I know. They promised to come see me before their train. We've been having some lovely chats. They are wonderful people."

Her parents had been spending time with Frank? How did she miss that? "Lovely chats? About what?"

"Let's see . . . *you*, the weather, the canyon, *you*, how excited they are to move here, and did I mention, *you*?"

There was that look again. It made her stomach flip. So much for neutral ground.

# 17

**FRIDAY, JUNE 25, 1909**

"M iss Anniston!" Emma Grace waved at her friend across the Rendezvous Room.

Ruth smiled, but it was wary. Because of all the people around?

Emma Grace worked her way around the guests and stepped beside Ruth. "How are you?" She gave her a brief hug.

"I'm doing all right. Very busy."

Why did her eyes look . . . different? "Do you have time for a quick chat?"

Ruth blinked several times, but her pupils were much larger than normal. What did that mean? "I'm sorry. I can't." She glanced over her shoulder.

Emma Grace understood her friend enough to see that something or someone was making her uncomfortable. Was it those two men chatting over by the check-in desk? Wait. Weren't those the two auditors? For some reason, Ruth didn't seem all that at ease around them. Maybe she was simply worried about her position?

"I need to get back to my office. I'm sorry. We'll talk soon, and I'll catch you up on everything."

There. Behind the troubled brow, Emma Grace saw her friend. She pasted on a smile. "That's all right." She leaned in for another hug and whispered in Ruth's ear. "Just remember that I'm here if you need anything. You don't have to conquer the world all on your own."

Later that evening, Emma Grace couldn't get rid of the nudging to pray for Ruth. She sat down at her little kitchen table and lifted up her friend to the Lord.

Sipping a cup of chamomile tea—something Ruth had suggested years ago to help calm her nerves—she stared out the window to the starry night.

Every time she'd tried to get time with Ruth, Emma Grace had failed. Perhaps it was time to try something different.

She padded over to the desk and pulled out stationery, her pen, and ink. As moonlight streamed through the window, it hit the crystal candlestick holders Ray had bought for her last birthday and sent little prisms of color dancing across the desktop.

The words began to flow.

*Dear Ruth,*

*It seems like ages since we were back in the hotel, sitting on the bed in our stocking feet, and talking about all the shenanigans of the girls. Now I deal with the daily shenanigans of a two-year-old. And, of course, Ray. But even though I fall into bed each evening exhausted, I am consumed with joy from the Father.*

Emma Grace's heart poured out in apology and regret for not taking the time that she should have to check on Ruth during her recovery. Even with a newborn to care for, she could have come to see her more often. Her words turned to her concern and love for her friend. Before long, she had three pages filled. She dipped the pen back into the ink, searching for the next words she longed to share.

But how did one share with a person how much they'd meant to them? Ruth would never know how she'd impacted Emma Grace's life. Or how treasured her friendship was.

And then Ruth's own words came back to Emma Grace's mind.

She bent back over the paper.

*You once told me that families protect one another. You said we were family, my friend. And you are definitely family to me. I know you are going through a lot, and there are many responsibilities weighing on you right now. But friends and family help to carry one another's burdens.*

*If you don't have time to chat, perhaps you can write me back. Let me know how I can be praying for you, and I will lift you up to the Father.*

*I love you,*
*Emma Grace*

She set her pen down and reread her words. The sudden urge to pray for her friend overwhelmed her, so she went over to the window, lifted her face to the stars, and prayed for Ruth.

Rubbing the cream into her leg, Ruth realized the jar was half gone. What would she do when Mr. Goodall left?

He was only there for the summer. So how would she get more once he was gone?

The thought wasn't a pleasant one. She'd have to talk to him as soon as she could and order several jars. She had a good bit saved and set aside. Surely it wouldn't hurt to spend it, especially when it would help her get better. And that was the whole point, right? To be able to walk normally again. To be rid of the scars.

After the cream was absorbed, she wiped her hands on a towel and made herself a note for tomorrow. She'd have to request an audience with Mr. Goodall again. Prayerfully, his goodwill would continue to extend to her.

She'd taken the elixir a few minutes ago because she'd felt so tired, and now she was wide awake. Her mind spinning. Her conversation with Frank the other day popping up.

But she needed to push that back. She didn't understand these feelings. Couldn't have them. Shouldn't. Because she cared far too much for Frank Henderson.

And she was crippled. Deformed. Unworthy.

She leaned her head against the wall behind her bed. Before the accident, she didn't grapple with that word.

Unworthy.

Why did it keep coming back to her? Deep down in her heart, she knew that she'd been made worthy by what Christ did on the cross.

Why was she feeling unworthy now? Because of the scars? Because she wasn't the same able-bodied, pretty woman that she'd been before?

Logically, she knew her emotions were all over the place.

She'd made a lot of progress lately—at least she thought she had. She hated these doubts that kept creeping in.

Tessa's words from a few weeks ago had echoed through her mind time and again. *"It's like trying to count the stars. We can't do it. I think the part that is unfathomable is that we want to do something for it. To somehow earn God's favor. So that we feel worthy. Because we are unworthy until . . . His grace. And it's completely and utterly by His grace alone. That any of us are here. That we are breathing. That we have the chance at eternity with Him."*

Grace plus nothing.

Frank had made a good point. Did she know where the storehouse of grace was? Could she ever—no matter how hard she tried—find the key to unlocking it?

No. God's grace truly was unfathomable. Every time she asked Him why this had happened to her . . . why He hadn't given her a husband before it happened . . . she felt guilty.

Ruth picked up her Bible. Frank had pointed to Job and how he questioned God after all the loss and had to listen to his friends tell him it was *his* fault that the bad things happened. Maybe it was time she revisited the book.

*Heavenly Father, You know my struggle. Please help me to see whatever it is that You want me to learn. I'm so tired of the constant war in my mind. I want to understand . . . I do. Please help.*

For two years she'd prayed for healing. Prayed for guidance. Prayed for understanding. And yet she still felt the same way. It was enough to drive her crazy. She knew better than this. Didn't she?

Flipping through the pages of her Bible, she found Job and started at the beginning.

In the first chapter, it showed Job's great wealth and large family. And how all of it was taken away. At the end it said, "In all this Job sinned not, nor charged God foolishly."

It made her examine herself. Had she charged God foolishly? The thought made her a bit sick to her stomach. Job's loss had been so much more than hers. . . .

In the second chapter, Job was afflicted with boils. Not only had he lost everything except his wife, but he was miserable and in great pain. And yet, there it was again, "In all this did not Job sin with his lips."

Enter his friends. Which granted, they were good friends. They came to mourn with him and comfort him. They sat with him for seven days and seven nights without saying a word.

Then Job spoke and poured out his heart in grief. Then his friends spoke. And oh, did they speak.

The speeches went on and on. Man trying to figure out the mind of God. Man trying to justify themselves before God.

Ruth hadn't remembered the harshness and judgmental nature of these three men who said they came to mourn and comfort him. Did they think they were better than Job because they weren't afflicted?

That made her heart sink.

She'd been thinking worse of herself because of her injuries. Thinking that everyone else was too . . .

Shame filled her. "Oh, God. I'm so sorry. I've been so blinded by my own grief."

Ruth read on. By the time she made it to chapter thirty-one, she was in tears at Job's words, "For what portion of God is there from above? And what inheritance of the Almighty from on high? Is not destruction to the wicked? And a strange punishment to the workers of iniquity? Doth not he see my ways, and count all my steps?"

It was like her heart was on the page in front of her. She'd questioned her heavenly Father just like this. But Job acknowledged that God was God, and Job was not.

Ruth had wallowed in her shame and feelings of unworthiness. *God, forgive me.*

She continued to read. Job's friends continued to lecture. But then?

God spoke. "Who is this that darkeneth counsel by words without knowledge? . . . Where wast thou when I laid the foundations of the earth? Declare, if thou hast understanding. Who hath laid the measures thereof, if thou knowest? Or who hath stretched the line upon it? Whereupon are the foundations thereof fastened? Or who laid the corner stone thereof; When the morning stars sang together, and all the sons of God shouted for joy?"

As she devoured the rest of the book, she noticed exactly what Frank had said. Job asked a lot of questions. But God didn't answer them. Instead, He responded with more questions. Helped Job—and his friends—in their humanity and finite minds to see that they couldn't understand everything here on earth. *He* is unfathomable.

*His love for us is unfathomable.*

And His grace, oh, His beautiful grace.

Unfathomable.

Ruth closed the book and held it against her chest.

Grace. Plus. Nothing.

"I get it now, God. I do."

Rather than relying on her own strength, her looks, her skills, her knowledge—any of it—she needed to rely on Him. And only Him.

All her life, she'd liked order. Control. It's what made her so good as a headwaitress.

But maybe . . . just maybe . . . God took the comfort of

control out of her hands, so she could understand His grace more fully.

"Don't give up on me, God. I'm still learning."

As she set the Bible on her table, she smiled.

She couldn't wait to talk to Frank. Closing her eyes, she breathed a deep sigh of relief.

Why wait? Ruth grabbed her stationery box. She'd write him a long letter. Pour it all out. Then when they had time, once they solved the mystery at the hotel . . . they'd talk.

A real heart-to-heart.

Oliver wiped his hands on the towel. The place was filthy. Every time he came here, he cringed. But no one had discovered it. Which was exactly how he wanted it.

It had taken three weeks, but he now had every detail of the Harvey Empire that he'd wanted. Once he made a big enough shamble of their crown jewel, he'd move on to all the other Harvey Houses and destroy each one.

Mr. Smithey and Mr. Lovett—the real ones—weren't looking too good. But he really didn't care anymore. They'd run through their usefulness.

They'd originally cooperated because they wanted to go home. Saw it as their only way. But he guessed that they knew it wasn't a possibility anymore.

His men at the hotel were doing a fine job keeping everyone on their toes. The next phase of his plan had begun.

How many missing deposits would it take before good ol' Mr. Owens noticed?

When he called for the sheriff, well, things would really heat up. Oliver would make sure of that.

He turned to his hired men. "Stay here and keep them alive another month. Just in case I need anything else. Then you may leave. Your payment will be waiting. We don't want the coyotes and buzzards alerting the sheriff too soon, now, do we?"

With a nod to them, he headed up the stairs and out the front door for the last time. He couldn't wait to leave the dirty, cobweb-filled farmhouse behind him.

The night was dark. Clouds had come in and covered the moon and stars.

A storm was on its way. Literally and figuratively.

The El Tovar waited for him.

# 18

R uth woke up tired and sluggish. She rubbed at her eyes.

It hadn't been that late when she'd stopped reading her Bible last night, had it? Reaching for the elixir, she didn't even bother with a spoon and swigged out of the bottle. It was a good thing she had this on hand. She'd need all the energy she could get for the next few days. The hotel had two different birthday parties to host, on top of all the questions swirling about what was going on at the hotel. Mr. Owens had been right to feel something was amiss. He probably didn't think it would be anything of this magnitude, though.

Well, one thing was for certain, they weren't going to allow it to continue. Between her, Frank, their manager, and the man he'd hired, surely they could resolve it soon.

With a sigh, she stood and stretched. Her energy this morning simply wasn't there. She must not be sleeping well. Maybe she should go ahead and request to have Mr. Goodall come see her today. That way she could make sure that she had enough medicine for the next few months. After that, she would feel a lot better. The scars were already beginning to fade. At least she hoped that wasn't wishful thinking.

After writing the quick note, she got herself ready for the day and headed up to her office. The cream was great to use right before she went up the stairs, because then she could hardly feel the discomfort in her leg.

Mr. Owens was at the top of the stairs, waiting for her.

"Mr. Owens." She looked at the watch on her shirtwaist. "Did I miss a meeting?"

"No. No. I simply wished to speak with you."

"Oh."

"In your office, please."

They walked to her office, she unlocked the door, and then he closed the door behind them. "Miss Anniston, the deposit from last week never reached the bank."

She put a hand to her throat. "What?!"

"It's true. I spoke with Mr. Ackerman on the telephone."

What was going on? "Did Mr. Lovett say that anything happened to him along the way?"

"No. He has acted as if nothing is awry."

"Oh my goodness. What are we going to do?" Her mind raced in a hundred different directions.

"Nothing. At least not right now." Mr. Owens paced in front of her desk. "The bank manager promised me that he won't say a word. We need his help."

"Help to do what?"

"Catch whomever is behind this. Mr. Asbury believes we can set a trap. If they don't know we're on to them, they'll probably try it again." He stopped and crossed his arms over his chest. "I sent a telegram to Ford and Byron Harvey this morning. I'm convinced that Mr. Smithey and Mr. Lovett are behind this."

"But why would the Harvey Company have auditors who are crooks? It doesn't make sense."

"No. It doesn't. But I'm beginning to think that those men are imposters. Haven't you noticed that there have been a few times things have been . . . off?"

She gave a reluctant nod. "Even though I haven't spent as much time with them as you have, a few times things haven't felt right. Their presence alone strikes fear in all the staff, so maybe they've used that to their advantage?" It was too much to consider. "Where is Mr. Asbury now?"

He leaned closer. "Down in Williams. He has a lead on the order padding."

Too many things didn't add up. It couldn't all be a coincidence. "Do you think we need to be worried about people's safety? I mean . . . I hate to jump to conclusions, but the more we find out, the more nefarious it sounds."

"I don't know. Whoever is behind this seems to be after money. At least that's how it appears . . . but we need to keep our eyes and ears open. And somehow keep this place running in perfect rhythm as if nothing at all is the matter." His lips made an *O* as he blew out his breath. Then he lifted his shoulders and straightened his waistcoat. "I know this has been quite a burden for you to bear, but can I continue to count on you?"

"Yes, sir."

"How may I be of service to you, Miss Anniston?" Charles bowed to her. He knew exactly what she wanted. But he needed to use this to his advantage.

"Since you are only here for the summer, I would like to

purchase enough of the treatments to last for the next four months or so."

"That will cost a great deal. Are you sure?" He used the most sympathetic tone he had.

"I have money set aside." She flinched as she said it. "And the treatments seem to be working. I'm hopeful that a few more months will get me back to where I need to be."

"Certainly. I have some with me, but I will need to order a bit more."

"That's why I wanted to speak to you about it now. I know it takes time, and with our busy schedules, I thought it prudent to put in my request now."

"Very wise of you, Miss Anniston."

She turned and walked behind her desk. He took that time to peruse the room. There was a little book on her desk. Different from what he'd seen there before. Hmmm.

"Thank you for coming, Mr. Goodall."

"You are most welcome." He straightened his tie and cleared his throat, playing the part of the nervous suitor. "Miss Anniston?"

"Yes?" She lifted her gaze.

"I hope this doesn't sound too forward, but I have admired you for some time now. Is there any chance I could interest you in a walk along the rim some evening?"

Her eyes grew wide, and then she gave a modest attempt at covering her surprise by taking her seat and straightening some papers. "That is a lovely invitation, Mr. Goodall." She bit her lip as pink crept up into her cheeks.

"Does that mean you will accept?"

Blinking several times, she clasped her hands in front of her on the desktop. "I admit you took me by surprise. I would like to think about it, if that's all right with you?"

"Of course." Even if she declined, his feigned interest in her would give him an excuse to be around her more often. "I will take my leave. Rest assured, I will let you know when I have what you've requested."

"Thank you." The sweet smile she sent him gave him all the proof he needed that it was time to reel her in.

Charles gave a light bow again and left the room.

Such an innocent thing, Miss Anniston.

He almost felt sorry for her.

It was a perfect day to have off. Thankfulness filled Frank as he relished the morning air. Owens had already eased up on his strict schedule after the auditors finished their audit. Of course now the manager was pretty certain it had all been fake. So he'd instructed the staff to return to their regular schedules. Which gave Frank a bit of time when he wasn't in the kitchen to observe things.

They all knew something was off. But so far, no suspects. Now they waited. Again.

To make the most of his time, Frank knew some solitude would be best. The storm last night had rushed through with rain and freshened everything up. It seemed to have cooled the temperatures considerably too, which was a welcomed gift this time of year.

Then, to make everything even better, there was a letter in his box this morning.

He'd recognize Ruth's handwriting anywhere.

Hearing from her gave him a spring in his step as he walked out to his favorite spot at the canyon.

Of course, Ruth would never join him here because he

liked to sit on the very rim, looking down into the vast, rocky expanse. But Emma Grace had joined him here once or twice.

He opened the envelope and pulled out the sheets of paper. With a deep breath, he began to read.

*My Dearest Frank,*

*I know you have seen me at my worst of late. I am deeply sorry for that. But thank you for your friendship and challenging words. You've never been one to hold back, and I am grateful. Truly, you have been my best and dearest friend.*

*I read Job tonight. To say that God worked on my heart is to put it lightly. My prayer is that you and I may discuss all that the Lord has shown me through this time. . . .*

Ruth's struggle since her injuries had been apparent to all who knew her, and they'd tried to give her space and time to heal. But as she put more and more distance between herself and those she loved, no one had been able to get through.

Seemed like God did, though. As Frank read her heartfelt words, it was difficult to keep from jumping up and shouting his praise.

Through the Word and through discussions with her friends, Ruth had found some peace.

Finally.

He set the pages down in his lap. *Thank You, God.*

Perhaps now there was a chance that he could tell her again how he felt. He could speak to Mr. Owens about courting her. Maybe when her parents arrived? Wouldn't it be wonderful to share this precious time with them?

He read through the letter one more time, overjoyed at the words and the passion behind them.

Ruth was back. His Ruth. The woman he'd known for years. They had been through a lot together. Hopefully they'd journey through a lot more.

Frank hopped up from his seat and tapped the letter against his palm. They'd left things unresolved between them before. Perhaps it was time for a clean slate.

He took long strides back toward the hotel. He hoped she wouldn't mind an interruption from him.

But Howard caught him in the rotunda. "Chef Henderson, would you mind double-checking this order for me?" The man appeared nervous.

"Is there something you are concerned about?" Frank didn't want to give anything away. Did the young chef know that they had been checking into things with Patterson?

"No . . . no." He cleared his throat. "Just wanting to be thorough. It's been busy lately, and we are all tired."

"Take it back to the kitchen, and I'll be there in a little bit to look it over."

"Thank you, sir." Howard walked away.

Now what was that all about? Frank had been hesitant to think that his assistant chef could be involved in anything untoward—especially since lately, he'd been sure to dot all his *i*'s and cross all his *t*'s. Absolutely everything had been spot-on. *Too* spot-on. As if he had something to hide. And now the request to double-check the order? Frank let out a sigh. To him, that only confirmed that Howard was guilty.

He swiped a hand down his face. Later. He'd deal with it later.

Right now, he wanted to see Ruth.

When he reached her office door, he knocked.

"Come in."

He opened the door and peeked around it. "Hi. It's me."

A warm smile filled her face.

But he couldn't help but notice the crease in her brow. This summer had brought much more stress to her job than normal. If only he could take it away. "I came to thank you for your letter." He held it up and stepped all the way in.

"You've read it?"

"Yes." Their gazes connected. Words weren't necessary. She'd shared her heart, and he understood. "I was hoping you wouldn't mind me stopping by. I know you're busy."

"I'm glad you did." Her face went back to a serious frown. "Would you mind closing the door?"

He did, and his heart skipped a beat. "Something bothering you?"

Her long exhale conveyed that she was frustrated. "There's so much more to what's going on here. . . ."

"What's happened?" While he'd hoped to chat with her about their personal relationship, this took priority.

"It started with the discrepancies, then the newspaper articles, then the company sent the Harvey men here, right?"

"Right."

"Well, since they've been here, they said everything had been resolved. But we discovered the problem with the orders. *Then*, I've noticed that every night—*every night*—after I double-check the count with Mr. Owens, the ledgers are changed. By whom . . . I'm not sure." She pulled a small journal out of her desk. "But I know it's happening, because I've been writing the exact same number that I write in the main ledger in this little journal."

"Oh, that can't be good."

"When I first noticed, I told Mr. Owens. We came up

with a plan, and I started taking pictures with my camera . . . you know, for proof. And now? The last deposit didn't make it to the bank."

That was *really* not good. "Who took it there? I thought Mr. Owens always took the deposits in."

"He was about to when Mr. Lovett offered to take it. It's not like he could tell one of the Harvey auditors no."

"What a mess. How'd you find out about the deposit?"

She gave him the rundown on their manager's conversation with the bank manager and the telegram sent to Byron and Ford. Ruth placed her elbows on her desk and rubbed her temples with her fingers.

"What about the man Mr. Owens hired?"

"Still following a lead. He's hesitant to say until he has proof, but I'm pretty sure this all leads back to the auditors. There's no chance the Harvey Company would have crooks in their employ. As least not for long. And Mr. Owens said that when he asked about the men coming—before they came—he was told both of the men were highly respected and were dedicated to the company. For years."

"But the trouble started before they came. How could they have been involved?"

Her brow furrowed, and she thrummed her fingers on her desk. "I don't know. But they're up to something."

He didn't need to be throwing more trouble and doubt her way. Best to simply jump in and offer his assistance. "What can I do to help?"

"I don't think you can do anything at this point. Not until we hear back from one of the Harveys. We're keeping our eyes out for any trouble and keeping track of everything for proof in case we need it."

He stuffed her letter back in his pocket. He'd hoped to

clear the air with her about their last conversation, but that would have to wait. Besides, this was much more serious. "If you need me to do anything, let me know. Tell Mr. Owens."

"He trusts you, Frank, so if he needs anything, I'm sure he will. Right now, I think we're baffled by all of it and trying to figure out what is going on without jumping to too many conclusions. If we have imposters or thieves or whatever among us, we've got to stay on our toes."

"I can't believe that someone would—"

Suddenly, the door opened behind him, and he turned to see Mr. Owens. His face was white.

Their manager removed his glasses and looked to Ruth. "I'm sorry to barge in. . . ."

"That's perfectly all right. I was just filling Frank in on the latest. Did something else happen?" Ruth came to her feet.

"I'm sorry, Ruth. You received a telegram." He walked toward her and set the telegram on the desk. "I'm so very sorry."

Frank's gaze went to Ruth as she read the telegram.

She collapsed into her chair. "No . . . no . . . They were just here. . . ."

---

The ache in Ruth's heart grew like nothing she'd ever felt before. Tears burned her eyes. "They were just here. . . ." she repeated.

Frank and Mr. Owens were still in the room, standing. Watching her.

She glanced up and, with a shaky hand, handed the telegram to Frank.

Without breathing, she watched him as he read it. Maybe this wasn't real. It would go away. A bad dream?

Then his eyes lifted to hers. Tears shimmered in them. "Oh, Ruth . . ." He set the paper down on the desk and came around beside her. He crouched down beside her chair and put a hand on her arm. "What do you need? Anything. I'm here for you."

She released her breath, and the tears flowed then. It wasn't a nightmare. This was real.

Sobs burst from her as she shook.

Frank wrapped his arms around her and held her as she cried on his shoulder.

Her father was dead. An automobile accident. The cab was taking them home from the train station when it happened.

Mother was seriously injured. Aunt Mae said she was having another surgery on her arm. Whatever that meant.

Mr. Owens cleared his throat. "Would you like me to send a response, Ruth?"

She shook her head and pulled away from Frank's comforting arms. "No. I'm sure Aunt Mae will wire when she has more news. Wait. Yes, please ask her if any arrangements have been made for my father." Swiping at the tears all over her cheeks, she swallowed. "I might need to help her. . . ." Her throat closed on the last words. "But the hotel? All the problems?"

Frank stood and gripped her shoulder.

The manager's face was full of sorrow. "I will send a telegram right now. Take as much time as you need, Ruth. Family is much more important than any crisis here."

"Thank you." She choked on a sob. "Could you please let me know as soon as you have a response?"

"Yes, of course." Mr. Owens stepped out and closed the door.

"Tell me what you need. I'll do anything." Frank knelt at her side again. He took both of her hands in his.

"I think I need to go to my room." She pushed to stand, but the room spun. Closing her eyes against it, she tried to steady herself with her hands on the desk. But it didn't work. Her breaths came in short gasps.

Strong arms lifted her up. Pressed her head against a warm shoulder.

"I've got you. Don't worry."

# 19

Ruth blinked. Couldn't get her eyes to focus. She blinked again.

And again. Until shapes at least emerged. Looked familiar.

She forced her mind to remember all that had happened.

"Ruth?" A voice beside her.

Charlotte.

Ruth licked her lips. "What day is it?"

"It's Saturday. The third of July."

That meant a week had passed since the telegram had arrived.

Memories fell into place.

The first telegram. Telling her about the accident.

Then another . . . stating that her mother had lost an arm below the elbow. After four surgeries, they'd had to amputate.

Tears stung at the corners of her eyes and then began to flood and stream down her face.

She'd never see her father again.

248

Her mother would never be able to play the piano with two hands again.

Dad's body had been sent to a crematorium. For some reason, he'd said that was what he wanted. Aunt Mae had followed through.

Ruth didn't understand.

Not any of it.

Aunt Mae wired that Mom's wish was for Ruth to stay put. Because she would still be moving to the canyon soon. Aunt Mae had decided to come with her. They might be delayed a little while her mother healed. But this was what Mom wanted. There was to be no argument. How could she when she'd demanded they stay away two years ago?

Those first few days passed in a blur.

The blur of waiting for news. Receiving the news.

Not knowing how to deal with it.

Then apparently, she collapsed in the hallway in the middle of the night. In her nightgown.

Tessa had found her and called for help.

She remembered being carried away from the El Tovar and into a carriage. Dr. Collins had asked her a lot of questions.

Now Ruth lay in a bed at his house.

"Do you need anything?" Charlotte stood beside her.

"Some water?"

Her friend's smile was full of relief. "I'll get you some."

Footsteps approached. "Ah, you're awake."

Ruth looked up and saw Dr. Collins. "What happened?"

"Well, let's see . . . you've been asleep for three days straight."

That wasn't what she expected to hear. How had she slept that long? "Three days?"

"Mm-hmm." His gray hair stood up in several places. But

it was always a bit of a mess. "And I heard that you made a visit to Doctor Newport. Is that where you got this?" He lifted up her bottle of elixir as his eyebrows raised in question.

Ruth licked her lips again. "Um, no. But Doctor Newport did show me some exercises I could do for my leg." Not that she wanted to accuse Dr. Collins of anything, but she didn't want to have to talk about the treatments from Mr. Goodall.

"Well, I think this"—he held up the bottle—"is part of the problem."

She tried to push up in the bed and sit straighter. "What do you mean?"

"I'm not certain what's in it, but if you've been taking this regularly, that's probably what caused the collapse and your sleeping for three days."

"Could it not be that I'm grieving and tired?" Oh, how she wished that were true.

"No, my dear. I'm sorry. We tried to wake you. Had to force water down your throat just so you wouldn't be dehydrated. Something of a *narcotic* nature must have caused this."

She reached up and rubbed her temples. What had she done?

"I'm going to take this bottle and send it to a friend of mine. Hopefully they can tell me what's in it and make sure we don't need to counteract anything else."

"Counteract?"

"Dear, if you have narcotics in your system, they could do serious damage to your organs. I want to be thorough." He headed back for the door.

"Doctor?"

"Yes, Miss Anniston?" He looked over his shoulder at her.

"Do you think it's all right for me to do those exercises to strengthen my leg?"

"It will take time for the scar tissue to break up. That will be the most painful part. But I think it's fine for you to do the exercises." His smile didn't reach his eyes, but the man looked weary. Possibly because he'd stayed awake the three days she'd slept.

Charlotte came in as the doctor left. She held out a big glass of water.

"Oh, that looks wonderful." Her mouth was so dry. "Thank you, Charlotte." She took the glass and let the cool water flow through her lips and over her parched tongue.

Thoughts of her parents kept pressing for an audience, but she tried to push them back. Not that she didn't love her parents, but because her heart couldn't take it right now.

When did everything take such a sour turn?

Frank always loved the Fourth of July, one of their busiest days of the year. It meant he had the privilege of creating hundreds of new and exciting dishes for the guests to ooh and aah over. Their pastry chef was producing a flurry of red, white, and blue–themed masterpieces. Cakes, pies, cookies. Even ice cream this year.

Many people visited from Williams on this day to celebrate at the canyon. Fireworks would be shot off later at the rim. Food would be plentiful. And people would picnic out in the sun, enjoying the beautiful day.

But it did mean that he was a little bit more frazzled than usual. His lists were pages long. About ten times more than usual.

Add to that, he couldn't keep his thoughts from turning to Ruth. His worry for her and not only her health but also the depth of grief she was going through. He wouldn't wish that on anyone. They hadn't had the chance for a long chat since she found out the news. But the doctor had kept him and Mr. Owens apprised.

"Chef!" Louis called from the corner. A pot was boiling over. Not something that usually happened in the El Tovar's kitchen. But today everyone had their eyes on more than one thing and their minds had to keep up.

Averting the crisis, Frank headed back to his station in time to see Mr. Smithey and Mr. Lovett enter. He let out his breath. If these men were the masterminds behind the thefts, he wanted nothing more than to punch them right then and there. But just last night, Mr. Owens told him that Asbury was close. And the only way to stop them was to catch them in the act. So, Frank put on a smile and went to greet the men, pretending nothing was out of the ordinary. "How can I help you, gentlemen?"

"Well, seeing as we are here to audit and we haven't been in the kitchen for a couple weeks, we thought it would be good to observe today and ask questions."

"This isn't the best time. It's our busiest day of the year." Frank attempted to usher them out, but he failed.

"What better day to be here than today? We can assess how your kitchen handles pressure. Watch the men. Quiz them on their knowledge. Harvey demands the best, you know." Lovett's smile seemed fake. Of course, everything about these two now appeared fake.

No matter, Frank was not happy they chose today of all days to do this.

Was it on purpose?

For sure it was. Of course.

Today was going to be a very, very long day.

Sweat gathered under Frank's chef hat and under his arms. The kitchen had heated up to about three times its normal temperature. At least it felt that way.

Smithey and Lovett had circled like hawks.

Making the men nervous. Asking ridiculous and frivolous questions. Interrupting and keeping the men from doing their jobs.

All with smiles on their faces.

Which only built Frank's ire.

Fury began to build. Once they knew for sure that these men were criminals, he would like nothing more than to throw the two out of the hotel himself.

But that wasn't very Christian-like. In fact, most of his thoughts today hadn't been.

*Lord, help.*

God knew what he was up against. The simple prayer would have to do.

Thankfully, they'd averted several disasters today, but that didn't mean they were without mishap. Several dishes had to be started over. Every man in the kitchen had some sort of food spilled down the front of him. And every single one of them looked like they could use a good dunking under a cold hose.

But the food kept going out to the guests. And that was what mattered.

The only thing that kept him going was the note that Ruth had delivered to him that morning. She was hoping to venture out to see the fireworks and hoped to be able to chat with him. He'd responded by saying he'd love that.

If he could make it to that point. At this rate, he was thankful to survive each hour.

Almost all the cooking for the day was finished, and they only had to complete a few more things. Then the cleanup could commence and he could head out to see the fireworks with everyone.

"Frank!" Mr. Owens' voice cut through the kitchen, and Frank had to search to find him. It had to be really important if he was calling him Frank.

He wiped his hands on a towel and hurried over to the man.

His face was red. His eyes wide. "Something's wrong with the food."

"What do you mean?" His heart dropped like a rock.

"I've had reports that almost half of our guests are sick."

"What about the people from town?"

"A good many of them too. We're trying to find buckets and cool washcloths for everyone, but this doesn't look good."

Frank looked around the kitchen. He'd never had any of his food make anyone sick. Never. What had happened?

Smithey and Lovett headed their way with vile smiles. Smithey nodded at Frank. "I think we've done all we can do today. It was good to see your men in action." The two exited.

Mr. Owens' face fell. He looked utterly defeated. "Never in my day have I seen anything like this."

"I'm sorry, Mr. Owens." He croaked out the apology. "I can't understand what happened."

"I don't think this was your fault, Frank." His gaze followed the men who'd just left. "How long were those two in here?"

"Almost all day, sir. I tried to get them out, but they said they needed to see us in action and under pressure."

Fury spread across the manager's face. "I don't believe for a minute that it was the fault of anyone here in the kitchen. But I do believe that someone did this on purpose, and I intend to get to the bottom of it." The man began to step away and then stopped. "Cancel the rest of the food for the day. You might as well go ahead and clean up." He came closer to Frank and lowered his voice. "Make sure everything is scrubbed from top to bottom. I don't know what they put in the food, but we need to make certain it is gone."

Frank couldn't believe that people could be so deplorable. He pushed the words out through clenched teeth as his temper rose. "Those sneaky reprobates!" To think that they had been in his kitchen all day. Tainting the food.

Owens stepped closer. "Calm down, Frank." His eyes darted around. "We don't want anyone else to know our suspicions."

Right. Certainly no one in his kitchen assisted with the foul play? He was tired of this whole mess. It had gone on too long. Frank lowered his voice. "Has Asbury found anything?"

"I'll speak with you about that later. For now, I need to go help the good doctor deal with all the sick." The man walked out.

Frank looked at his men, who had grown silent with the exit of their manager and stared. How to tell them that all their hard work today had done nothing but get a crowd of people sick?

Another thought made him feel sick to his stomach. Were any of his men involved?

Two hours later, Frank sat on a bench with Ruth.

The fireworks had been canceled because all the guys who knew how to shoot them off had gotten sick. People lay on blankets all along the rim outside the hotel. The train was delayed in leaving for Williams because the entire crew had eaten at the festivities and *they* were all sick as well.

"I don't know what could have caused it." Frank sat hunched over his knees. Thankful he hadn't eaten because he'd been too busy, and he was more than grateful that Ruth had eaten with Mrs. Collins. "But I'm assuming Smithey or Lovett did something while they were in the kitchen. They had access to all the food we were preparing."

"This is not your fault, Frank." Ruth's voice was soft.

"I'm sorry to come out here and complain about my day. That wasn't my intention. You have enough weight on your shoulders right now."

"Anything that has to do with the kitchen or dining room falls under my responsibility, remember? Besides, it's been good to get my mind off my troubles for a while."

He turned on the bench to face her. "Are you heading out to be with your mom?"

Ruth picked at her skirt. "No. She told me to stay put. Aunt Mae decided to move with her, and they will be heading here soon. I don't know how my mother is handling all of this. But maybe that's the point. Maybe she can't deal with my grief on top of her own?"

"Your mother is a strong woman. Maybe she wants to get out here as soon as she can so she can be with you."

"But with her own healing? I can't imagine what she's gone through. Aunt Mae says they are doing well, but I'm not so confident."

Frank lifted her chin with his finger. Made her look him in the eye. "How about you? How are *you* doing?"

"One day at a time. I still can't believe my dad is gone and I'll never see him again. He was so excited to move out here." As she blinked, tears slipped out.

"I know. He was full of smiles thinking of moving closer to his little girl."

"Oh, Frank." The tears came out in a torrent now.

He put his arm around her shoulder and pulled her close. He didn't care if anyone saw. No one could judge. Ruth had lost her father. She deserved to be able to grieve.

———— ┤ ├————

His little game of chess was going better than he'd even planned.

Amazing what crushed rhubarb leaves could do to a bunch of food. Even more people than he'd imagined were sick. No thanks to that sniveling Howard. The man could be so infuriating. But Oliver needed him for one last chore.

Good thing he'd planned to stay somewhere else for a few days. He didn't want to be at the El Tovar right now with all the people sick and probably scrambling to get away as soon as possible. As much as he'd like to see that, it was best that he wasn't present.

All of his telegrams had been sent. Every major newspaper in the country would be running with the story. Hundreds of people were sick from Harvey's food.

At their best hotel, to boot.

The young man at the telegraph office came back to the counter. "All done, sir."

Oliver handed him the money for the telegrams, then gave him another twenty dollars. A small fortune for a young working man. "And the other matter?"

The young fellow looked around him and then back to Oliver. "Yes, sir. I took care of it. They haven't been sent."

He tapped the counter and smiled. "Good." He slipped another ten dollars across the counter. "Keep up the good work."

"Thank you, sir."

Oliver left the office and headed to the brand-new Fray Marcos Hotel—another Harvey House—in Williams. It wasn't elaborate like the El Tovar, but he wanted to keep his eyes and ears open. Because this would be his next target.

He'd stay here a couple more days and wait. Then head back to the canyon for his final play.

# 20

Opening the door to her office, Ruth took a deep breath.

So much had happened since the last time she was in here. And since she hadn't slept well last night, she wanted to clean up her office and desk in hopes she could convince Mr. Owens that she wanted—no, needed—to get back to work.

She closed the door behind her and stepped toward her desk. A lovely envelope with Emma Grace's beautiful script lay on top. Their friendship had seen a lot of mountains and valleys over the years. A deep valley this past year, that's for certain.

She settled into her chair and reached for the letter opener.

As she read the long note from her friend, her heart cinched. She couldn't allow Emma Grace to take the blame for the lull in their friendship. Ruth had just as much responsibility. In fact, she probably had more. Because she'd gotten really good at pushing people away. Shutting out everything. Holing up in her office and ignoring the world.

Oh, how she longed for things to return to how they'd been. Ruth folded up the letter and tucked it inside her desk. But things would never be the same again.

Never.

But in the words of Job . . . *the Lord gave and the Lord hath taken away; blessed be the name of the Lord.*

She had no idea how to bless the name of the Lord yet. But she would try.

Lifting her chin, she pulled out a sheet of stationery, her pen, and ink. The least she could do was let Emma Grace know that she loved her, that she was coming out of the fog from the past two years, and that she treasured their friendship. It would take time to heal. But she was more than ready for healing.

Another wave of grief crashed over her with the force of a loaded freight wagon. *Why, God, why?* As soon as she'd made forward progress, she'd been thrown back to the ground with fresh wounds.

Her father's voice drifted through her memories. She closed her eyes and could see him sitting before her. "*The enemy will come at you from every side when you are trying to live a life for Christ, my dear. Don't let him win. 'For we wrestle not against flesh and blood, but against principalities, against powers, against the rulers of the darkness of this world, against spiritual wickedness in high places.'*"

The memory passed, and she opened her eyes. "I won't let him win, Dad." She choked back fresh tears.

Focusing on her job would be good for her mind and heart. It was the best she could do until her mother and aunt arrived. So, she finished straightening her desk, clearing it of everything so that she could start fresh.

Her back ached as she noticed the time. How long had

she been sitting? What she needed was some fresh air. She could come back in an hour or so. After she cleared her head. After she'd gotten permission from the manager to come back to work.

But for now, she'd go splash some water on her face, redo her makeup, and then get something to eat. The only way to get past this was to focus on something else.

And there was plenty for her to do.

What she wouldn't give for a sip of the elixir right now. But the thought that it had caused her to sleep for several days banished the urge.

Thankfully, Dr. Collins hadn't told her to stop using the creams. They were working, and Mr. Goodall had a stellar reputation among his clientele.

Maybe continuing to take the elixir—but in smaller amounts—would still be okay? It must have been all right since countless others took it. Mr. Goodall said so himself. And Dr. Newport had heard good things as well.

The debate continued in her mind. She simply had taken more than she'd been directed. He'd said it was all natural and contained the highest-quality ingredients. Maybe it wouldn't hurt. After a few more days of rest, of course.

An hour later, she was back at her desk. She'd told Mr. Owens she couldn't handle one more day being cooped up and watched by everyone. She wanted to be busy. Working. Helping.

All the people who'd gotten sick were now better, but they'd had over half of their guests leave early. She couldn't blame them. Not after such a nasty episode. Two days ago, they'd been gearing up for the festivities of the year. Now look.

A single letter was on the desk in front of her. Her mother's handwriting.

With a breath for courage, Ruth opened the envelope and pulled out the letter.

*My dearest daughter,*

*Words cannot express how my heart aches for your father. And yet, I am overjoyed that he is with his Savior. I cling to that fact and rejoice in it. Even though I miss him desperately.*

*There's something your father wanted to tell you in person, and well, now that he's gone, I feel it is time. He wouldn't want you to mourn him, sweetheart. Even though I know you do, as I do.*

*Last year, he was diagnosed with cancer. Since it had spread, the doctors didn't give him a lot of time, but he'd hoped to hold it at bay as long as possible. His greatest desire was that he wouldn't suffer like so many others we have watched go on before us. He wanted to live out his last days doing all the fun things he could and spending time with "his two girls."*

*I'm sorry we didn't tell you while we were there. But I want you to know that your father was ready. And even though this tragedy has been horrible to endure, I'm thankful he didn't suffer.*

Several dried spots were on the page. Probably from her mother's tears. Sniffling back her own sobs, Ruth read on.

*I can't tell you how happy he was on our trip there, and on the way home he told me that it was the best time of his life.*

*So take that to heart. Cling to it as I have. Know that your father would want you to go on living your life to the fullest. For him. Because he wanted that for his little girl.*

*My arm is healing nicely. The phantom pains are real and quite a nuisance, but I pray myself through them. Your aunt Mae has been by my side every day. I think she's as excited about moving out to the Grand Canyon as I am. We are eager to be on our way.*

*The doctor told me he thought I should stay here for a few more weeks, but there's no infection and there's nothing to do here. My music, piano, and all of our things are already headed there. I'd much prefer getting there and asking your doctor to help me keep an eye on my healing.*

*Every day, I am reminded of and recite my favorite verses in James. I do count it all joy, Ruth.*

*Every moment with your father. Every moment with you. The trying of my faith definitely worketh patience. Just like Scripture says.*

*"But let patience have her perfect work, that ye may be perfect and entire, wanting nothing."*

*That is what keeps me going. And the thought of seeing your beautiful face. We allowed too much time to pass without getting to hug you, and for that, I am so very sorry. But I rejoice again in the fact that your father was able to see you one last time.*

*I'm itching to play the piano again and see what I can do with one hand. If anything, your aunt Mae can fill in the other hand for me. Won't that be a sight? We haven't played together since we were children.*

*Oh, the things to look forward to.*

*I am overjoyed.*

*I can't wait to see you soon. I'm sure we will shed*

*many tears together, but your father would want them to be tears of joy. Because he isn't suffering. He's in the presence of God Almighty.*

*I love you, my dear, and will be there soon. Aunt Mae will wire once we've purchased tickets.*

*Love,*
*Mom*

After reading it twice, Ruth mopped up her tears with her handkerchief and tucked the letter back into its envelope.

Why hadn't her parents told her about Dad's illness before? Was it because of her own selfishness? Because she'd wallowed in her own pain and injuries?

If she hadn't denied her parents coming two years ago, she could have had more time with them. Precious time that she could never get back. If she hadn't kept them away, maybe they wouldn't have seen the need to keep his illness from *her*.

Even as the ugly, hateful voice inside her head taunted her, she calmed. Because once again, she wasn't fighting against flesh and blood.

*Lord God . . . help me. Help my unbelief. My doubts. Forgive me, Father, for all the mistakes I've made. The hurt I caused my parents by pushing them away. But thank You for the time we had. Thank You for Mom and Aunt Mae being able to come soon. Please, O Father God, keep them safe.*

As her thoughts turned to trying to find joy and thankfulness, the voice quieted. It would be so wonderful to have her mother here.

Joy practically oozed out of the letter. How her mother

did it, well, it simply had to be supernatural. Ruth needed that same joy. But it was hard to find through the grief.

Ruth tucked the letter into the pocket of her skirt. Work would help her get her mind off all the memories. And she wanted to make sure she kept them close. Those last days with Dad were more than precious to her. But right now, they hurt too much. Made her cry at every turn.

How many times had she reached for the elixir, needing a little boost? Too many. But Dr. Collins had taken it.

She hoped against hope that it didn't have anything like narcotics in it. She wanted to ask Mr. Goodall about it, but he had been gone for a few days.

A tap at her door made her paste on a smile before she called, "Come in."

Charlotte peeked in with a tray in her hand. "I brought coffee and tea. Which would you like?"

Ruth slumped back in her chair. "How did you know I needed something?"

"I don't know." She shrugged. "Just thought I could do something for you. It's so much slower than usual."

"I've heard. Mr. Owens is supposed to come see me in a little bit so we can discuss all of this."

Charlotte set the tray down, and Ruth poured herself a cup of strong tea. Perhaps that would help.

"Ruth?" Charlotte picked at one of her fingernails.

She took a sip and then set her cup down. "Yes? Is something bothering you?"

"Well . . . I need to apologize. You were right to question Mr. Denton. He ended up being a cad." She sniffed. "And even after my little tantrum, you still treated me with love and grace. I haven't known how to say anything. The hotel was so busy, and then your father . . ." She hiccupped and sniffled again. "I'm sorry, Ruth. You are one of my dearest friends, and I respect you more than anyone else here. I should have never spoken to you that way."

"It's all right, Charlotte. Truly. All is forgiven." She looked down at her hands. "You know, the fact that you said I treated you with love and grace . . . that wasn't me, Charlotte. That was obviously God at work in me if you saw that. I haven't been myself for a long time, and I've been struggling . . . more than you probably know. So thank you for loving me too. I need your friendship, and I'm sorry if I've pushed you away over the last two years." Ruth stood and walked around the corner of her desk.

Charlotte met her there, and they hugged.

"I needed that."

"Me too." Her friend lifted her shoulders with a big breath. "Well, I'm going to get back to work."

"Thank you, Charlotte."

The girl's black dress and white apron swirled as she turned and almost ran into Mr. Owens in the doorway.

The two nodded at each other as they passed.

Her boss came in and shut the door. He stepped over to her desk and plunked down some papers. "Over fifty cancellations for next week."

She'd braced herself for it but found she wasn't ready.

"Then there's these." He tossed several newspapers down.

"I don't want to look, do I?"

"I'll give you the gist. Someone told every large paper in the United States about our outbreak of sickness. And every single one of the papers cites a source that says the food at the El Tovar on America's Independence Day was tainted, spoiled, and shouldn't have been served." Instead of his usual

266

pacing, Mr. Owens stood very still, his eyes gazing out the window behind her.

"I'm so sorry, Mr. Owens. What can we do?"

"We can find whoever is doing this. I haven't heard a word from Ford or Byron, which makes me think they must be furious. They could very well be on their way here now. To fire all of us."

She flinched. Hopefully that wasn't true.

"No. They are very generous, kindhearted men. But this is unlike them not to communicate. The last deposit also went missing. Both of our *auditors*"—his voice dripped with disdain—"offered to bring it in. I kept up our little ruse but arranged with Mr. Asbury to be at the train with Sheriff Andrews to follow Lovett and Smithey when they arrived, but I haven't heard a word from him since before the Fourth. Mr. Ackerman told me that no one has even come into the bank on behalf of the El Tovar."

"Looks like we now know who's behind all this." Ruth couldn't believe that people could be so horrible. "Mr. Smithey and Lovett? It has to be them . . . right?"

"That's the thing. They're still here. Walking around as if nothing is wrong. Oh sure, they expressed their disappointment about the sickness—they even acted sick themselves, but it didn't seem nearly as severe as everyone else. Why are they still here? I don't understand it. Especially if they know all I have to do is give the bank a call. And how did they arrange everything before they arrived? It's hard to imagine that Howard pulled all of this off. We aren't even certain he's been a part of it."

"Do you think they're waiting to see how much they can steal? It's pretty bold to do it right under your nose."

Mr. Owens shook his head. "Maybe? I don't know. But for

some reason, my gut tells me that there's something else behind all this. Something bigger. Maybe that's just pessimism talking because this has been one nightmare after another."

"But with people canceling, with the deposits missing, and now with this"—she lifted up the papers—"is there a chance this will ruin the El Tovar?"

"That, Miss Anniston, is a very real possibility. One I hate to even entertain. I've poured my life into this place. Not to mention all of you. And the Harveys. The railroad. That's why we have to do everything we can to stop it. I'm going to travel to Williams tomorrow and give the sheriff a visit. See if I can find out what happened to Mr. Asbury. But don't say a word of it to anyone, all right? I won't be gone long. Perhaps I won't be feeling well and we can tell people that . . . ?"

Two hours later, Frank sat across from her.

"I've only got about fifteen minutes before I need to be back in the kitchen," he said.

"All right, I'll try to be quick." She filled him in on everything that she and Mr. Owens had spoken about earlier.

"Wow. It doesn't sound good."

"No. It doesn't." With a hand to her forehead, she weighed all the thoughts in her mind. "Let me ask you a question. I know that you trusted Howard—said he was loyal and all—but is there any chance he was the one who tampered with the food? I mean, we have our suspicions he was the one behind the orders, right? I wish I would have kept those receipts and orders he gave me." But Smithey and Lovett had it all now. Had they covered it up? How was it all connected?

"I have to admit, I didn't think he was the kind of man to do it, but the evidence suggests otherwise. Howard has been more helpful and supportive than ever, which has made me second-guess everything. Mr. Patterson told me that the orders have gone back to what they were, which makes me think Howard must've gotten wind that we were checking into it. But it couldn't have been him on the Fourth."

"Why not?"

"Because Howard wasn't here. He cut his hand pretty deeply the day before and was in Williams with the doc."

So much for that theory. "How convenient." She hated to sound so discouraged, but this whole thing was a big, tangled mess. Why did people insist on doing bad things?

"Don't worry, Ruth. We'll figure this out. Somehow."

"I hope you're right. When Mr. Owens told me he hadn't heard from Mr. Asbury, I have to admit I felt like we were back at square one. I had hoped that the investigator would figure it all out and then swoop in with the sheriff and arrest all the guilty parties and everything would go back to normal."

"I hope nothing has happened to him." Frank shook his head. "But if something has . . . ?"

Her heart sank at the look on his face. "You don't think that someone would actually hurt people? Aren't they just after money?"

"Whoever they are didn't seem to mind making hundreds of people sick. Someone could have easily died." The words hung in the air.

Dread and unease swirled inside her. "We have to get to the bottom of this, Frank. Before anyone else gets sick or hurt or disappears."

"Agreed. So what do we do?"

# 21

SUNDAY, JULY 11, 1909

Frank sat outside with Julia and her husband, Chris. Emma Grace and her husband, Ray, were nearby while their little one napped in the sunshine on a blanket. Chasing the dragonflies must have worn the little girl out.

More than anything, he wanted to discuss everything that was going on with the men and get their input, but Mr. Owens didn't want anyone else to know.

The manager had found Mr. Asbury laid up in Dr. Newport's home. He'd been hit by an automobile on the way to the sheriff's. Normally not one to be cynical, Frank couldn't help but think it wasn't a coincidence. The news from Sheriff Andrews' office hadn't been any more encouraging.

Thefts had been happening all over town, and the sheriff and his men had been running ragged to keep up. What was going on? Things like that hadn't been normal in Williams. Nor at the El Tovar. Why was it that all of this was happening at the same time? Could it be connected? But how?

270

"Thanks for coming everyone." Julia's voice broke through his thoughts. She looked straight at him. "By the deep frown on Frank's face, I think it's safe to say that we all need a pick-me-up." She held one of those fancy new clipboards in her lap. "I know we have been very busy, and there's been a good bit of difficulty lately."

If they only knew the half of it. Frank put his best effort into listening. This was for Ruth, after all.

"I know we all love Ruth and want to do something special for her. She's been through a lot the past couple years." Julia brushed at a tear that slipped down her cheek. "And now with the loss of her father, I think it's even more important that we rally around her and celebrate her."

Frank leaned in. "This is exactly what she needs. At this point, she's trying to stay busy to help her through her grief." If they only knew about the other burdens she was carrying right now. "If we can give her something really joyous, then I know that will lift her spirits."

"Okay, good. This is what I think we should do." Julia started going down her list.

Emma Grace and Ray would get the rest of the Harvey Girls recruited for decorations and party games. Julia would help Frank with the food.

Now all they had to do was pray for a sunny, beautiful day. And no disasters.

---

**TUESDAY, JULY 13, 1909**

Oliver crouched below the open window outside Miss Anniston's office. The oppressive heat the past few days had been fortunate for him. Something in the way Mr. Owens had looked as he rushed to her office made him wary. So, on impulse, he'd come out here.

"Frankly, Ruth. I'm worried." The manager's voice sounded tired. "With Mr. Asbury out of commission, and everything else that has gone wrong, I think we should do something ourselves. The sheriff said he would look into it quietly, but since we haven't heard from the company, and I didn't have any proof to show him, I don't think he'll do much. Williams has gotten bigger and busier, and it sounds like his hands are full with a lot of thefts too."

"But we do have proof, right? I've kept track of everything in my own ledger and have photographs of the books side by side to show him. The money. The ledger. All of it."

"How are we supposed to prove that Lovett or Smithey took the deposits to the bank? It's our word against theirs."

Something tapped against the desk. "The train tickets. Wouldn't they show who went?"

"Yes. But couldn't they say that they didn't have the deposit? That it wasn't their job to take it?"

"Oh. I see."

"That's the problem. They're supposedly Harvey Company employees. When they tell me they'll take the deposit in, I'm not supposed to argue with them. The only thing I know is that the bank hasn't received two of the deposits. I'm personally taking the one tomorrow."

"How do you think Smithey and Lovett will respond?"

"I don't know. But I guess we shall see. At this point, I'm not taking no for an answer."

Huh. So they were suspicious of Smithey and Lovett. That shouldn't surprise him too much. The men had seemed a bit too comfortable and cocky lately. They liked the power that their pretend positions gave them. Oliver shifted and tried to get closer, but then the window abruptly shut.

Staying as still as he could, he waited. But no one came after him. Best to wait until the light went out before he moved.

Straining for all he was worth, he could hear their muffled voices but couldn't make out the words.

His mind spun with all the possibilities. He could speed up his timeline. That wasn't a problem.

The problem was their proof.

Somehow he had to get to that ledger of Miss Anniston's. And find the photographs.

Once he had those, he could finish things off. No need to stretch out the game of chess any longer. The damage had been done. And the newspapers were eating out of his hand.

With a couple more well-placed blows and a little time, the Harvey kingdom would fall.

⊣ ⊢

SUNDAY, JULY 18, 1909

Thirty-five.

Ruth stretched on her bed. That's how old she was today. Thirty-five.

The thought was a bit surreal. So many years. So much life lived.

But she definitely felt it. That's why she'd come back to her room for a quick nap. Sometimes that was her favorite part of Sunday.

She reached for the jar of cream. After she examined the long scars on her leg, she looked up at the mirror and turned her head a bit. They did look better. And whatever was in that cream sure did make it more tolerable to do the exercises.

Yesterday, she'd decided it was time to start them up again. They hurt. But she could do it a little bit at a time. Perhaps each day try a little more. Dr. Collins said it would have to break up scar tissue. Just the thought made her cringe.

She'd intentionally not said anything to him about the creams. Since they were working, there couldn't be any harm to them, right? Not like the elixir that she'd taken internally. It had taken her days to rid her mind of the craving for it. She had prayed about whether to take any more and decided it was best to wait for what Dr. Collins found out.

After she had the cream thoroughly rubbed in, she dressed again and washed her face. Turning her face to see the scar in the mirror, she grimaced. It was still there.

Of course it was still there. It couldn't be erased. But there were days when she wished she didn't have to see it. That no one did.

She picked up the powder and began to cover the scar and her face with the first layer. It took time to blend it all in, but at least it helped her feel more presentable.

A flurry of knocks sounded on her door as she laid down the makeup. "Happy Birthday!" was shouted by more than one voice.

A smile stretched across her face. They remembered. As she caught her reflection, for a second, she saw her old self.

Happy and confident.

It propelled her to the door. As she opened it, she was pushed back by a pack of girls squealing and all trying to hug her at the same time.

Tessa grabbed the walking stick, placed it in Ruth's right

hand, and then grabbed her left hand. "You, Miss Anniston, are coming with us."

The whole flock of Harvey Girls traipsed out the basement door and then around the back side of the hotel. Ruth got caught up in the chatter and laughter. It felt good to be with them.

The sea of black and white in front of her kept her from seeing where they were headed. At her short height, she could rarely see over anyone's head.

Oh well, hopefully it wouldn't be too far. And the crowd was moving slowly enough that she could keep up.

But then, in the distance, she heard even more cheering. After several more steps, the sea parted, and she saw her friends. The Watkinses, the Millers, friends from church, other staff members, and . . . Frank.

For a moment, she allowed her gaze to linger on his face for a few extra seconds. Her heart did a little flip. Then his words reverberated in her mind. ". . . *it's time you accepted the fact that you are loved—exactly the way you are. You were loved before. You are loved now. You are a beautiful woman of God that needs to stand up on the two wobbly legs that she has and let Him take control.*"

Dare she believe that he could love her the way she longed to be loved? The way she . . . loved him?

Swallowing down the admittance, she blinked and looked away.

"Come on! This party is for you." Tessa led her forward, and she saw a beautiful picnic laid out.

Two men from the kitchen carried a beautifully decorated cake large enough to feed a crowd of a hundred or more.

"One, two, three!" Frank's voice boomed.

Then everyone shouted, "Happy Birthday!"

Julia and Emma Grace approached her first. Julia held out a small box. "This is from us."

Ruth opened the package to find a gorgeous broach, necklace, and earrings that all sparkled in the sunlight. The blue stones took her breath away.

The crowd around them oohed and aahed when Ruth held them up.

"We wanted you to have something to match your beautiful eyes. And to show you how much we love you." Emma Grace came forward and wrapped Ruth in a hug. She whispered in Ruth's ear. "Family sticks together through thick and thin. I love you."

Words still wouldn't come. She'd never in her life received anything so special. Blinking back tears, she smiled at her friend.

Julia rushed them both and wrapped her arms around them. "I don't know what I would have done without you two."

Emma Grace winced as she scrunched up her nose and raised a hand. "I know. Stayed out of trouble?"

Laughter bubbled up. It felt good and right to laugh and tease with these two. She didn't care about her scar or her limp. *They* didn't care about them either. It was time to let Ruth Anniston be herself again.

"Me next!" Tessa pushed through the crowd with her gift.

The afternoon passed in a pile of gifts, cards, good food, games, and lots of hugs and warm wishes. Her heart was fuller than it had been in a long time.

"It's time to cut the cake." Frank pulled her to her feet and walked her over to the gorgeous masterpiece that was beginning to melt in the July heat.

He whispered in her ear, "Happy Birthday, Ruth. I hope it's the best year yet."

Handing her the knife, he put her in charge of cutting the cake while the girls scurried back and forth delivering pieces to everyone.

She had so much frosting on her fingers that they looked almost like she was wearing thick winter gloves. It made her giggle.

What a wonderful birthday. And to think that they had all planned this surprise for her.

It had been just what she needed.

In her mind, she heard Dad's voice. *"Happy Birthday, sweetie pie!"* She looked toward the sky. *Thanks, Dad.* She blinked away the tears and pasted on a smile. Her mom would be here soon enough. And they could grieve and heal together. Tell stories about him and talk of how much they missed him.

A rumble sounded behind her, but with all the laughter, games, and excitement, she kept cutting the cake.

But then screams filled the air.

Several huge boulders tumbled through the party, knocking people over and crashing into others.

Ruth sat on the front steps of the hotel and watched the carts carry the wounded to an area where Dr. Collins was working on them.

Nothing seemed real.

How had this happened?

Sure, rockslides were common down in the canyon. People were always warned to be diligent on the trails.

But she'd never seen anything like this. The slope down to Bright Angel Trail wasn't *that* steep.

Someone must have put those boulders in motion. She was certain of it. Too many bad things had been happening for them to be a coincidence.

Mr. Owens came and sat beside her. "I'm so sorry, Ruth. Not the way any of us planned your birthday party to end."

She twisted the handkerchief in her hands. For over an hour, she hadn't been able to move. Just sat. Waited. Hoping to hear some good news. "How many are hurt?"

"Twenty-two people total. Two of the kitchen staff have broken arms. Eight of the waitresses have broken arms or legs. The rest are bruised and cut up."

Her breath left her in a huff. "I guess it's a good thing our guest numbers are down right now." She hated to even say it out loud.

"Ruth . . . both Louise and Tessa have broken legs."

Both of the headwaitresses.

"I know it's a lot to ask, but I'm going to need you out on the floor until they can return, or until I can find someone else."

As supervisor of the kitchen and dining room, that should have been her call. But she wasn't thinking straight. All the fears of falling down in front of people, of little children pointing and asking questions, or people staring at her hideous limp assaulted her at once.

But deep down? All she'd ever wanted was to be able to get back on the floor again. To show that she was capable. To feel worthy of the job again.

"Ruth? Did you hear me?"

She shook her head. "I'm sorry, Mr. Owens. I heard you.

Yes, I will go back out on the floor. I'll go to my office now and prepare. I should find my uniforms as well." They'd been buried deep in her wardrobe last time she checked. The long black skirts and the white shirtwaists with black ribbon at the neck were the signature of the headwaitress.

"Of course." He stood from the steps and offered her a hand up. "I guess I'll see you first thing in the morning. I'm going to go help with the wounded. Make sure no one else needs transport to Williams."

"Yes, sir." She took his hand and stood. "Mr. Owens?"

"Yes?"

"Could you tell Frank that I'll see him tomorrow?" She pointed out to the crowd. She'd been watching Frank go from one person to another and offer them water. Pray with them. Or just sit with them.

The manager nodded.

She climbed the last few steps to the doors and limped her way to her office. How would she survive the long days on her leg?

Shoving the doubts and questions aside, she clenched her jaw. They needed her. And she wasn't about to let them down.

Back in her office, she went to the first cupboard that held her notes and journals from all her years as headwaitress. Grabbing the most recent one, she sat at her desk and flipped through the pages. It brought a smile to her face to go back to the familiarity.

The clock struck eight in the evening, and she stretched. Goodness, she'd forgotten to count the lockbox with Mr. Owens. He probably hadn't been inside yet anyway. She could do it and save him that step.

She unlocked her drawer and reached for her ledger.

But it wasn't there.

Riffling through the papers and other items, she couldn't believe it wasn't there. She always put it right on top.

Every night.

But . . . it was gone.

# 22

The morning had come all too soon.

Last night, after tearing her office apart, Ruth stayed up and tore her room apart as well. But the ledger was nowhere to be found.

Then the money still had to be counted. So, she took care of that and collapsed into bed two hours later than she should have. Worried about the implications of the missing ledger. Tossing and turning over the coming day's challenges. Sleep—that she desperately needed to be able to face a day on her feet—eluded her at every turn.

But here she was.

Back in the dining room as headwaitress.

Her black skirt, white shirtwaist with the black ribbon around her neck, and bow in her hair made her feel like the old Ruth. She'd slathered on an extra layer of the cream this morning, hoping and praying that it would help keep the pain from standing all day at bay.

After giving what she hoped was an inspiring speech to all

the girls, she'd set them to work. They were shorthanded. But things could still run smoothly.

Frank had waved at her this morning as he passed through. But two other men vied for his attention, so she didn't blame him for not coming to say hello. Maybe later in the day they could compare notes.

She could do this. This was what she wanted to do. She could earn her place. Feel valuable.

*"Grace plus nothing."* It was Tessa's voice that she heard in her head. It made her stop in her tracks.

Here she was again. Trying to control things and do it all on her own. Trying to earn favor.

Ruth went over to the nearest chair and sat—something a Harvey Girl was never supposed to do. But she needed the seat. Needed the humbling.

She couldn't do this on her own. Didn't need to try and be stronger than she was. She could ask for help.

For a little grace.

Charlotte walked over to her. "You all right, Ruth?"

"Yes, I'm fine. Could you go ask Frank if they still have that stool in the back of the kitchen from when Chef Marques sprained his ankle?"

Charlotte's eyes lit up. "Brilliant. I'll go check." She raced off around the large buffet that was the waitresses' station and into the kitchen. In a minute, she returned. "Found it!"

"Perfect." Ruth took it and placed it in the spot where she normally stood. She could still be the headwaitress and watch over the room and not put too much strain on her leg. This way, hopefully, her leg wouldn't have reason to give out from under her.

The dining room was about to open for breakfast. Ruth took a long inhale, sent a prayer heavenward, and smiled.

By the time luncheon rolled around, she was back in the swing of things. As long as she didn't stand for too long or try to walk too far, her leg felt pretty stable. She'd hoped to make it downstairs and apply another layer of the cream, but there hadn't been time.

Even though the hotel had cancellations, it seemed plenty of other people had arrived, which kept them all scurrying.

The first hour of lunch went surprisingly well. But the scents from all the delicious food had sent her stomach into wild hunger pangs. She should have had more breakfast, but at the time, she'd been so nervous that it had made her queasy.

Charlotte approached her, frowning. "The two auditors are asking to see you, Miss Anniston."

"Do you know why?"

She shook her head. "No, they haven't even ordered. I don't think they have anything to complain about, but they were quite adamant that I get you straightaway."

"All right." Ruth dared a glance around the buffet. The room was crowded. She'd have to choose her steps carefully and take her time. But something didn't seem right. Her mind flashed back to her missing ledger. Had one of those men broken into her office and stolen it? Did they know they were on to them? Thoughts darted around as she tried to remember if she'd seen them anywhere else they shouldn't be.

"Let me go with you." Charlotte walked beside her. She didn't hold her arm or do anything to make her feel like an invalid, but it gave Ruth an extra boost of strength and encouragement.

When they arrived at the table, Charlotte spoke first. "Miss Anniston." She stood there with her hands clasped.

"You may go." Mr. Smithey waved their waitress away.

This made Ruth's eyebrows shoot up as she grabbed Charlotte's arm. "Miss Rand stays. Is there a problem, gentlemen?"

Both men's gazes drilled into her. But she refused to let them intimidate her. This was *her* dining room. She was in charge here.

"We heard there was quite an incident yesterday afternoon." Mr. Lovett leaned forward. "At your birthday party." What was it about his tone? It was almost . . . menacing. Or was she imagining things because deep down she suspected they were up to no good?

Since they didn't ask a question, she chose to bite her tongue. Exactly what was he implying?

"More than twenty people were injured." Mr. Smithey added. "We're going to have to report that."

"No need." Mr. Owens appeared at the table. "I've taken care of it already."

The two men swiveled their heads. "As you should have. But we will have to submit our report as well." Mr. Smithey took a sip of his coffee.

"That is not the protocol in these situations, gentlemen. Something you should know as experienced auditors." Mr. Owens' tone was sharp, and his words were daggers aimed at the men.

Smithey came to his feet. "You should know that this isn't a typical audit. *Protocol* or not, we will be submitting that report."

Ruth eyed the room. Too many people watched the exchange. She cleared her throat. "If that will be all, Miss Rand will be glad to take your orders." She didn't give them a smile but raised her eyebrows.

Mr. Lovett's arm shot out to stop her mid-turn. "Happy

Birthday, Miss Anniston. I hope no one else gets hurt." The last words were hushed.

She glanced at Mr. Owens, who frowned and moved toward her. Had he heard? Had Charlotte?

Fear prickled at her neck. As she tried to step hastily away, Mr. Lovett pushed his chair back and stood.

Her foot caught on the chair and down she went.

In front of a dining room full of guests.

Frank stood outside the kitchen with Ruth. "Are you sure you're all right?"

"I'm fine." She twisted the ribbon at her neck. "It's my pride that was hurt. I might have a few bruises tomorrow, but it really wasn't that bad."

"Come on, Ruth. This is me. Be honest."

She turned her face away and twisted the ribbon around her finger again and again. "I feel so unworthy. Deep down all I ever wanted was to get back out on the floor. That was my identity for so long. I can't tell you how wonderful it felt to be out there today. I even realized that I needed to ask for help and had Charlotte grab the stool. All in all, I was feeling pretty good about myself. And then those men . . ." She growled. "The way they looked at me . . . the way they spoke to me. It's like they wanted to put me in my place and tell me that it was all my fault that everyone was injured."

"I'm glad Mr. Owens showed up when he did."

"Me too. It made me feel so . . . dirty. Ashamed. Unworthy."

"That's not from God, Ruth. Remember that." He couldn't help it, he gripped her shoulders. Needed to touch her.

"I know. I hate that they made me feel that way."

He ran through his mind what she'd told him. "Why do you think Lovett said what he did?"

"I don't know. But I was hoping someone else overheard it. It sent chills up my spine."

Frank shoved his hands into his pockets. "I think it was a threat."

"What do you mean?"

He lowered his voice. "I think they know you are suspicious of them. Why would your ledger be missing otherwise?"

The back door opened behind him. "Chef Henderson?" Kenneth's voice squeaked. He was the newest of the staff and still a bit scared of him. "We need you in here. Howard ran out a bit ago. We thought he needed to . . . excuse himself. But he hasn't come back, and the orders are piling up."

"I'll be right there." He rolled his eyes at Ruth. "They can't live without me." His attempt at humor was met with a frown.

"Where do you think Howard went?" She tugged on his arm. "Something is going on, Frank. Please . . . be careful."

They stepped into the kitchen, and then Charlotte burst in. "Frank! And any other men! Come quick!"

"What's happened?" The foreboding in Ruth's stomach grew.

"It's Mr. Owens. He fell into the canyon."

Frank turned to her, a new intensity in his eyes.

"I need to go hide the photographs," she whispered. "It's all the proof we have left."

"You be careful. Please?"

With a nod, she watched the kitchen empty as men dashed out the door.

She limped her way through the dining room, though no one was watching her. They'd all gathered at the windows once word had spread.

What was happening? And who was behind it all?

———— | |————

Oliver smirked as he glanced over his paper. The chaos confirmed that Howard did his final deed. Good for him.

Staff members darted here and there. Word must've gotten to them about their beloved manager.

After all this time, the end was in sight.

He'd sent out another slew of telegrams about the El Tovar this morning. After the press got wind of this, there was no way the hotel would survive.

No one was the wiser that he had been posing as Charles Goodall for years. Mr. Goodall, wealthy philanthropist who had access to the rarest and finest medicines in the world. In all actuality, he was nothing but a salesman. Oh, but he was the best. All those charlatans who peddled their wares from town to town didn't know how to do it.

But he did. Use fine ingredients . . . things that actually worked, at least for a little while. The real secret was in making sure the customer knew how to come to him. Make them think it was something they couldn't possibly have or afford and they wanted it even more and would do whatever it took to get their hands on it.

Over the years, his reputation had grown so that his name was whispered in the highest of circles. He never went anywhere as a salesman. Every resort he visited, his cover was simple: He was on vacation from his very time-consuming *work*.

He'd made a fortune.

But it wasn't just for him. There'd always been an end-game in mind.

The O'Brien family had faced shame and ridicule for far too long. It was time to turn that around.

He set his paper down and picked up a large satchel. Time to go see what Miss Anniston had up her sleeve. Since she was in the dining room after the little picnic tragedy, he should have plenty of time.

Shaking his head as he sauntered toward the hall where her office was, he couldn't help but pride himself on his schemes. His most brilliant plan had been to befriend the woman and gain her confidence. Because she would never suspect someone who was helping her, right? Making her beautiful again? Poor thing, she was a good person and didn't deserve what was about to happen. She would lose her livelihood, after all.

He shook his head. He'd become calloused a long time ago. This was no time for sympathy.

He picked the lock and opened the door. Now where would she keep those photographs? The cabinets along the east wall didn't have any pictures in them. But her camera was sitting on the shelf in the corner.

He checked the desk next. But two of the drawers were locked. Well, he hadn't let that stop him before. Charles pulled the pick back out of his pocket.

"What are you doing in here?" Miss Anniston's shocked voice made him jump to his feet. Had she seen what he was doing?

"I came to see you." He reached into his satchel. "I looked for you earlier and couldn't find you, so I thought I'd leave these in here for you." He pulled out several jars of cream and set them on her desk. "I tripped as I came around the desk. Hopefully they didn't break." He pretended to examine the jars.

"Oh." But she didn't sound convinced. She crossed her arms over her chest. "How did you get in?"

"Your door was unlocked, so I was hoping you wouldn't mind. I didn't want to leave such expensive creams out where anyone could take them." After all the jars were on the desk, he put a hand through his hair and then dusted his pants. "How embarrassing. Tripping over my own big feet. I hope I didn't damage your desk." He looked at the corner as if he was truly concerned.

She squinted at him. Studied him.

Perhaps he should sweeten the deal. "I don't want to make you uncomfortable in any way, but I've had a generous benefactor come to me. I helped his wife through a terrible bout of diphtheria last year. He wanted to pass on his thanks, and he gave a large amount to the fund that I keep for benevolence. So please accept these jars and know that someone else has wanted to extend grace to another."

Her face softened at that. "Grace," she whispered under her breath and then limped over to her desk and picked up one of the jars. "That's indeed very generous, Mr. Goodall."

With that one word, he'd won her over. Charles bowed and headed toward the door. "I'm glad to be of help. I'm sorry I don't have the elixir right now, but it should be here shortly."

"No need. I'm feeling much better." Was there a hitch in her voice?

"Have you considered my invitation for a walk?" This would help him. Surely.

Pink tinged her cheeks. "I am flattered by your attention, Mr. Goodall, but I must decline."

The look on her face told him she truly was flattered. Exactly what he'd hoped for. "Well, perhaps another time?"

"Perhaps."

"Thank you, Miss Anniston. I will pray for your health to be fully restored."

With quick steps, he left and headed toward the main staircase. That had been a little too close for comfort. And he still hadn't found the photographs.

He couldn't risk another try.

# 23

Frank led the other men and raced to the rim. He tore off his chef coat. If Owens was down there, he had to help him.

He leaned over the edge and saw where his boss lay, then whistled under his breath. He prayed the man was still alive after a fall like that. "Everyone stand back. We don't need anyone else falling in." By this point, a good crowd of people had gathered to see what was happening.

"I've got rope!" Blanche Kolb's voice drew his attention toward the west, where she ran with little Edith in her arms. Before she even made it to him, she tossed the sturdy rope.

Frank caught it and had three of his men whom he trusted from the kitchen anchor it around them. "All right, I'm relying on you guys to hold me. And that's not an easy task." His attempt to lighten the mood at least helped the panic on their faces turn to determination. "Once I'm down there, I'll need your help to get Mr. Owens out."

The men nodded, their faces solemn.

With the rope around his own waist, Frank gripped it with both hands, backed up to the rim, and then started to walk his way down the sheer rock face. It didn't take long for him to reach Owens.

Untying the rope, he called out, "Mr. Owens, can you hear me?"

He went to the man's side and leaned over him. He was at least breathing. Good. "Greg. Can you hear me?"

Nothing.

He patted the man's face. "Greg, I could really use your help."

The man's eyelids fluttered. "Frank?"

"It's me."

"How—" He gasped.

"I have a rope, sir."

Owens closed his eyes for a moment. "No. How . . . ard."

Frank pursed his lips. "Howard did this to you?"

A long blink. "Asked . . . me to speak . . ."

"We need to get you to the doctor."

Owens' arm seized Frank's in a viselike grip. "Said . . . he knew . . . who was stealing . . ."

"You followed him out here?" Frank could picture it. The younger chef saying he needed a private word. "Then what?"

"Pushed." The older man closed his eyes.

"Stay with me, Greg. I'm going to get you out."

At the moment he wasn't sure how, but he would do it. From the looks of it, the manager had broken bones, and if he put the rope around the man, that would probably do more damage as they pulled him up, since he wouldn't be able to help. If Frank carried the man, the weight of the two of them would be too much for the men to hoist.

He scanned around him and looked up at the men waiting for his cue. "How many men do you have to pull?"

Heads pulled back behind the rim. Then Emery Kolb's

face appeared. "We've got ten strong men. There's a pencil-thin trail to the west of you, but I don't think you'd make it carrying him. Let's give it a shot with the rope."

If the wiry photographer said to try it, Frank was all for it. Emery alone could probably haul the two of them up if he had to. He was just that kind of man who needed a challenge. The thought made Frank chuckle. "All right, Greg. This might hurt—in fact, I'm pretty sure it will. But I'm going to be gentle and lift you over my shoulder. I'll hold you as best as I can while these fellas do their best to haul our backsides out."

The man groaned but nodded. "Hurry. Please."

Once he had the rope securely around him once again, Frank gingerly lifted Owens and positioned him over his shoulder with his torso and head in front of him so that Mr. Owens' weight wouldn't topple them. He shifted a few times to get a solid grip with his left hand on the injured man and then gripped the rope with his right. Not the best climbing mode, but he'd have to rely on the guys up top to help. He raised his brows at Emery and let out a big breath. "All right. Give it all you've got!"

Frank held tight to the rope and listened for the command from the men and stepped up the wall as best he could to help.

"One, two, three, pull!" Another couple steps. Then another. And another.

His arms screamed at him from the full body weight of Owens and the grip he had on the rope. He knew better than to look down. But he would make it to the top. He would.

Pushing with his feet, he gritted his teeth. The rope burned his palm and fingers.

But he wouldn't let go.

"One, two, three, pull!" The last tug got him eye level with the rim, and several men rushed him and grabbed Mr. Owens.

Frank dragged himself the rest of the way up and then collapsed, sweat pouring from his brow.

⎯⊣ ⊢⎯

### WEDNESDAY, JULY 21, 1909

Ruth stood at the platform, walking stick in hand, and waited for the morning train.

Aunt Mae sent a wire yesterday that she and Mom would arrive this morning. They'd tried to make it for her birthday but had been delayed along the way. Which had been a good thing.

As much as she wanted to see them, she worried about bringing them into such a mess. Was it even safe? Were any of them safe?

Mr. Owens was alive but seriously injured. The wound to the head was what Dr. Collins was most concerned about. So far, he hadn't woken up since he'd spoken to Frank, and the good doctor was worried that he might not. Or that he might suffer memory loss. What would they do without him?

Frank told her that the manager had said Howard pushed him. But why? Was it true?

The so-called auditors had been in the dining room when it happened. Charlotte confirmed it. Ruth wondered if their whole little scene in the dining room right before Mr. Owens' fall was on purpose. To what end? Prove they weren't the ones who pushed? Did they know Howard? Was it all connected?

Then there was the crazy disappearance of the assistant chef. No one had seen him since. The fact that her ledger was missing made her wonder if he had taken that too. But that's where her mind went now. Always trying to figure out this impossible puzzle.

One thing shoved its way to the front. She did *not* want anyone else to be hurt.

The only person she'd confided in was Frank. He'd looked as concerned as she was. But his hands were full with Howard gone and two of his other men injured. What were they going to do? With Mr. Owens out, running the hotel fell to her. Especially since the auditors hadn't shown their crooked faces this morning. Even though she was glad they hadn't.

The train whistle blew. Ruth took a few moments to breathe deep. The melody of "Amazing Grace" ran through her head. As much as she hated the things that were happening, they were all sinners. In need of grace.

---

**SATURDAY, JULY 24, 1909**

Ruth sat on the stool in the dining room behind the head-waitress's station and tried to juggle the paperwork she needed to do for the front desk and keep everything running with the Harvey Girls. It wasn't easy. Thankfully, Charlotte was trying to learn everything she could to help as a head-waitress, but Ruth tried to be on hand during the busier times.

Thankfully, Mom and Aunt Mae kept themselves busy settling into their new home. Ruth had seen them every day, but not as much as she would like.

Sheriff Andrews had come and gone. Multiple times. Right now, he was looking for Howard. The rest of the chaos at the hotel had taken a back seat.

No one had seen Howard Monroe. No one had seen him at the train station. No ticket had been purchased by him.

Then there were the auditors. Who also had disappeared.

It had been five days since Mr. Owens had fallen into the canyon. Ruth was exhausted from trying to keep everything running.

She'd sent a wire to the Harvey Company and hadn't heard a thing. That wasn't right.

As soon as the lunch rush was over, she was going to call them herself. Not that she would ever think of doing something so bold, but these were dire circumstances.

The dining room began to empty, and she caught Charlotte's attention. "I'm going to head to the office for a while."

Her friend nodded.

Ruth carried the paperwork with her to Mr. Owens' office and went straight to the telephone. She told the operator what she needed.

"I'm sorry, Miss Anniston. But right now, the long-distance lines aren't working all the way to Kansas. They've been having trouble with them."

Of course. "Well, thank you. Can you patch me through to Mr. Jefferson at the telegraph office?"

"Yes. Hold, please."

Mr. Jefferson answered almost immediately. "Hello?"

"Mr. Jefferson, it's Miss Anniston at the El Tovar."

"How can I help you?"

"I need to get an urgent message to Mr. Ford Harvey and Mr. Byron Harvey." After she told him what to wire, she felt better. It hadn't fixed anything, but at least she felt like she was doing something. "Mr. Jefferson?"

"Yes, miss?"

"You're certain no other wires have come through from the company? Mr. Owens has sent several and never received any word."

"That's odd." Shuffling sounded. "I haven't sent any telegrams to the Harvey Company on behalf of Mr. Owens."

"None?"

"Let me check the books." It sounded like pages were flipped. "Nope. Not a single one since May."

She flopped back in the chair. "Will you be there tomorrow, Mr. Jefferson? I have some urgent business to speak to you about."

"After church, I'll be here all afternoon. Anything I can do to help, miss."

"Thank you."

After they hung up, Ruth let her mind spin with all the different possibilities. No matter what, she was going to sort it out. She owed Mr. Owens that much.

Michael was at the front desk as she left Owens' office. "Let me know immediately if any telegrams come in."

"Yes, Miss Anniston."

There were a million things on her list that she needed to accomplish today. But as she reached the rotunda, the strains of Chopin's "Waltz in E minor" reached her ears. She smiled. She hadn't taken time to see Mom today, and she'd promised that she would make family a priority. Shifting to the stairs, she headed for the Music Room.

Mom and Aunt Mae had done a wonderful job of settling in without her. Once she'd shared all the horrible things that had happened, they both had promised to stay together at all times for their safety. Even though they'd only arrived three days ago, it had done wonders for her heart and mind simply knowing they were here.

Mom was dealing well with the loss of her husband and the loss of her limb—better than Ruth ever handled her injuries. It was sobering.

Her mother wasn't hiding in grief or in her disfigurement. Good grief, she'd been in the Music Room playing the piano—with one arm—every single day. And that had to be hard. But playing the piano was her passion.

The thought of not being able to do it with both hands . . . well, it made Ruth ashamed. She probably would've pouted. Wallowed. Complained.

But not her mom. No.

As Ruth entered the Music Room, she spotted her mother and aunt sitting on the piano bench together, giggling like little girls.

"No, now I want to try the right hand." Mom shoved her sister off the bench and Aunt Mae had to go around to the lower keys.

"Okay, I'll play the left with my right hand. Just to make it fair."

"Deal. One and two and three—"

The two took off like they were in a race. Laughing the whole way through the first section.

Ruth couldn't help it. She laughed along with them.

Both heads popped up when they heard her. "Ruthie!" Mom stood and stepped toward her. "Your aunt and I are trying new ways of playing."

"I see that."

"Aren't you impressed?"

"Well, of course I am. You have always impressed me."

Aunt Mae came over and hugged her. "Sweet girl. Love covers up all the mistakes, doesn't it?"

"Yes, ma'am." She winked at her aunt.

Aunt Mae pointed to the door. "I am going to give you two a few blessed minutes of chat time while I go find a cup of coffee. I'm going to need it if I'm to keep up with your mother."

"Come sit." Mom tipped her head toward the piano bench.

Ruth sat and tinkered with the high treble keys. She'd taken lessons from Mom when she was younger, but it wasn't her gifting. Not like her mother's.

"I can see you've got a lot on your mind." Mom's words were gentle, yet they prodded her to open up.

"I'm sorry. I know I haven't had a lot of time lately."

Mom leaned in and tapped shoulders with her. "That's okay, sweetheart. You have your hands full. That's the wonderful thing about my living here. When you need me, all you have to do is come find me."

She rubbed her forehead. "I'm a mess, Mom."

"We all are, honey."

"Thanks for the encouragement." She let out another laugh with her sarcasm. "And for the humor. I needed that. This year has been the toughest one yet. Every time I think I'm making progress, I feel like the rug gets yanked out from under me. And now that I'm facing an obstacle larger than I ever imagined, I don't know what to do. I want to run away and hide."

"Sweetie, you've always struggled with not being able to control every aspect of your life. But, Ruth, you've been blind to all the people around you who love you and want to help. There's nothing wrong with having help or asking for it. We can't do everything. We can't be perfect."

"Look at me. I know I'm not perfect."

"Stop it with the scar references and the woe-is-me because I'm injured. Just stop it." Mom rarely got stern, but when she did, it was time to be quiet and listen. "Stop feeling sorry for yourself and live your life. It's the only one you've got. Stop wasting it."

Every defensive nerve in her body came to attention. And then she deflated. "I was always the one to help everyone else. During those years of being headwaitress, all the girls would come to me. And then when I had to go through the hard days myself . . . I didn't know how to handle it."

"Faith had been easy for you, Ruth, because life had been relatively so. But this was a trial you've been challenged with so that you could persevere through it and grow. We are called to 'count it all joy.' And no matter what comes, I intend to do just that. It's about your mindset, your attitude . . . your choice. It's about becoming mature and complete. You have to choose joy. Live a life filled with grace."

There she was again, trying to add something to grace to make it better. Like she could help it along somehow. Ruth placed her head on her mom's shoulder. All the treatments in the world couldn't make her feel like this. Being loved. Unconditionally.

"Ruth, there's a man out there who loves and adores you, and he's waiting for you to wake up and see him there waiting for you. So hurry up and figure out who is behind this whole mess so you can tell him you love him too."

Once again, Mom understood better than even Ruth did. The thought of Frank loving her made her heart soar. Deep down, she knew it to be true. She raised her eyebrows. "You know how I feel about Frank?"

"Honey, it's written all over your face."

Mom gave her a little nudge off the bench, and Ruth stood, determined.

It was time to solve this mystery.

———| |———

"Frank?" Ruth's voice in the kitchen caught him off guard.

Wiping off his hands, he went to her side. "Everything all right?"

"I sent a telegram to Ford and Byron Harvey. Is there any chance you can have someone else in charge of the kitchen tomorrow, since it's Sunday and a bit less of a strain? I think you and I need to go to Williams and talk to Mr. Asbury. Doctor Newport called and said he was awake and alert again."

He looked around at the men he had. "Of course."

She stepped closer, and his heart picked up its pace. "Do you have a minute now to talk?"

With a nod, he headed toward the side door and held it open for her.

Even once they were alone, she stayed close.

He didn't mind it one bit.

In a whispered tone, she said, "Mr. Jefferson hasn't sent any other telegrams."

"What does that mean?"

"I think we're in real trouble here. Someone has gone to great lengths to keep us isolated and without help. Is that why the new bookkeeper got sick and there hasn't been a replacement? And who are Smithey and Lovett, really? And Howard? I've arranged with Mr. Ackerman to allow me to bring the deposit tomorrow, even though it's Sunday. I simply don't trust anyone else to bring it in."

"Did the sheriff say anything else while he was here?"

"No. He was very concerned about what happened to Mr. Owens, and when I took him aside and told him everything else that has happened this summer, he was shocked. He's sending two men to pose as customers and try to see what they can find out."

Frank shoved his hands into his pockets. "Did Doctor Newport say if Mr. Asbury had said anything?"

"No. Just that he refused to talk to anyone but Mr. Owens. The doctor said he'll tell him about what happened to the manager tomorrow when we get there. Then hopefully Asbury will open up to us."

"It's worth a shot."

She placed a hand on his arm and peered up into his eyes. "This has been terrible since it started, but with my mom and aunt here, I'm pretty worried. I don't want anything to happen to them. The sooner we figure this out, the better."

He covered her hand with one of his own. "I'll be with you every step of the way. I won't let anything happen to them."

# 24

The train ride down to Williams had been too short. Ruth had brought a new notebook with her, the photographs she'd taken of the ledgers and money, and plenty of pencils. Today needed to be productive. For Mr. Owens. She just knew if she could go to him in his bed at the doctor's house and tell him that they caught whoever was responsible that he would wake up. Everyone had been praying for their manager, but Dr. Collins was losing hope as time passed.

"What else do we know?" For the past three hours, they'd gone over every detail they could remember, trying to put it in a timeline order. Then on one page, Frank had written names, drawn circles around them, and tried to see if they could connect them somehow.

But there were too many missing pieces to their puzzle.

"I think we've written down everything, Ruth." He placed his hand over hers.

With a huff, she snapped the book shut and leaned her

303

head back. "You're right. I'm praying that Mr. Asbury has something else to give us a clue of where to look next."

The last few minutes of the journey, she hadn't moved her hand. Allowed it to be held by Frank. He didn't say a word, simply stared out the window.

She studied his profile. His thick red hair was tousled a bit, while his mustache was neatly trimmed close to his face. The green eyes watching the landscape pass had been a source of great encouragement to her over the years. They made her feel safe. Comfortable. At home. And yet they seemed to pierce her very soul. The freckles that dotted his nose and cheeks made him look much younger than his thirty-seven years.

That boyish grin.

She looked down. The strength of his hand. The strength of . . . him.

The train slowed, and Frank looked at her. "Well, are you ready?"

"Yes." In fact, she was ready for more than just today. But she'd tell him that later. Soon.

They disembarked from the train with Frank keeping her hand tucked neatly in the crook of his arm. As they walked to Dr. Newport's office and home, she'd never felt more secure and strong.

Anna opened the door for them. "Perfect timing. He's had a bit of broth and is awake." She held the door. "Please, come in."

Ruth's heart picked up its pace. But she lifted her chin, licked her lips, and headed inside.

Dr. Newport gave a small smile. "You are looking wonderful, Miss Anniston. It's good to see you."

"Thank you, Doctor." She entered the room he motioned to.

Poor Mr. Asbury lay bruised and broken in the bed. Schooling her features, she inhaled for several seconds to calm herself. "Mr. Asbury, I'm Ruth Anniston. I work for Mr. Owens."

The man barely dipped his chin in a nod. "Doc told me."

"This is Mr. Henderson. He's the head chef at the El Tovar. We need to ask you some questions. Is that all right?"

Another small nod.

"Before you were injured, were you able to find out anything to help Mr. Owens?"

The man looked around the room. "Please tell the doc and his wife to come in and shut the door."

They did, and Anna stood near the door as Dr. Newport came to his side. "Are you feeling all right?"

"Shut the window. And the drapes."

Ruth couldn't help but lower her brow. The man was clearly fearful.

Asbury swallowed. "Doc, I'm sorry. I didn't want to bring any danger to you or your wife."

The doctor's shoulders lifted. "Tell the truth. We will be fine."

The man in the bed closed his eyes. "I followed a couple of suspicious-looking characters to an old farmhouse outside of town. In the basement, there were two more, and they had the real auditors tied up. I know because I overheard them talking about how Harvey hadn't missed them yet, so the plan was working. The whole group of thugs was planning on leaving them there at some point . . . to starve and die."

Ruth covered her mouth with her hand for a moment and then grabbed her pencil. She needed it all written down. Word for word if she could.

"I tried to get out of there as fast as I could so I could fetch the sheriff. But they must have heard me. I thought I lost them when I came into town. But as soon as I dismounted my horse and tried to skirt around buildings so I could make it to the sheriff's, that horseless carriage ran me down. They tried to back up and hit me again, but a group of people saw me in the street and raced to help. When I woke up the other day, there was a note in my hand. It said they would kill the doc and his wife if I said a word to anyone."

Frank stepped closer. "Do you have the note?"

Asbury blinked in affirmation.

Ruth looked to the young doctor. He had his arm around his wife. "Do you have someplace safe you can stay for a few days until all of this is over?"

"I don't want to leave Mr. Asbury unattended."

Frank nodded and looked to the injured man. "Do you know where the farmhouse is?"

The man gave directions. Ruth wrote those down as well.

"Is there anything else?" She looked up, but Mr. Asbury was asleep again.

"Sorry, folks." Dr. Newport waved them toward the door. "I'm sure that was pretty taxing on him. He may not wake up again until tomorrow."

As they left the room, Frank stopped the doctor with a hand to his shoulder. "We're headed to the sheriff's right now with this information. I'm going to ask him to send over someone for protection, just in case."

"No need." The doctor walked into another room and came out with two shotguns. "My wife and I are pretty handy with these, if it comes to that. But I will lock the doors and windows tight."

"Sounds like a plan."

Ruth went to Anna and gave her a hug. "Thank you. I'll come back to visit soon." For some reason, Ruth couldn't get the hairs on the back of her neck to cooperate. Maybe it was what Mr. Asbury had told them, but everything about this made shivers race up and down her spine.

With her notebook shoved down into her bag, she took hold of Frank's arm. "Is there a faster way to get to the sheriff's office?"

"Take our buggy." The doctor tipped his head toward the back. "We just got back from church, so it's all hitched up."

"Thank you."

Frank helped her up into the buggy, took the reins, and set a brisk pace to the sheriff's. She clutched her bag to her chest. Fear clawed at her and she kept looking over her shoulder.

Then, a familiar face in a boardinghouse window flashed right before the sheer curtain fell back into place. They'd been watched.

"Frank, hurry!"

He flicked the reins, and the horses picked up their pace. Frank yelled, "Watch out!" as people scattered along the street.

The unmistakable sound of an engine made Ruth turn around. *God, help us!* She tugged at Frank's arm. "They're coming after us."

Frank urged the horses again. But they would be no match for a motor vehicle.

Ruth laid a hand on his arm and closed her eyes.

"It's going to be all right." Frank's voice was calm. Soothing. "We're almost there."

She counted to ten and tried to calm her breaths. Then, all of a sudden, the carriage jerked to a stop. Frank climbed over her and jumped down. He lifted her off the seat and ran straight into the sheriff's office with her in his arms.

"What's happened?" Sheriff Andrews eyed them with his hands on his hips.

But she couldn't tear her gaze from the window. She held her breath as she watched the car speed by.

———| |———

**MONDAY, JULY 26, 1909**

"Chef Henderson?" Sheriff Andrews stood in the doorway of the kitchen.

Frank stepped forward and wiped his hands. The man nodded at him, and Frank followed. The time had come.

The sheriff headed out the door, through the dining room, through the rotunda, and into the Rendezvous Room, where a lot of people were gathered.

Two men stepped toward him. They both held out their hands.

"Ford Harvey."

"Byron Harvey."

Frank shook each of their hands and nodded. "It's nice to meet you both."

"Chef Henderson, it's *our* privilege to meet you." Ford gripped his shoulder.

Frank scanned the room and saw Ruth standing near the edge with a huge smile on her face.

Ford Harvey clapped him on the back. "We hear we owe you a debt of gratitude for all your help this summer. Mr. Owens told us everything you've done to help keep the El Tovar afloat."

"Thank you, sir."

Ruth had been correct. As soon as they'd returned from Williams and she went and sat at the manager's bedside and relayed the story, the man had woken up.

Ruth. Strong, courageous Ruth. Her smile grew as he stared at her.

He wasn't sure what the sheriff had planned, but he prayed this was the end of the trouble at the El Tovar. The question was, had they caught all the parties involved?

He glanced around the room. Then took a second glance. "Howard?" His assistant chef's hands were tied, and the man wouldn't look at him.

"We caught him at the train station. Buying a ticket to California." The sheriff placed his hands on his hips. "Yes, he's the one who pushed Mr. Owens. He's also been selling your recipes to a competitor in exchange for becoming the head chef at a new restaurant. Padded the orders too, but you already knew that."

Byron Harvey stepped forward and pointed. "So Howard was behind all this?"

"Far from it. He was just a pawn." The sheriff steered the Harvey brothers toward the two men who'd been at the hotel all summer. Mr. Smithey and Mr. Lovett. "Along with these two. Found them hiding in a boardinghouse."

"Those men don't work for us." Ford frowned and narrowed his eyes.

Frank wanted to punch the imposters for the way they'd humiliated Ruth that day in the dining room.

"No, they do not." Byron stepped forward. "But thanks to you and Miss Anniston, the sheriff figured out what was going on and found the real Mr. Smithey and Mr. Lovett yesterday afternoon."

"Are they all right?"

"They will be. In time. They'd been beaten and starved. Left for dead." The sheriff shook his head.

"Wait a minute. So who was behind all this?"

The sheriff pointed to another man. Handcuffed. With a scowl on his face.

"Mr. Goodall?" Frank exclaimed.

"Otherwise known as Oliver O'Brien."

Frank was livid now. That man had gained Ruth's trust. What had he done to her? He charged at him. "You . . . How dare you! What was in that elixir you gave her?"

The man sneered. "A lot of sugar, even more caffeine. Oh, and a hint of opium."

Frank got within a foot of grabbing the guy by his neck when the sheriff pulled him back.

"Now that we have arrested everyone, it's about time I take them back to Williams and let them stand before a judge." The sheriff went over to Ford and Byron. "Thank you for coming."

"Thank Miss Anniston over there. If she hadn't informed us, we wouldn't have known." Byron pointed to Ruth.

She stepped forward. "Apparently, there was a young man who worked for Mr. Jefferson at the telegraph office." Her gaze was pointed at Goodall. "I'm guessing it was you—Mr. O'Brien—who paid him to intercept any telegrams from us and make sure that none of Mr. Owens' wires were sent to the company."

"How did you figure it out, Sheriff?" Ford asked.

"I didn't." The man pointed at Frank and then at Ruth. "These two did."

The Harvey brothers still looked confused. Ford held up a hand. "Someone is going to need to explain."

Ruth stepped over to Frank's side and smiled up at him. "This might help untangle the mystery for you. We discovered that Mr. O'Brien is the nephew of the O'Brien who was partners with your father back in the 1860s. His uncle told him that Fred Harvey stole all the money out of their till one night, every cent they had from their restaurant and saloon. Which wasn't true. It was the other way around."

Frank watched O'Brien's face. "That's a lie! Harvey stole it!"

"Settle down." The sheriff shoved the man down into his seat. "You'd do well to listen."

Ruth shook off the interruption. "O'Brien didn't fare too well after that and always blamed Fred Harvey. And when he saw Fred Harvey build a huge empire and become a wild success, he got madder and madder." She looked to the man who had posed as Charles Goodall. "Is that about right?"

He narrowed his eyes at her.

"I'll take that as a yes. To try and sum this up simply, all these years, he—Mr. Charles Goodall—made a name for himself as the purveyor of specialty treatments to the rich. Granted, they do have fine ingredients in them, but he charged a small fortune for each one. It really was quite a lucrative business. Because wealthy people will pay just about anything to feel younger and more alive, right?

"But good ol' Charles—or should I say Oliver—promised his uncle that he would avenge the O'Brien name and make everything right. So, for years, he's been studying the Harvey Company, trying to find a weakness. Then he put his plan into motion. He hired Howard to sabotage us here. He was ordering scads more for the kitchen, having the hotel pay for it, and then selling the extra out the back door for a tidy profit. O'Brien sent letters to newspapers saying that Harvey had financial troubles. So the Harvey Company sent two men to audit. Mr. Owens had already seen the discrepancies but couldn't figure out where they were coming from.

"Mr. O'Brien kidnapped the two auditors and replaced

them with his own men. He held those men captive and tortured them to find out the workings of the Harvey Empire. Because once the El Tovar was ruined, he would go after the rest. All for revenge. The imposters stole the deposits, changed the books, and even put crushed rhubarb leaves in the July Fourth food so that people would get sick." Ruth took a breath and shook her head at O'Brien. "We found a paper bag full of crushed leaves in their room. And let's not forget my birthday party. Howard gave you up on that one. Said you saw it as the perfect opportunity to make even more chaos." She took a step closer to Frank.

"Mr. O'Brien, why didn't you come and speak to us?" Byron had his arms crossed over his chest. "We aren't unreasonable men. We would have happily spoken to you about the partnership your uncle had with our father."

O'Brien spat at Harvey's shoes.

Frank wanted to throttle the man for all the pain and suffering he'd caused. But instead, he stepped toward him and said, "All these years you've been chasing revenge—all for a lie."

O'Brien jumped out of his chair, screaming obscenities at Fred Harvey's sons. The sheriff and his deputies gathered up the gang of criminals and headed out for the train that waited to take them back to Williams.

In that moment, Frank turned away from the chaos to look at Ruth. He wanted to kiss her more than anything else in the world. She looked so cute standing there, proud of herself for helping with the mystery. And now everything would get back to normal. The El Tovar would continue to thrive—especially after the papers printed the whole elaborate, sensational story—and the Harvey name would continue to stand for good service, honesty, and integrity.

All was right with the world. Except for one thing.

"Ruth Anniston." Frank dropped to one knee. "I'm tired of waiting. Our world has been topsy-turvy for too long, but I know you love me. And I love you. Will you marry me?"

"But what about—"

His kiss to her fingers must have shocked her into silence. "Wait . . . I—"

He stood and kissed her on the forehead.

"I have one question," she whispered.

He raised his eyebrows and waited.

She paused and let out a long breath. "How about tomorrow?"

Frank wrapped his arms around her waist and twirled her around the room, his laughter reaching to the rafters.

# 25

They walked along the rim, Ruth with her walking stick, and Frank content to watch her.

"I've made a decision." She snuck a glance at him. The adoration in her eyes made his chest swell. "All right."

"I'm going to stop wearing powder and makeup to try and cover up my scar."

There was obviously a lot of thought behind her statement. "What brought you to that decision?"

"To be honest, the scar still bothers me. I don't like how it looks. But I was reminded that it is part of who I am now. I never want to get caught up in treating the symptoms and not the real problem. It's a good spiritual reminder to me."

"A good lesson for all of us. Man looks on the outward appearance while God looks on the heart."

"Exactly. Do you think it's a good choice?"

"Of course I do." It's not that he wanted to tread carefully, but he also didn't want to hurt her in any way. He was good at sticking his foot in his mouth. "Whatever you want to do. You're beautiful no matter what."

314

Ruth swatted at his arm and shook her head. "You're just saying that."

"No. No, I'm not." He held his hands up and turned serious. "Look, your scars make you who you are. I think they're beautiful. Just like you." He leaned down and kissed the scar on her cheek.

She tilted her head and studied him. "You know what . . . everything I was trying to do to get rid of the scars?"

"Uh-huh?"

"Well, I had a thought. Jesus carries His scars, doesn't He?"

"From what we see in Scripture, we can assume that, yes."

"It makes me think of His unconditional love in a whole new way. It says that we'll be made new in heaven. But He will carry those scars forever. They are marks of grace and mercy."

"Forever a reminder of what He did for us on the cross."

"Wow." She wiped at a tear. "He's Almighty God. Perfect. And He's willing to carry those scars. For you and for me."

Frank stopped and let that sink in. "I love how you make me think, Ruth Anniston."

"And I love you, Frank Henderson. I can't wait to be your wife."

"Tomorrow, my love. Tomorrow."

**SATURDAY, AUGUST 7, 1909**

"Sweetheart, you look beautiful." Mom flittered around her, fluffing her skirt here, tucking the lace there.

"Thanks, Mom." Ruth couldn't believe that she was marrying Frank. Last night, as they'd walked at the rim, she'd giggled and asked him, "Why didn't we decide to do this a long time ago?"

He'd hugged her and kissed the top of her head. "I was ready years ago. It took you a bit longer because you had to see this frog turn into your prince."

In reality, Frank had always been her prince. Patiently waiting.

She turned to Mom. "I miss Dad. A lot. But I know he would want today to be full of joy."

"Yes, dear. He would. This was his greatest desire. To see you married and happy."

"And to have grandkids." Ruth rolled her eyes. "Dad always talked about how he couldn't wait to be a grandpa."

"That he did." Mom's eyes sparkled. The way she'd adapted to only having one arm was a wonder. She never once complained.

Aunt Mae came into the room. "Oh, you are breathtaking."

"So are you, Aunt Mae. And look at how cute you two are wearing your matching gowns."

"We used to dress alike all the time growing up. We rediscovered how much we like it." Mom shrugged. "So Miss Chapparelle in Williams is making us several more outfits." The merriment in her face took years off her. It was so good to see the smiles. Hearts full of joy.

"Can we pray together before we go to the Music Room?" Ruth reached for Mom's hand and one from Aunt Mae.

"Perfect." Mom led them in a beautiful prayer dedicating Ruth and Frank and their marriage to the Lord.

Ruth blinked back tears the whole time and kept looking to the ceiling. She wasn't sure what heaven was like and if those who had gone on before could see them, but she hoped that God would give Dad a snippet of today.

The beautiful Music Room at the El Tovar had been transformed into a wedding venue.

Frank hadn't wanted anything big. Neither did Ruth. Her two requests? She wanted her mother to play the piano, and she didn't want to have to walk far down the aisle.

Easy enough.

He simply wanted to marry her.

After all these years. Today was the day.

He stood there in his finest suit beside the pastor from Williams. Sweat beaded on his upper lip and on his hands. Why was he so nervous?

Deep breaths. That's what he needed.

They'd invited their closest friends. All the while, the hotel hummed around them with guests from all over the world and the Harvey Girls serving them in style.

"It's time," Ruth's mother whispered from the piano. She caught his eye and winked at him. "I'm proud of you."

His heart swelled as she played a beautiful arrangement of "Amazing Grace."

The doors opened, and Ruth walked in with Emma Grace on one side and Julia on the other. Her dress was white with lace all over it. Simple. Elegant. Beautiful. Just like Ruth.

He couldn't help but beam at her.

Sniffles were heard around the room. Mr. Owens had tears streaming down his cheeks.

So did Charlotte.

At one point, Ruth wobbled, and her two dear friends shored her up. They stood for a moment while Ruth got her balance and then continued to him. It wasn't more than twenty steps total, but he couldn't wait for her to be here. With him.

Then . . . there she was. Beside him.

He took her hand, and they faced the pastor together.

"Dearly beloved, we are gathered together today to join Frank Henderson and Ruth Anniston in holy matrimony. To begin the service, the couple has chosen for a special song to be shared."

Tessa—sweet, quiet Tessa—came to stand beside Ruth's mom at the piano. Mrs. Anniston played an introduction and then Tessa sang their favorite song. One that had more meaning to them with each passing day.

> Amazing grace! how sweet the sound,
> That saved a wretch like me!
> I once was lost, but now am found,
> Was blind, but now I see.

The room was spellbound by the perfect clarity and tone of Tessa's voice. Many were moved to tears. Frank had never heard anything more beautiful.

The ceremony was simple. Exactly what they'd asked for. Neither one of them wanted Ruth to have to stand and be nervous in front of a crowd, even if it was a small one. Of course, he ended up being the nervous one. Funny.

Frank did his best to pay attention, but all he wanted to do was take Ruth in his arms. She was finally his! After all this time. After all the waiting. *Thank You, Lord!*

"Frank?" Pastor nudged him.

"Hm?" Uh-oh. What did he miss?

Quiet laughter filled the room.

"Do you take Ruth to be your lawfully wedded wife?"

"Oh yes! I do."

"Whew. I was worried there for a moment." Ruth winked at him.

More laughter.

But it helped ease his nerves.

After a few brief sentences of advice and blessings, the pastor said, "I now pronounce you husband and wife. You may kiss the bride."

Frank didn't hesitate. He pulled Ruth into his arms and whispered against her lips. "I have loved you since we first met, and I vow to love you more each and every day." As they came together for their first kiss, a fire lit within him that was passionate and hungry and made him feel whole.

The applause around them made him pull away, but then he went right back in for another kiss. Cheers and laughter filled the room. Ruth was his.

She was worth the wait.

# Epilogue

Happy Birfday, Mama!"

"Happy Birtday, Mama!"

The twins raced toward Ruth's legs. At three years old, they were showing more and more of their father every day. Red hair and all.

She braced for impact as her two boys plowed into her and hugged her tight. Then she collapsed onto the blanket with them in a fit of giggles.

"Forty years old never looked so good." Frank cuddled up next to her on the blanket and kissed her cheek. "In fact, if I were to be honest, I'd say you don't look a day over thirty." He winked.

"Forteeeeeeeeeee!" the boys chimed together and jumped up and down. Frank had been teaching them all week that Mama was about to be forty. It was their new favorite word.

She grabbed them and put her hands over their mouths.

"Well, yes, but let's not shout it to the world." Not that it mattered. Everyone knew this was her fortieth. That's why they were having this party, after all.

She turned to her husband. "And stop your lying, Frank Henderson. I feel like these two have aged me ten years."

"Oh piddle-posh." Mom held her parasol over her head. "They're keeping you young. Me too, don't you know? That's the secret to staying young. Children and grand-children."

It was wonderful to have her mother here. Grandma to her children. Piano teacher to many. The woman could play with one hand better than most could with two.

"Thanks, Mom." The words got caught in her throat as she choked up.

"For what, dear?" The innocent look in her eyes sparkled with love and joy.

"For teaching me to grab on to joy. Each and every day."

Her mother shrugged. "Your father taught me that, Ruthie. And he learned it from the best source." She poked her parasol toward the sky.

The lump in her throat grew. She told her boys about their grandpa every day. They knew him from his photograph and all the stories they told about him. He would be proud.

Frank sat up and pointed. "Watch out. Here comes the rest of the party."

Ruth stood up and clapped her hands together. Emma Grace, Ray, and their three little girls all carried baskets. Julia, Chris, and their brood of four walked with them. The kids were all waving streamers and skipping. Oh, and then a line of Harvey Girls walked arm in arm, carrying a huge banner that read, *Happy Birthday, Ruth!* Tessa and Char-lotte were on each of the ends.

Chuma, Sunki, Humeatah, and a dozen or so of the Hopi people came from the Hopi House, their traditional celebratory garb a gorgeous array of colors.

One of the new men from the kitchen pushed Mr. Owens in his wheelchair, and a crowd of others followed behind. The strains of "Happy Birthday to You," sung to the tune of "Good Morning to All," began to build and echo to the canyon.

Her one request for the day had been for everyone to gather for a group photograph. There had been a few grumbles and complaints from those who didn't like having their picture taken, but no one could refuse her. It would take some doing, but the Kolb brothers had promised to come and help. All in all, there were more than fifty people to try and squeeze in. She wanted to try and capture the El Tovar and the canyon as backdrops.

Her family.

Her home.

Nine and a half years ago, she'd come here with a head full of dreams and a heart searching for love. While she may have guided and mentored hundreds of young women over the years, it had taken her coming to her own crisis of faith to change her whole view.

She didn't have to *do* anything but believe. Plain and simple. There was no earning it. No good enough. No worthy or unworthy.

Just like Tessa had said, it was grace plus nothing. The most beautiful, simple, and complex idea she'd ever had to grasp.

*Thank You, God. For Your grace.*

With a hand from her husband, Ruth got to her feet again and went to welcome her friends. Years of exercises had helped to strengthen her leg, but the limp was still there.

So were the scars. But they too were marks of His grace. A blessed reminder. Funny how that worked.

Unconditional love. It was a beautiful thing.

# Note from the Author

In 1861, Fred Harvey's business partner in real life from their restaurant/saloon, William Doyle, took off with all the money they had. Doyle was pro-slavery, and Harvey was against slavery. After their political argument, Fred never saw his partner, nor all the money, ever again. It was this event and other tragedies in his life that catapulted Fred Harvey into building the Harvey Empire.

I didn't want to cast aspersions on the Doyle family, but the villain in this story is loosely based on the premise of what Doyle did. It in essence gave me the motivation for Oliver O'Brien. So I changed the family name.

Chef Marques was a real historical chef at El Tovar. I don't know how long he served at the hotel, so for the purposes of this story, I fictionally had him leave so that Frank could take his place.

It has been a joy to bring you this series at the Grand Canyon and El Tovar. These Harvey Girls stories are some of my favorites.

I hope you'll join me for my next series with Tracie Peterson—JEWELS OF KALISPELL—starting with *A Heart's Choice* in May 2023, and the start of my next series featuring dinosaur bones and women in paleontology coming in September 2023.

Until next time,
Kimberley

# Acknowledgments

Every book, I share with you how many people it takes to make this possible. I'm sure I miss some each time, and I'm so sorry about that. But here's some of the people I'd like to thank for their love, support, and help to put *A Mark of Grace* into your hands.

Jeremy—my best friend and soul mate. You are my hero!

Josh, Kayla, Ruth, and Steven—my kids and their spouses. I wouldn't be able to make it without your support and love.

Tracie—my dearest friend, partner in "crime," mentor, prayer partner, and fellow chocaholic. I am so very blessed to have you in my life.

Jaime Jo Wright, Jocelyn Green, Jayna Breigh, Becca Whitham, Tracie Peterson, and Darcie Gudger—my mastermind group and fellow Eating Our Words founders. I love you guys. Thanks for being there through thick and thin.

Jackie Hale and Carrie Kintz—two of my very favorite people on the planet. Your friendship means the world to me. I love you.

Jessica Sharpe and Jennifer Veilleux—my editors. Thank you for all that you do.

All the amazing people at Bethany House. You guys are wonderful. What a blessing to work with you all.

And to my readers—I pray for you as I write each book, and I hope that you are blessed by these stories.

To God be the glory!

**Kimberley Woodhouse** is an award-winning and bestselling author of more than thirty books. A lover of history and research, she often gets sucked into the past and then her husband has to lure her out with chocolate and the promise of eighteen holes on the golf course. She loves music, kayaking, and her family. Married to the love of her life for three decades, she lives and writes in the Poconos, where she's traded her title of "Craziest Mom" for "Nana the Great." To find out more about Kim's books, follow her on social media, and sign up for her newsletter/blog at kimberleywoodhouse.com.

# Sign Up for Kimberley's Newsletter

Keep up to date with Kimberley's latest news on book releases and events by signing up for her email list at kimberleywoodhouse.com.

---

## More from Kimberley Woodhouse

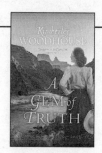

Longing for a fresh start, Julia Schultz takes a job as a Harvey Girl at the El Tovar Hotel, where she's challenged to be her true self. United by the discovery of a legendary treasure, Julia and master jeweler Christopher Miller find hope in each other. But when Julia's past catches up with her, will she lose everyone's trust?

*A Gem of Truth* by Kimberley Woodhouse
SECRETS OF THE CANYON #2

# You May Also Like . . .

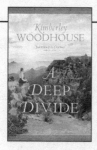

When her father's greedy corruption goes too far, heiress Emma Grace McMurray sneaks away to be a Harvey Girl at the El Tovar Grand Canyon Hotel, planning to stay hidden forever. There she uncovers mysteries, secrets, and a love beyond anything she could imagine—leaving her to question all she thought to be true.

*A Deep Divide* by Kimberley Woodhouse
SECRETS OF THE CANYON #1
kimberleywoodhouse.com

On the surface, Whitney Powell is happy working with her sled dogs, but her life is full of complications that push her to the edge. When sickness spreads in outlying villages, Dr. Peter Cameron turns to Whitney and her dogs for help navigating the deep snow, and together they discover that sometimes it's only in weakness you can find strength.

*Ever Constant* by Tracie Peterson and Kimberley Woodhouse
THE TREASURES OF NOME #3
traciepeterson.com; kimberleywoodhouse.com

Haunted by heartbreak and betrayal, Addie Bryant escapes her terrible circumstances with the hope she can forever hide her past and with the belief she will never have the future she's always dreamed of. When she's reunited with her lost love, Addie must decide to run or to face her wounds to embrace her life, her future, and her hope in God.

*Remember Me* by Tracie Peterson
PICTURES OF THE HEART #1
traciepeterson.com

◊ BETHANYHOUSE

# More from Bethany House

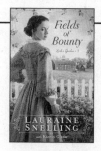

Lilac Nielsen must learn to balance her new courtship with the young Reverend and her pursuit of another dream—the publication of her artwork in a New York newspaper. But when a family crisis back in Ohio shakes the Nielsen sisters, can they continue the new life they've begun in Nebraska? And will Lilac be prepared for what God has in store for her future?

*Fields of Bounty* by Lauraine Snelling
LEAH'S GARDEN #3
laurainesnelling.com

When midwife Catherine Remington is accused of a murder she didn't commit, she flees to Colorado to honor a patient's dying wish to deliver a newborn to his father. But what she doesn't bargain for is how easily she'll fall for the charming sheriff, or how quickly her past will catch up with her and put their love and lives in danger.

*The Last Chance Cowboy* by Jody Hedlund
COLORADO COWBOYS #5
jodyhedlund.com

After being left for dead with no memory, Maria Stover attempts to rebuild her life as she takes over her father's blacksmith business, but the townspeople meet her work with disdain. She is drawn to the new diner owner as he faces similar trials in the town. When danger descends upon them, will they survive to build a life forged in love?

*Forged in Love* by Mary Connealy
WYOMING SUNRISE #1
maryconnealy.com